Neil Carpenter

Killing
You
Softly

ISBN 978-1497420557

Acknowledgements

In recent months, there are so many people for whose support I am grateful: Peter Carter at the Royal College of Nursing; Peter Fisher at the NHS Consultants' Association; Rachael Maskell at Unite; and Martin Rathfelder at the Socialist Health Association.

In preparing the book for publication, Philip Kennedy's cover design has made up for all the gaps in my visual imagination and Scott Newland has been unbelievably good-humoured and meticulous in his formatting of the novel.

At a much earlier stage, I am indebted to James Oliver for patient and painstaking advice on the book's medical content and to Lauren Bayfield for making the younger characters and their language sound genuinely young. Any failure of authenticity in either area is my responsibility, not theirs.

Within my family, thanks to the next generation down for ironing out my frequent bungling on the computer and for always giving that invaluable second opinion; and, above all, thanks to Vanessa for her constant encouragement.

April 2014

1

Becky Goldsmith listened as her father's car left the drive.

"If you're going to muck about with Wikipedia, you'll have to be quick. He's always forgetting things and he often comes straight back."

"Okay, okay." Sarah King's finger pointing at the computer screen brushed away her friend's concern.

"Look – this bit's Dave. I told you it was. *'Chameleons' main purpose when changing colour is not camouflage ... it signals their intentions to other chameleons ... Chameleons will show darker colours when attempting to intimidate ...'* Don't bother with the rest of it. It's him, isn't it? It's just like his red face. The bullying, all that."

She waved a scrap of paper at Becky whose tentative nod was ignored.

"This wouldn't fit in, though, but it might ... " She had turned back to the screen. *'Chameleons have many parasites including threadworms ...'* That's it - it'll fit there."

"You sure you know what you're doing? Anyway, it's not going to work. It'll be on there for the rest of the day, if -"

"So what!" She placed her hand on Becky's fingers to still her agitation. "It's a bit of a laugh, anyway."

Her fingers keyed in the addition.

'On occasions, the chameleon has been known to transmute itself to human form, especially to humans in positions of influence. There have also been reported instances, as yet uncorroborated, of traits of the chameleon being passed on, virus-like, to over-zealous followers of the influential male.'

" 'Zealous' doesn't really fit my dear father but to hell with it. Leave it on." Hastily, she shut the computer down. "See what happens."

2

Colin Goldsmith, despite Becky's fears, had not forgotten anything. He had not gone back home but wished he had.

It was the second day. The second day of who knew how many. Most of them were retired and could keep it up indefinitely. They stood blocking the entrance to the surgery itself and all the reserved parking spaces, including the one he had used for over twenty years - an unwritten agreement which, like so many informal understandings, had had its uses. He sighed.

It wasn't the eighties, perhaps only because of the village's size: there were no massed battle lines; there was no spitting, no venom in the swearing. Yet by local standards it was unsettling although and because he recognised all the faces.

He reversed out on to the road and found himself a space. His posture was naturally a little stooped and so, briefcase in his hand, he drew himself up, an appearance, he hoped, of confidence, not arrogance.

"You know why we're here, Dr. Goldsmith. I know she's not one of yours but why isn't Amy Goddard getting treated properly?"

"I don't know the detail but I'm sure -"

"But there are people coming here from Penmerrin, one from Reskeel, forty miles or more, and they're getting treatment. How can that be right?"

He felt his shoulders dip and tried to keep his eyes up.

"You know I can't discuss other patients' circumstances."

"No, but we can discuss your car."

The words were audible but only just. He edged awkwardly away from the sudden envy. To him, it was no BMW but only a family car - spacious, admittedly, and almost brand-new.

He walked, unobstructed, to the door and let himself in.

* * * * *

The school and the corridor were their usual chaotic selves, although the bell had sounded. Some ran and pushed their way while others walked, turned and chatted. Someone tripped or was tripped and the laughter surged through the door, barged open, of the briefly silent room where the conscientious ones - Becky had dragged Sarah, for once, into that category - were already waiting.

"Come in and sit down. I'll find out why you're late in a moment." There was an edge to Emily Pollard's voice but they seemed to expect and accept it.

With two more interruptions, she completed the register.

"Can you stand up, please? Yes, we've got an assembly. Will you put your chairs under and file out as usual?" The groans subsided. "Not you three, no."

The subdued jostling funnelled into the calm of the hall, policed at all three entrances. She followed, shepherding her three stragglers, and, at a glance from Stuart Fletcher, pulled the doors softly shut behind her.

4

"Good morning, everyone." Fletcher paused, the protracted hiatus an assertion of his headteacher's authority, not an orator's flourish. Most of his audience sat looking down, uncomfortably cross-legged, while a few raised their eyes in an appearance of attention. For them, his bloated face and swollen stomach had been so comprehensively looted for potential jokes - 'Toad' had been his nickname from the first day - that few anticipated even the limited light relief of examining his face and ponderous movements closely.

"My theme today is protest. We live in a time when protest, internationally and at home, has become increasingly common - but what makes it legitimate or, in simple terms, reasonable and fair?" He paused again and perhaps, in a younger incarnation, he would have looked for a response from his audience. Not now.

"History provides us with many examples but to take just one - the uprisings against the Communist regimes in Eastern Europe some twenty-five years ago. Many of you take for granted basic freedoms such as freedom of speech but for people in countries such as Hungary and Czechoslovakia none of this existed. And it was the people peacefully but in their thousands - what is now known as 'people power' - that overthrew those oppressors."

He meandered on, no concrete examples, no sequencing to create even a hint of suspense, no awareness of isolated and whispered staff comments that dismissed this sanitised version of the past.

"And so any change that protest produces is only as good as the methods that have brought it about."

His pause in ending was as long and portentous as in opening. Any impact, however, intended rather than actual, dribbled away in fragmented notices from staff - two or three miscreants who needed to stay behind, the time for cross-country training …

Sarah, thanks to an elbow in her ribs, observed the hall's silence until they had all passed through the doors.

"That's all right, then, Becky. Flowers in tanks always do the trick."

Pollard, at the door, smiled to herself as the girls pushed and laughed their way down the corridor.

3

"Just call in the surgery - it's all set up."

Mobile to his ear, upright and alert, Martin King evaded the mid-morning shoppers bustling towards and past him. "About a hundred yards past the pub, on the right." His voice softened. "No, for now, just get yourself registered. Leave seeing Goldsmith for a while."

He stopped outside a shop window to let a young woman and her buggy pass. "Anyway, I've got to go - nearly there now. You still all right to come round later?" He listened, his eyes scanning the street. "No - it shouldn't have happened like that but Sarah won't be there after school today."

The call over, he adjusted his tie, facing a mannequin who stared past him. Pushing back his shoulders, he crossed the road and stepped into a black archway and up its barely-lit steps.

The contrast with the brightly-lit office on the first floor could not have been greater. The weak sunlight of a cloudy day was complemented and overwhelmed by an array of spotlights and table lamps. The girl at the computer terminal next to the door was as bright as her surroundings, her smile as confident as his.

"He should be ready to see you, Martin. I'll just check." He fixed his eyes on her even though her head was thrown back as she used the phone. "Yes - just go on in," and she returned immediately to her screen.

Such attachment to a computer was not for James Marriott. When King came through the door, he was beckoned to look at an email - as if it might disappear as suddenly as it had arrived.

"See there. They must be getting their sums wrong on a lot of this." His long finger, an older generation, stabbed at the words on the screen. "Central Office is getting in a lather over these botched reforms. That death in Winchester has put the wind up them and so they're going to throw more money at it - good news for the likes of you. All covered in redundancy costs, according to this."

"Ought to be good for you as well. None of my business but you're performance-based, I suppose? You'll make a killing too, won't you?"

The smile in reply was languid. "After a fashion, but for me - and there's no reason this should be true for you - it matters whether we, as Conservatives, are perceived as a shambles. I suppose I'm the lifelong England cricket supporter at Lord's and you're the man off the street, turning up for his first ever match. There is still the concept of loyalty for some of us, although it's becoming strained."

"Bad comparison, I'm afraid. Never did like cricket - can't stand the game." Incredulous despair flooded into Marriott's eyes. "Not even sure what I'm supposed to be loyal to."

An angry stare fixed him briefly. "At least I know where you stand - but that's probably enough disillusion for one morning."

He swivelled his chair away and then back, to look directly across the desk at King. "Back to business, which is your raison d'être: the money is there for people like you to spend, with a delightful absence of regulation - and just as well because who knows where it's come from."

* * * * *

From King's upstairs window, before he rearranged the bed covers, he watched her hips sway as she hurried to her car. No pining look back - only a hurried opening of the door and an equally rushed driving off.

The traffic noise obscured the closing of the back door. Footsteps in the kitchen and then a sequence of sounds when Sarah's bags dropped on the work surface and the cups were shunted to one side. He smiled to himself and, after opening the window a fraction, went downstairs.

"You're back early?"

"My bit was done first. Then he just laid into Sophie - she had to keep doing her scene at the end so several of us could go."

"What's the play?"

She scanned the drab kitchen. The two coffee cups could have been left over from breakfast but, to create a good impression, he had cleared away the rest. No muesli box, no encrusted dishes decorated the surface. Last night's glass, the crisp packets - all had been spirited away.

"Same as yesterday or last week or the last six weeks." She touched one of the cups and rubbed her fingers. "If it'd been a new one, I'd have told you." She unzipped her bag, piled up her books and emptied the day's letters into the bin. "God, even this has been cleaned."

"All part of my exciting life." His teeth pulled at his bottom lip as she stared at him in disbelief. "Not every day, I suppose." He nodded towards the bin. "Don't throw all that away - it might be

9

life changing."

"Whose - mine or yours? I can choose for mine, thank you. Everything tidied away upstairs as well, is it?" She continued to stare at him and his eyes dropped instantly.

"I just thought it would -"

"For Christ's sake, don't patronise me. I know what's been going on. The same as last week and God knows when else. You think I'd be here if I'd anywhere else to go? I just felt like crap and needed a bit of space. My own space."

"Sorry I was in the way." He attempted a self-pitying smile that misbehaved itself into a grin for a photographer. "It's just work's light at the -"

"Oh God, you're doing it again." She glared at him. "I know what is going on," each word enunciated separately as if she were still on the stage. "And I can't stand it. Nobody else's father is doing it all the time - not openly anyway, working his way through a queue." A flicker of self-congratulation in his eyes made her worse. "You've no idea, do you? What it's like?"

He reached for the cupboard door. "Let me make you a nice cup of coffee."

She rubbed her hand across her forehead, calmed - or numbed - by the banality of his suggestion.

"Surely you must say something better than that to them?" She paused. "Look - it's not about me needing sympathy. Can't you understand that? It's not about me at all."

Across the silence, the phone rang. He scuttled away, his voice suddenly animated for what she knew was a female caller. When he returned to the kitchen, she had gone, his rediscovered jauntiness wasted.

4

Another late afternoon and Sarah realised she had nowhere in particular to go. If she went through the village, she was bound to meet someone from school; if she walked down to the cliffs, she would look odd on her own. Older people, the dog walkers sealed in an anonymity of routine, in their wholeness, in their having passed curiosity and questions, could do it. Envy crowded briefly in until her father - and her mother, for very different reasons - filled her consciousness and drove it away.

She swore to herself. She hadn't even changed from her school clothes: another reason to find somewhere to go; another reason for the usual solution. Becky's would be ideal to escape the labelling - no cars, just the back lanes and the park.

Over the fence, she could see Liam Bennett working with his father on another extension to his house. 'Working' was an overstatement: they were holding at an angle some timber that would help add another room to their Lego-like house. She had been in it once and remembered its ramshackle sprawl and the way Liam's father joked at him and with him. It was probably the same now: she thought she could see Liam's grin, his strong face framed by floppy, unruly hair - and his father, making a few jokes.

Shielded by trees, she stood watching - it was too abstracted to be a stare, her finger on her upper lip - until sounds behind her made her move on.

She crossed the park and, after a moment's self-consciousness, hurled abuse back at some young kids who were spilling drinks and dropping crisps over the swings.

"You could be a policeman" - Becky was tugging at her sleeve.

" What - and join the other women? No, I'd be too wound-up for that." She took Becky's arm. "Perhaps not - perhaps that's what I need. I'd be a great careers' adviser, wouldn't I? Why you so late getting home?"

"Went to Liam's."

As they approached the drive, she had already taken a key from her pocket. Her opening the door, shedding her coat, taking Sarah's, hanging them both up, scrutinising a detailed note that had been left under a coffee cup, set a boundary to the conversation.

Sarah took in the sudden peace. There was a physical warmth, the lightest touch, barely perceptible, as far from being oppressive as the rest of the house. The colours - greys, light browns and soft greens, subdued but unfashionable - and the small-paned window looking out onto the back garden reassured her: she was out of the public eye, a wound was less exposed.

"Mum's going to be late - so I'm doing tea." She tucked the note and its recipe back in place. "You could do it with me - show me how it's done."

"Don't know about that."

"You could stay as well, if you want." She brushed Sarah's hand lightly. "Mum and Dad wouldn't mind."

"No - I'm fine now." She rubbed her hands up and down over her face. "No thanks - but I'd like to help." She took the vegetables that Becky passed her. "God, you don't know what it's like to have the stuff you need. There's always plenty in the house but it never fits. If I want pasta, I've got potatoes. He'll always go out and get more - it's not that bad - but that's not the point."

She stopped and saw Becky, attentive, a hesitant smile, her hand - a split-second gesture frozen into a sequence of stills - reaching towards her own arm. She rubbed her head again.

"I'm sorry to go on, although I haven't really got going, have I?" She squeezed Becky's hand before gently pushing it away. "Not like the other night. God, that bloke was an idiot. How these new courses would open up job after job. Didn't your dad say to you it was like National Service? Put up with something pointless for two years and then get back to what you wanted to do in the first place. If Liam wasn't so laid-back, he'd be tearing -"

The door bell rang, drawing a trace of impatience into Becky's eyes.

"Back in a minute."

A blurred, unfamiliar male voice followed the opening of the front door.

"No, I don't know why they told you that. I'll just check at the surgery that he's there."

The breeze carried through to Sarah from outside.

"Yes, he is. He's expecting you but he might be tied up with a patient. You'd better ask reception first."

The voice sounded untroubled and the door closed.

"Another mess-up - him coming here, I mean. It's Dad's car he wants - the windscreen's been cracked, he thinks."

* * * * *

13

Goldsmith was far later than he had planned. Forty minutes spent attempting to thrash out a detail of financial arrangements that had changed yet again after another revised government directive. Phone calls to his insurance company to sort out the car repair had taken another twenty. More apologies to patients than usual for being late.

Mary kept saying that something had to give and she was probably right. With things as they now were, he had started to sense that he was losing the determination - and the mental clarity - to argue his case.

In the past, there had never been anything fundamental on which to take a stand, only changes to the practice which in hindsight seemed minor - or issues, normally delays, to take up with the Royal. In those contexts, arguing had been an exercise in organisation and, occasionally, intellectual precision; in the current context, self-interest muddied everything. Not a problem with the outside agencies they had to deal with - that was their raison-d'être - but with colleagues, some of whom he classed as friends, it was increasingly difficult. When even Ian could see an argument in favour of what Sheila - he smiled at her stubbornness - refused to call 'reforms', he found it hard to counter his suggestions without impugning his motives.

His own irritability was another problem. It may have been hidden from view, at work and at home, but he knew he had to release it - and not through the whiskey bottle he had just bought.

He passed the cluster of yobs that had gathered at the entrance to the park. They stood, prematurely stooped in adolescence, one or two of them glancing his way. He knew calling them 'yobs' was unfair - he would have argued the point with anyone else who pinned that label on them - yet, once in a while, it was cathartic.

Not cathartic enough because his unease at the huddled group registering his existence lingered. Those teenagers were now alive in three dimensions, not a mere part of the village backdrop - and only since the demonstrations outside the surgery. He recognised the early stages of paranoia: hardly enough to warrant the term but his morbid self-awareness was undeniable.

He remembered long phases at school when he had yearned for adulthood, for being valued for his brain rather than being despised in nicknames he had rarely understood at the time. He remembered a day's stares as the faces turned outwards, followed by perhaps a week when his route around school was neutral concrete against clear blue skies that profiled the overhanging trees - until another day of implicit threats arrived without any apparent logic.

The same sensations now - even if the circumstances were different. Not the "yobs" but the patients blockading his approach to the surgery - the logic of their actions was inescapable, returning, an inflated abstraction, whenever any mental light relief had ebbed away.

He turned onto the drive and winced at the sight of Sarah beside Becky at the window. A little bit of peace would have helped. Becky on her own was so good at that, so undemanding with her quiet humour. Like anyone at that age, though, someone else could set her off.

He paused before withdrawing the keys from the ignition. It would be childish not to follow his own time-honoured advice to patients to keep things in perspective and so he lifted his head to reclaim his smile, before walking up the drive.

He pushed the front door open until it stuck.

"Sorry, Dad, you've got nowhere to put your case."

The bags left in the hall had tested his equilibrium; her face flushed slightly at the failure of her jibe, the mutual predictability that he normally enjoyed.

"No, it's not a problem. Hello, Sarah." Eyes distracted, he scrabbled in his pockets for his phone. "Ah, got it. You two wouldn't have that problem, would you?"

"Only twice a day." She waved behind her into the kitchen. "Sarah's done tea. Cut above my normal efforts."

"I don't know about that. We can both take the blame for it."

He smiled reassuringly. "I'm sure there'll be no blame. It smells very good indeed." Turning to open the cupboard above the kettle, he held his head still before he took out a glass.

"Would you both like some?" He stretched out the orange juice in his other hand and, at their nods, again, as he turned to the cupboard, he hesitated before reaching for two more glasses.

"Are you -?"

"Yes, fine - no problem. Head just going around a little." His face took on its professional veneer before his voice was raised from a whisper. "All your work done again?"

"Yes. Nothing new today." Her mouth taut, she tried to fix his eyes. "Not like you, by the sound of it. Did that bloke manage to sort out the car?"

"A little confusion to start with but then it only took twenty minutes. About the time your homework takes."

The tension lingered in her face.

"But how did it get cracked?"

"More than a crack. A stone. Must have been thrown."

"You're joking."

"No - unfortunately not. Someone overstepped the mark near the surgery. A part of me can't blame them, though, to be honest."

He put his glass in the sink and edged towards the stairs. "Are you okay to finish that off?"

"It's all done, really. We had another careers' talk today - social care this time."

"They seem to multiply in inverse proportion to the number of jobs available." Goldsmith looked at Sarah in surprise as she continued. "It sounded good, I suppose. I know it's all because they've now got to recruit more in the U.K. but, despite the bureaucracy, it is still with people."

He forgot whatever he had intended to do upstairs. "You need to watch it, though. Bureaucracy seems almost harmless from the outside but when it's combined with growing numbers and shrinking resources, it becomes a means of enforcement." He tried to bite back the tone of implied superiority but it had not put her off.

"It's got to be better than being one of the enforcers, doesn't it?"

"If you're strong enough, yes, because it's all part of passing the buck further down the line. Unless you're in the middle and can make enough money out of it."

He glanced at Becky whose eyes had picked up the subtext and were willing him to change tack.

"Talking of passing the buck -" Her words did no more than fill the air.

"It's like my father. I probably shouldn't say it but he's making more money now, I think, than he ever did, at a time when everyone else is struggling." Although the content was confessional, perhaps because she had grown used to seeing a doctor, her open face, her upright head gave her words a declarative confidence that he had not expected. "If it's a market working, it's not working properly."

"When did it ever?"

"But if everyone's subject to competition, it's at least

consistent. Instead the way some people are profiting makes a farce of all their pronouncements."

"I don't know who else is coming in to see you but," and he smiled, "I should think you've got a political career if you want it."

As she nodded tentatively back, he remembered his tact, his duty to his daughter who felt much the same way, if not so articulately.

"You two could do whatever you want. Science is probably at the back of the queue, isn't it? Too impersonal?"

"At the moment, yes." She paused as if she were gagging herself, to allow Becky to continue.

"In school it is but what you've done with it isn't. Who knows? I could follow in your footsteps."

"A lot of work to be done first." He raised his eyes and clenched his teeth lightly. "Anyway, I won't start on. I'll leave you to it but you will stay for some of this lovely meal you've made?"

5

"Fucking hell, we're going to be late."

"So what? It's only if we want to do it anyway."

The four of them stumbled through the sand that pulled at their feet. The spring morning retained some of the night's chill, their breath momentarily a haze in front of them. Cold faces, warmth inside their coats.

"Ben." Sarah's voice screeched. "Emerton - for Christ's sake, I've got to slow down! Malcolm's seen us already. We won't get much more of a bollocking. Where's Liam anyway?" Her face had gone red with the exertion.

"You're meant to be as fit as I am." Ben somersaulted through the air. "Look - no sand in my hair. No reason you can't do it as well."

"Oh, give it a rest. Walking across here is hard enough."

His face froze in simulated shock, before an exaggerated smile spread across his face. "I get it. You're like her back there, whatshername, Andrews, the fat ..." Brief concentration threw out the Christian name. "Kirsty - that's all she's ever after. Some gentler exercise with my dick. You as well - that's it, isn't it? And it's hard enough - see, you even get a what-you-call-it, a pun, thrown in, as well." He pulled theatrically at his zip. "Perhaps not. Second thoughts. A bit cold."

"Thank God for that. We haven't got ten minutes while you look for it."

"Is that all I'm going to get – a load of abuse ?"

"Yeah – and if it's not enough, your help-yourself variety'll keep you going."

Becky nudged her. "Is that Liam coming out the front door?"

"Ah, it all fits. Sarah helping herself."

"Oh, Christ, you know who I was talking about."

"I can picture it now. You lying there alone but not alone -"

"Don't push your luck."

His eyes bulged at Sarah in mock hurt before he ran on, leaving the girls to follow, with Kirsty trailing behind them. Waiting for her, they ignored his shout, the word "useless" reverberating, the sound otherwise imperfect.

"He's right. Even a monkey would hit that nail on the head. They don't ever let us do anything."

"Of course they bloody don't, Kirsty."

"So what are we doing this for?" She persisted, already talking to the backs of the other two girls. "God, I wish I could lose some weight." She tripped from the exertion, brushing stray hair temporarily back in place. "Wait for me, can't you?"

"Please don't moan." Becky stepped back and tugged her forwards. "You can see why they think we're useless."

"Look. My mum would say how beautiful this is if she were here. I know she isn't. That's the subjunctive, isn't it? Slow down, for fuck's sake." Kirsty almost stopped the three of them. "It is beautiful, I suppose. Perhaps that's why we're here: sensitivity, artistic appreciation."

"Oh, Christ, don't - you're playing into their hands again."

As they plodded on, they could see beyond the life-saving club hut, dwarfed by the banks of wind-driven sand, to where the beach extended for a quarter of a mile until the sea at low tide broke, soundless, in the tiniest of waves. Two horses galloped, echoing from the rutted wet sand. A stray shout, delayed by the distance, from one of the riders, penetrated the silence.

From the village, a tractor emerged, a speck at first. Slowly it grew, its steady rumble audible, like an actor talking in the wings, about to take his place on the stage. At the high tide mark, below the club hut, it stopped, incongruous clogged mud on its wheels, before reversing over the wet sand. Its ponderous momentum gradually slowed to nothing as it hit the deepening dry sand. Three of the juniors sat on the rim of the trailer, feet on the concrete blocks, laughing at each shuddering jolt.

"Fuck me. We're hardly late at all - and it is Liam." He was one of five dropping shovels by the front door and heading down the beach. "Hang on - wait for us."

Kirsty's shout was greeted by raised eyebrows from two of the boys and an angrier shout from the squat, older figure standing in the doorway.

"Don't waste any more bloody time." Malcolm O'Donnell waved the boys on. "And what time do you call this?" He had forgotten again to put in his front tooth, harshening the glint in his stare that a newcomer could never interpret.

"Sarah said the clocks were changing." Ben shouted, running backwards and laughing. "She wasn't sure which week, though. So we came half an hour late in case it was half an hour early."

"Bloody clever dick. One's too many - and a whole bevvy with him. Still, there's loads of tea to be made" - and he waved them on towards the others who were already unloading the blocks and carrying them, one at a time, towards the hut.

"Can't you take two at a time?" Ben's taunt raised a quiet smile from Liam.

"In a minute, I expect."

They joined the small queue at the trailer.

"I can't carry one of those on my own."

"Why not? You're big enough."

Kirsty grimaced. "That's uncalled-for, you prick."

"Well, pair up with someone. That's what we're doing."

"But they don't need help - they can all manage on their own. So what's left? I'll go and make the tea, I suppose."

She glared at the cheers that came from the trailer but trudged off. Sarah and Becky followed, carrying a block between them.

"This is a bloody stupid way to do it. Why we all walking so far?" Sarah's voice was raised. "Why don't we form a chain? Loads quicker."

There was no response apart from Ben bellowing "Daisy chain" and snorting. She shook her head.

"Don't argue. There's no point." Becky's words were laboured, her breathing strained by the effort of walking sideways with the block.

"It's just so stupid."

As they reached the hut, they were deafened by Malcolm's shout, aimed over their heads at the trailer. He was red-faced and staring. "Do I have to sort out everything for you? Use your brains, for God's sake. You, the bloody monkey down there." Ben stopped swinging on the open tractor door. "Make a chain or we're going to be all day. Girls, you go in the middle. Come on - get a move on."

Taking their places in the uneven curving chain, Ben smirked at Becky.

"Right again, smartasses."

"Not me - she's the one to grovel to."

"No problem. I'd get down on my knees for either of you." He paused. "Anyone, in fact."

"You know, Ben, sometimes you don't even deserve to be patronised."

They looked away as a droning sound grew, a drill penetrating the atmosphere. The dot in the distance over the sea grew into a small plane, trailing a banner behind it.

"Keep it going - the idiots've got their seasons wrong again."

The otherwise empty beach appeared to confirm the accuracy of Malcolm's words but their gazes stayed distracted. As the plane banked over the beach, the banner's words, bold in red and blue against a white background, were plainly visible: 'The Big Society'.

Even for Malcolm, it had been worth stopping. Through the cacophony of derision around him, he clearly enjoyed his rant. "What does that cost them in fuel? Five times what we get in a year. Stupid stunt. I thought they'd given up that nonsense. Big Society, my ass."

The plane banked again over them and, as it straightened, a shower of leaflets cascaded down on them. In the still air, the drop had been surprisingly precise. They stood, festooned in glossy red, blue and white paper, while the plane retraced its path out to sea.

6

Becky held back until Liam's father was out of earshot.

"I really don't mind. I don't want to get in the way. I can wait in the car or go for a walk."

He clearly hadn't thought about it and could not see any of the sensitivity that lay behind the offer. He muttered "No", accompanied by a light shrug of his shoulders, so she followed up the drive.

The house would have been impressive in its time. A steeply sloping roof, massive windows and a front door which they passed, church-like in its size and coloured glass - all were the signs of past wealth. Now there were the signs of scrimping, of relative poverty: the rusted rail behind the car parking area, the boulders that could have been a rockery piled haphazardly in a corner, the unpainted plaster around the doorframe.

She closed the door quietly and through the open, glass inner door saw Liam's father talking to a woman sitting at a large kitchen table. She sat a little awkwardly but was surprisingly young, her eyes animated under shoulder-length hair. Her mouth was distended on one side, her speech hard to decipher.

Liam's father stood with his arm across her shoulders. "Betty, you haven't got any for me then?"

Becky caught a word in reply, probably "Wednesday". The woman reached from the table a piece of card on which was written a list of prices and offered it to him.

"So I need to get my days right next week if I want my Maltesers?" He looked at her, a bold, mock-flirting stare.

She laughed raucously and he kissed the top of her head before, with a wave, moving into the hallway, past two young women, one in a nurse's uniform. Becky followed him, her uncertain smile and wave a rare imitation of what Liam, in his hesitant way, had just done.

Liam's father had already signed her in but pointed to the hand wash. "I should have thought to tell you as well - you're a bit overdressed. It's hot enough here and you wait until we get upstairs."

The stairs creaked as she pulled off her fleece. She quickly adjusted her shirt that had come untucked but neither Liam nor his father had noticed. They weren't talking, as their quiet self-absorption seemed to preclude any curiosity in the outside world, in her - even, in a relaxed way, in each other. One of the glass panes of the door they went through was covered by an apocalyptic warning of the dangers of fire, the horrors highlighted by an exclamation mark for each sentence.

An alarm rang on the floor below, a light flashing on the numbered panel as Liam's father knocked quietly on a door on the other side of the landing, simultaneously pushing it open.

"Hello, Mum."

Liam's gran turned a fraction towards them. At first, Becky assumed it was indifference but, once they were fully in the room and facing her head-on, her face broke into a full, gentle smile. Her eyes looked uncertainly at the girl, her hand lifted and pointing - perhaps at her, perhaps past her.

"This is one of Liam's friends, Mum. It's all right for her to come in, isn't it? We didn't want to leave her in the car."

"Oh, no." The words were slurred but, from the nods and the continuing smile, intended to reassure.

"She's doing a project as well on food," Liam forced himself to add as he kissed his grandmother. Holding on to his hair, she, in turn, muttered something.

"She said you need it cut. Quite right, too, Mum."

She had let go of Liam and waved in the direction of the window.

"Did you want it open, Mum?"

"No." The word was clear enough.

"Do you want the picture moved?" Just as Mrs. Bennett, on their arrival, seemed to be working through a range of tiny chores and concerns that had accumulated since their last visit, so Liam and his father seemed to be responding with their own range of moves, as predictable as the opening gambits in a game of chess.

"You're mucking us about, aren't you?" as another guess failed and her eyelids closed in frustration.

"Is it the flowers?" Becky suggested and realised, as the old woman's mouth unclenched, that she was getting warmer. It was like the finding game she had played as a child. "Do they need water?"

The assenting nod was clear.

"Well done, girl. Good job somebody's got some brains. No, don't you worry - I'll do it."

Crossing the room on a diagonal from sink to window ledge would have taken no more than three of his normal strides but in his way were a commode, the corner of the bed, the alarm cable and the small table beside Mrs. Bennett's chair.

"Flipping obstacle course, Mum. They'll be asking to run the Grand National around here soon - and they'd get planning permission. No problem. Would keep the crowds down, though. Who's been moving your pictures, Mum?"

She looked blankly at her son. Becky could not tell if it was because Mrs. Bennett couldn't understand or because of her hearing or both. He waved at her the photograph of three women in military uniform and a switch was flicked in the old woman's eyes.

She stretched her arms, as far as she could, horizontally and then vertically; her voice was blocked in the mouth's confines, with only random words escaping.

"... man ... black ... "

"One of our coloured friends?"

Her head went down, her mouth tightening again. She rallied her determination for another effort. She tugged at her son's jumper and then, looking at Becky, with partially unclenched fingers waved her closer, near enough that she could touch the girl's patterned waistcoat.

"Was he wearing something like this?" Mrs. Bennett's eyes were pleading, teetering on the edge of a depressed resignation. "A suit?" The smile was immediate confirmation. "A man in a black suit?"

They all looked at each other. The concrete had been exhausted; the abstractions, the reasons for the presence of the man in a black suit in the room, his demeanour, his conclusions, were as inaccessible as if they had been locked behind a door with no key.

The chess game seemed to have reached stalemate: moves had dried up, the players temporarily sealed in immobility. Hands were poised but frozen, minds becalmed. In reality, no more than a second had passed until a knock on the door came as a reprieve.

27

Becky noticed how the conventions of normal life were suspended here - the knock was not followed by a delay to allow for a response, the permission to enter, but instead a small, cheerful man, perhaps a Filipino, pushed gently in with a tray and a nodded apology to the three of them.

He cleared a space on the table for the meal - fish and chips, cut into small pieces, a bowl of jelly and a mug of tea.

"Sorry. You like cup of tea?"

"No, no, we're fine. You've got enough on your plate."

If the pun was intended, it fell on deaf ears. The man smiled, backing out through the door, his foot stretching behind him to keep it open, and was then gone.

Mrs. Bennett was already using her fork as her son spoke to her.

"I hope it's all right, Mum, if Becky goes downstairs to see the cook. She's doing some school work on food and she needs some evidence on what they do here. To poison you."

"It's on nutrition, on how to achieve a balanced diet for different people - and that looks lovely."

Mrs. Bennett made no response to either of them, another convention that was suspended. Her energies were concentrated entirely on her food, on lifting a fragment of fish onto her fork and opening her mouth, eyes closed, to receive it. There was no room for the politeness that Becky was sure would have been there, even a year earlier.

As she walked down to the ground floor, she thought of her own grandfather and how, ten years younger probably than Mrs. Bennett, he would have been rushing down these stairs to escape the artificial heat. Ten years would make a huge difference to her, a teenager; ten years might alter his life irreparably.

The cook talked to her in chaotic detail while she cleared up, letting Becky take photographs of everything, giving her copies of fact sheets and guidance notes from a bulging cupboard, drying her hands repeatedly as she reached for something new.

At the top of the stairs, Becky stopped to gather a leaflet that had dropped on the floor and to rearrange the others that were about to head in the same direction. After the landing door closed behind her, she could hear Liam's voice through the wall, quiet, probably repetitive although the words themselves were indistinct, saying more in a short time than she could ever remember him doing. She knocked and, at his father's reply, pushed the door open.

In front of her was Liam feeding his grandmother, with - even in his hand - the jelly trying to slip off the spoon. Mrs. Bennett reminded her of a baby bird: passive, only the mouth insistent in its opening and shutting. Liam stood silent, eyes averted from the open door, the edge of a self-conscious smile just visible.

7

"Oh, no." Pollard stood in the open door. "I think I'm going to try this again." She allowed the door to close behind her and, in the corridor, despite its start-of-the-day bustle, took a deep breath and suppressed a smile.

Her second entrance was greeted by a rare but expectant silence. All the tables had been pushed to the side and the whole tutor group sat in a snaking line of chairs in the centre of the room.

"We're on a bus, miss." Ben was at the front as driver. "It's a single decker. Don't ask me why it's wiggly. All part of the cuts, I suppose. Can't get metal any more." He stared at her to gauge her reaction. "Toad -"

"Ah, ah, ah."

"Mr. Fletcher told us we had to sort out our behaviour on the buses or we'd be banned. So we thought we'd have a practice."

Her face, angular and tanned, gave no hint of what she was thinking.

"Where's your money, then?" She strode towards him, hand outstretched. "Don't give me that stuff about your bus pass. I haven't seen it any day this week. Cough up or you're off." She sniffed the air. "You've been smoking again, haven't you? You can see the sign as well as I can." She pointed at the thin air beside him.

"It's no good, Miss, he can't read."

"What do you mean, 'Miss' ? Are you questioning my masculinity? I drink ten pints a night and never touch any of your veggie muck." There was a giveaway, reciprocated flicker in her eyes as she glanced at Sarah. "And you? How come you're condescending to join us today? What's on after school, then? Another demo is it? Against the rising cost of eye shadow? Dear God, if I was your teacher, I wouldn't let you in with all that lagged on your eyes."

"But it's so expensive, Sir. It only looks lagged because the same stuff's been on there all week. It's either that or my six brothers and four sisters wouldn't have anything to eat. Show a bit of kindness, Sir."

Her mouth turned down, her eyes clenched in as close a simulation of crying as she could manage.

"All right, but get some new stuff for -"

The door opened behind her. Thankfully, it was neither Toad nor one of his recent appointees but Jim Siddons who was too tired to be officious and who, in any case, despite his age, retained a resigned measure of humour. Like a parent who finds his son in bed with his next door neighbour's wife and merely asks them to make the bed properly when they've finished, he looked at her.

"I need to see your School Council reps, just before the bell, in the hall." He looked past her, authority intact in the broad sweep of his eyes over the class, too broad for any individual eye contact, and then walked out.

"Come on, can't you see - we're nearly there? Oi, you, keep your litter on you - take it into school. Yes, you."

Liam, who had been doing or saying nothing, looked up at her and smiled.

"Right, we're there." Her voice changed pitch. "O. K. Back to reality. Two minutes to the bell. Room back to normal, please. Jerry and Kirsty off to the hall. Without any chat, the two of you, please."

As the rush subsided, she walked up and down the room, adjusting the position or the angle of tables. "Sit at your own table, please, once it's done."

She had ten seconds to savour the room's restoration before the bell rang out. A handful, mainly girls, stayed for their first lesson of the day, changing seats to get their favourite positions. As the rest trooped out, Ben grinned at her.

"Good laugh, Miss."

She nodded, reassured, and smiled back.

"That's it for the day now, mind. It's out of your system - I don't want any complaints about my winding you up."

He looked back at her.

"Please."

Break-time would tell her if he had taken any notice.

8

"What am I supposed to do then? Defend what they're doing? And there's another half-assed demonstration on the way. Do I go?" Kirsty sat, bolt upright in the chair, her hands clenched. "That sounds pathetic, doesn't it? But I'm no bloody economist and some of them are such smartasses."

"Come on, it can't be that many." Her mother smiled as she cleared the table. "I can think of two at most who've got the brains."

"Yeah but as well there are the others who pick up the slogans - and I agree with them. It all just seems fucking stupid."

"Kirsty!"

"Sorry - but it's all right for you. People you work with," she anticipated her mother's disagreement, "or some of them anyway, must want to say things but instead keep them buttoned-up. One of the advantages of being old."

There was no trace of humour in her voice. She picked at a loose thread in her sleeve, missing her mother's glance back over her shoulder, the eyes raised, resigned to not making any protest that would disrupt the girl's flow.

"The worst thing is Sarah clamming up on me. I come in and they don't all look away - there's nothing personal about it - but when they rant on about whatever new horror has just blown up, all agreeing with each other, Sarah just stays quiet. And she would've been the one to start it off, I know she would. Not against Dad, she wouldn't do that, but the issue in general." She grabbed her own hair and shook her head. "And I just say nothing. Yes, it does happen," her smile was in response to her mother's, "and it would be nice, wouldn't it? Oh, shit!"

"You don't have to tow the family line. You know that, don't you?" She had left the dishes to sit opposite Kirsty. "Mainly because there isn't one. We both want you to think for yourself and if that means taking a different position from Dad's, so be it."

"But what is his position? We hardly ever see him - I know what you're going to say and I know why we're here and not in London for the good of my education and because he's committed to the comprehensive system and all the rest of it -"

"And all of that is true."

"I know, I know, and it's not a great laugh for you either." She paused to see the strain in her mother's eyes. "I know it's harder now being a Lib Dem MP and all that stuff - but what is his position?"

"It depends."

"Oh God. That's what they all say."

"No, not that, not that at all." There was a first hint of impatience in her voice as she stood up and tidied a tea towel away. Her eyes stayed fixed on the open drawer. "It depends entirely on the issue."

"Sorry. He's not ... like the rest of them. Sit down again, will you?"

She stretched her arm out towards her mother who started

talking as she squeezed Kirsty's hand. "I could give you a list - what he thinks they're right on and where he thinks they're wrong. That would give you his 'position' if he's talking to me - or you - or the ones he's closest to up there. But he almost can't have a public 'position' any more. It's not like a marriage, no matter what they said at the start, with all that hysteria about honeymoons and the rest of it. He can say what he thinks, within limits - so can the party. But if he steps over those limits, it could be a resignation issue. Not that it's anywhere near that at the moment."

Kirsty looked at her, unsure if she was merely getting the standard parental reassurance. There was nothing garrulous in her response, subdued by the final ebb and flow in her mother's words.

"It can't be much fun." She laughed raucously at the banality of her own words. "Not like you or me." She saw her mother's face lighten. "Which brings me back to where I started. The thing they're still going on about is these NHS reforms. I probably know what I think but does Dad feel the same way?" She looked up with another laugh. "Nice and brief, if you can. All the organisational stuff is wasted on me."

9

It was three o'clock and Goldsmith was sitting in his chair at home with his eyes shut. He had considered lying down in bed but feared that sleep would take over. 'Fear' and 'sleep' were now inextricably linked. In the late evening, there was the fear of not sleeping that he tried to neuter by a range of tricks that he had talked through with patients; at two or three in the morning, there was the fear of not getting back off to sleep, the fifteen minutes with a hot drink and the light on, reading; and, on getting up, there was the fear of how he would manage the pressures of the day, how he would concentrate well enough to listen, retain his patience and not make a serious mistake.

Even now his fear of a smothering drowsiness kept pricking what could only be fifteen minutes peace behind closed eyelids. His mind conjured other disturbances: the cracked windscreen was pigeonholed easily enough but, in recreating his drive on his rounds through the countryside - the unevenness of the hedges that he could predict and therapeutically reconstruct, the sea at points as background to fields and slopes against which he could paint in houses, most of them whitewashed - suddenly a picture superimposed itself of a man dying in one of those cottages. Dying in a way which could not be alleviated, dying at a cost in his unproductive time that could no longer be justified against their 'business plan' - and the calm behind his eyelids was broken.

Broken, as well, by a sound that, at first, he thought was only inside his head. Like a letter dropping through the letter-box - but it was too late even for the postman and his shorts. Feet running away from the door which the postman would never have done, in case he missed a conversation to further delay the delivery. As he rose from his chair, he envied him that pace, that relaxation, a relic of a kinder time.

It was a letter of sorts in an unsealed, recycled envelope. His name was written neatly enough across the front. Inside, there were two juxtaposed photographs: one of a striking young woman in her early twenties, a mass of black curling hair framing a finely-structured, sun-tanned, thin but healthy face, with, underneath, the words, "Why not like this?"; the other he knew to be of the same woman but, without that existing knowledge, he would never have made the link. Amy Goddard had lost all her hair; her skin had a pallor that accentuated the delicacy of her jaw line and dulled the vitality of her eyes to a greyness. Below it were the words, "Why this?"

There was no accompanying detail but none was needed. Amy had become the local cause célèbre. Her family had been a running sore in the village for years. Her father had left shortly after the fourth child was born; her mother was a blowsy version of Amy, the defined facial structure overwhelmed by years of excessive eating and drinking. Her brothers and sisters were always blamed for any petty vandalism or theft. He remembered being called, not as a doctor but as a neighbour, to a disturbance in the park where, on the swings, Amy's older sister had been doing something unspeakable, one at a time, at a rate starting at ten pence, for a rapidly growing and increasingly rowdy group of adolescents.

Amy, somehow, without alienating her family, had bucked the seemingly inevitable trend, the route that both genes and conditioning had preordained for her. She had spirit aplenty - there were reports of scrapes in school - but most of it was channelled productively. She had worked hard there and had gone on to a degree course at Whitcross College. Not a time-filler either: she was within a year of qualifying as a paramedic when the cancer was diagnosed.

Now she felt she needed Herceptin and according to the policy - he could not recall who was now responsible for it - the drug was not appropriate for someone whose cancer had 'only' reached the stage of Amy's. To Ian had fallen the task of explaining this to her. He would have done it well, he had no doubt of that, but words behind closed doors were powerless to combat the combined forces that rapidly coalesced against them: the emotional vitality, albeit sentimentalised, with which Amy could convey the grimness of her illness; the organisational energy of her friends; the fury of her mother; the campaigning skills of older people who would, as a rule, have had nothing to do with the Goddards but saw in it a focal point for their opposition to the local impact of the reforms; and the growing furore in the national media as a succession of calamities emerged across the country.

In another time, he would have welcomed this upsurge in political activity in a normally passive and stolid community but not now, not in his present circumstances. And yet perhaps it was nothing to do with timing. Perhaps anything at any point in his older life that compromised his conscience, his sense of his own personal safety, would have had the same effect. What came first?

The mental and physical frailty or the pressure?

Standing with the piece of paper in his hand, the picture of Amy Goddard next to his thumb, he knew how different he had been at the same age - ready to take on anything, confident in his judgement and his ability to sustain it in the face of criticism, with a body and a mind that did not let him down.

Instead, now he stood, half-exposed by the panels of frosted glass, immobile until the merest glance at his watch reminded him that he was already late, not for a patient but for the preparation before surgery. He shook himself and reached for his case.

10

"They get better as they go on, don't they, Miss? Or is it just that they get closer to where we are now?"

"Wait till you see the next one - the last one - and then I'll explain what we did in the lessons you missed."

'Should I Stay or Should I Go' blared out as, on the screen, the pool game hurtled towards another victory for Levi jeans. Sarah grinned, despite herself.

"See - the one before that was more up-to date but that one wasn't."

"Yeah, yeah - I know what you mean about the setting but the way they're shot is different."

Emily Pollard nodded. Her Christian name was restored when she reached this time of day, the corridors quiet, apart from a scattered few like Sarah who were catching up.

"That was what we looked at when you were away. I ask myself 'Do I need to bother?' or will you tell me what you missed?"

"Sorry."

"No need to apologise but it's one reason you ought to be in class - you see things that a lot of the others don't." She paused. "I know we haven't had the note yet -" she held up her hand - "I'm sure it'll come but it wasn't because you were ill, was it?"

"I have got better - miles better than when I was in Year Eight and Nine."

"Look - your time's all but run out. 'Better' isn't good enough, is it?"

"I think it is, Miss. You wouldn't believe how easy it is to catch up. There's not a lot of thinking going on - English, a bit in History and that's about it."

They both smiled. "That's not the point, is it? And you know it. And you still haven't said why you were away. Not that you need to be a genius to work it out. February 25th - you're away, as are Tom Sanders, Richie Donniston and Lisa McMichael. Surprise, surprise - same pattern on January 10th. It's this anti-coalition group, isn't it?"

Sarah said nothing but nodded.

"What do you tell your father: the note he wrote last time; the note that'll be on its way soon? He wouldn't approve at all, would he?"

"No, but he doesn't know. He's hardly ever there so I tell him I've been ill and he writes the note." She shrugged her shoulders. "He never really asks - he doesn't care - and you know he doesn't think much of school, the way he had that almighty go at you last year."

"He would care about this, though, wouldn't he?"

She remembered the parents' evening when she had called Toad of all people because of King's tirade, the accusations of political indoctrination, the fist-banging on the table, her own tears, the weakness which she could not excuse or forget. So different from the year before when she had been made only marginally less

41

uncomfortable by his chair being pulled too close, the stare longer than necessary.

"Yes, but Mum knows and she thinks it's a good idea. She'd probably come along herself if she wasn't too old. You might just squeeze in, Miss, if you wanted to."

Pollard adjusted her top. "We're not talking about my political affiliations, are we?"

"We could do. You're the one who says every public action is a political one."

"I'd better keep it private then, hadn't I? Look, I'm being serious - you've got to do everything you can to make the best of what you've got."

"All right, I know." She looked at the frozen screen. "You're getting like them, though," and she pointed at the television, "dealing in clichés."

Sarah turned to gauge the teacher's reaction: only an exaggeratedly sharp intake of breath, a nervousness in her eyes - but no more words.

11

"There always has been a public foot path there, Mr.Andrews. My grandfather could remember walking down to the cove that way as a child himself and in the autumn there would be brambles, thick with blackberries, almost blocking it. Now, that was all right because it was natural and it would always be cut back in the spring" - she was capable of prolonging anything, an unwelcome guest who has opened the door to leave but still finds a new conversational triviality that balloons arbitrarily on the doorstep – "but this is utterly different. Under the old planning guidelines, they would never have got away with it because there is no way that building is intended just for commercial use. I know the developers can now do whatever they like but, the footpath, it's just plain dangerous for it to be rerouted onto the road."

What might have been bright, curious eyes in a young woman now had a hint of the obsessive. As she carried on, her stare was accentuated by a slight forward tilt of the head.

"Don't you agree?"

"I'm sorry. I don't quite follow."

Rather than appearing annoyed, she looked pleased that she

had caught out an MP, someone whose status was supposedly superior to hers. "It must be what you remember yourself - when you were a child."

"The traffic's certainly heavier." Tom Andrews nodded and smiled. If it was a guess, it worked. She resumed her narrative like the local bus service that meandered through every remote village rather than take the main road itself.

The obstructed footpath proved to be her sole reason for attending the surgery and she was placated by his promise to look into the matter and see her in a month's time. He saw her out, the last of the morning, the last of several preoccupied with local planning issues.

As he walked through to the office, he sighed. Of the rest, one had raised the threatened closure of the cottage hospital, one a reported new cut to the coastguard service and three, separately and apparently not part of any campaigning group, had raised the functioning of the health centres, one on behalf of a specific patient, the other two on behalf of the elderly and what they perceived as the likely impact of the centres' policies on such a numerically large group in the community.

"Had a good morning?" Graham Lewis pushed through the half-open door with an armful of folders. "Try again. Had a good morning?"

"Sorry - plenty of food for thought. Not bad, though." The response was tugged from him by the agent's energy: the filing cabinet, on top of which was a bowl of fading daffodils, was already open and the bundle of folders starting to diminish.

"Shouldn't need to do this, I know, but done it all my life and don't intend to stop now. You might want to look at that one. A few letters as well but the rest are saved on the computer." He looked up from his filing. "You wouldn't believe the abuse. Have you got to the bit about 'scum of the earth'? All over a footpath."

Andrews put the circular down. "I know. You've just passed one of them - the one you saved to the end as a treat for me."

"Puts you in a bit of a quandary - or, at least, it should do." Lewis laughed, shutting the filing cabinet door, his stomach protruding, his head just visible through the daffodils. "Although, as such an exemplary Lib Dem, you can't win on any of the national issues that are rearing their ugly Tory heads down here, you could make some gains on a purely local one - if there was one that was unifying. But there isn't. And if you take sides on this, you lose as many votes as you gain."

"Oh, come on, Graham," he gave him a warning glance, "you know I wouldn't touch it with a bargepole. Trouble is the ones that matter are the national ones when they become local."

"Can't do it. Even bigger quandary. Sitting tight and towing the line is a recipe for a lost seat at the next election. Kicking up a fuss is no better. Disloyalty is the cardinal sin until the final days when you might get away with it. But these days aren't quite the final ones, I hope. Some of us need the money."

He was staring out of the window. "If it's agreed policy, implemented nationally, yes. If it's not and someone else can be blamed, it might work. After all, we're supposed to be showing how we're different."

"Sounds surprisingly unethical for the noble local boy. If you can think of one, you ought to be doing Calamity's job. Coup from remotest Cornwall." He grinned. "Do something useful and look at those."

Andrews scanned one of the letters. Someone had unearthed an unspent surplus in a Devon consortium which, the writer claimed, had found its way into the pockets of the doctors and the company acting on their behalf.

45

"That's the one, isn't it, where you're asked to provide assurances that the same 'exploitation' isn't occurring here?"

He shrugged. "Another open goal for Labour. They probably sent it, anyway."

"Skip those. Two people saying the same thing - their treatment has been postponed for so long that they reckon it amounts to cancellation. I've done the replies - sympathy and not much else."

"Are they all about the bloody Health Service?"

"What do you think? That's another one there - but it's also about everything else under the sun. You know - whatshisname Oliver who runs the residential home in St. Budoc."

"Couldn't organise the proverbial piss-up."

"Can't organise his ideas, either. He keeps on about these immigration quotas that are leaving them short-staffed."

"Look forward to seeing what you're going to write about that. Another test for -" At the ringing of the phone, Lewis raised his eyes in exasperation.

"No, we do not have any problems with our computer. The only problem that we do have -"

Andrews clicked the red button. "Tact and patience - what you tell me normally. What about what he's saying here? That these criteria for Health support are not being applied properly?"

"He says there's the evidence - and he gives bits of it - but you'd have to take it with a pinch of salt."

"It does fit this area, though, doesn't it?"

"I know what you're thinking - and there's nothing like a solid citizen having to give up a home that a working life has been devoted to."

"Just draft a reply asking if I can come out to see him. Usual bland stuff - gets you out of any of the complexities."

"As long as you check it out properly. Get the facts wrong and it could blow up in your face."

"Another job for you, then." He waved towards the door.

"Most kind." Lewis backed out of the room in mock deference. "All the same, don't pin your hopes on it," and his wave became a salute.

Andrews replaced the letter on the pile and ignored the others. He sat, arms folded, staring into the middle distance.

"God, you look miserable. You haven't budged, not even the eyes, for about ten seconds. I need a coffee." Kirsty, standing in the doorway, laughed. "And I haven't got any money. My parents don't give me any."

"I'm a bit pushed … " He obviously thought better of it without a glance at her face. "Go on, then. Sparky's is okay and it's just around the corner."

He gave her a kiss before checking that the desk was tidy. "Come on." He put his arm around her shoulders. "I've got some money. Shame about your parents."

As he locked the door, his tone changed. "Your friend, Becky - you've met her father, haven't you? What's he like?"

12

A light jacket was draped across a kitchen chair, a handbag open, neat not careless, on the table. A shiny, imitation leather purse and a diary, blue with bright red and yellow overlapping circles, sat confident under her gaze. Sarah picked up each in turn. Both were light and insubstantial, not bulging with the weight of years - like her mother's, with its arbitrary receipts, the scribbled notes she had written herself. Perhaps it was her mother's scruples that she had inherited which stopped her from opening either purse or diary; perhaps it was a desire to shroud the squalid business in anonymity. Self-protection either way: a moral superiority retained; a person - or people, it didn't matter - more easily stored away and not protruding from bitter memory's pigeon-hole.

The sounds, too, from upstairs, were, in their inception, as anonymous as the intermittent rumbling of the dishwasher. A creaking, a movement in the bed, perhaps on the floor, followed by a silence. She looked around her for any evidence of haste. There was nothing, no clothes shed in a frenzy, no keys dropped to disturb the appearance of tidiness.

At the bottom of the stairs, she waited until the pattern of the sounds altered. The creaking resumed, accompanied by a groan that she recognised as her father's - but no sound from whoever she happened to be. She pondered for a moment - 'whomsoever' might have been a better literary choice for a better personal climactic point. It was only an instant of objectivity before her face tightened again at another male groan: so even that was no different.

She moved onto the stairs, stopping immediately, checking her silence as she shifted her weight lightly onto the front of her foot. And so, despite her growing anger, she edged, toes stretching, laboured in her forced patience, stair by stair, upwards. Two steps into her tightrope walk, she froze, when above her head a movement - at first, she feared it was feet on the floor - set the ceiling cracking. A faint female moan - she had to acknowledge it - was all that followed.

The creaking, the moaning heightened both the tension in her face and her confidence that any slight sound of hers would pass unheard until, two steps from the top, when his room was almost in view, she stopped. She realised she had no idea what she was going to do. If the door was closed, was she going to open it? If she did, should she scream at them or try to stay calm? If it was open ...

Her feet had decided for her, like a dog pulling its owner on regardless, and she found herself at the top, looking through the open door at the quilt piled on the floor - and at the bed. Diagonally across it lay her father, his calloused feet closest to her, a verruca below his big toe, the bare skin of his calf muscles, encircled by matted hair - and his buttocks, spotty and clenched, thrusting slowly into white thighs spread wide to let him in.

It was only a moment. Of her, she saw only her legs, white arms that ended in hands weighted by rings that cut into her father's shoulder blades - and black hair splayed from her averted head beneath his face.

She stepped back onto the stairs, out of sight, and leaned against the wall, a sudden smile on her face. Farce had removed all tension, a peculiar catharsis. The sound of her own breathing was masked by the growing creaking, the quickening bouncing of those middle-aged cheeks. Timing was all. She felt for the mobile in her pocket and carefully made her way back downstairs.

On the landline phone, she adjusted the ring volume to maximum and then, as the grinding upstairs appeared to be reaching climax, dialled her home number on her mobile. As those pallid hands upstairs might even have been clutching and covering his pimpled buttocks, the phone rang out, strident, long enough for them to hear before she answered.

"Oh, of course. I'll tell him. The next thirty minutes."

She put the phone down and shouted, unnecessarily as all was silent upstairs. "Dad! Speedyflow or someone like that. They're doing an inspection of the drains. Routine one. Reports of a blockage somewhere."

She did not know if her silence was any more secure than theirs. It might have been better if her anger had not been stilled in that momentary poise which left her vulnerable to doubt. If he charged down the stairs in a rage, that would be one thing; if he came down with her, a façade of permanence, how could she not shrink away in embarrassment?

Instead, it was neither. After a barely audible drone of conversation, light footsteps criss-crossed the ceiling above until they took a firmer course onto the landing.

She waited for the woman to emerge: her feet in the plainest of shoes, a full-length skirt that one of her young teachers aspiring to seriousness might have worn, a simple black top, a surprising absence of jewellery apart from the clumsy decoration of her fingers and shoulder-length hair.

Each step down the stairs was quick, each glance embarrassed. At the bottom, her eyes dropped to the floor and she muttered an apology before turning to the table and her handbag.

As she found her car keys, she pivoted back towards Sarah, lifting her head. She could not have been much more than twenty-five. She was pretty - it was obvious why he had picked her out, if selection came into it - but her clothes did not quite balance each other and her face was a little pinched from too much dieting.

"No, I do mean it. I am sorry. It can't be nice for you." She smiled tentatively like someone for whom apology and self-deprecation came naturally. Not very bright - "niceness" was a ridiculous understatement - but Sarah could not rouse any anger or spite against her. What was the difference between them? Not much in age, not much in vulnerability.

She felt tears coming and the woman stepping towards her, a hand with those rings outstretched.

"No, no, please, I'll be fine." She raised herself to her full height, hands pushing against the air in front of her. She tried to think of some feature to disparage, the legs, the arms, but nothing would come. It no longer seemed fair to either of them.

Her body language, though, must have been unambiguous, for the woman turned, taking her bag and jacket, to the door, with a final, apologetic glance back at Sarah before she let herself out. Even in that she seemed uncertain, pushing the door before pulling it.

"Bloody Speedyflow." His voice reverberated from the top of the stairs, his tone uncertain - it could have been anger or frustration or, on another day, grudging amusement at the wit of someone who, he knew, could rival him.

"I've seen it all now." He was still fastening his belt as he walked down the stairs.

"So have I." Her voice was flat, all defiance drained from it.

"Is this what you do in your Drama lessons, or whatever they call them now? Look at how to use a situation to embarrass someone?" He took hold of her face, firmly enough for her to realise how strong but fine her jawbone was. "How to find the humour in the everyday. Isn't that what one of your teachers said?"

"What if humour is the only way I can deal with it?" She sensed his grip slackening and pulled her face free, raising her eyes to him.

"I couldn't give a shit about all this pseudo self-analysis. I know we'll get the 'What about me?' bit in a minute but what about her? She's way past school, she hasn't got a job."

"So what are you? A bloody social worker? Such concern but not enough for you to stop swearing at your own daughter." She paused, cursing herself for her own stupidity. Why not have a full-blooded row? Why tarnish it, compromise it with self-pity?

Too late: her words had had their usual effect. He put his hands on the back of his head and stretched his elbows out as if his neck was hurting. "I just didn't think you were coming back at this sort of time."

"So -"

"No, I didn't mean it like that but I have to have some time clear for my work. Well, not work - you know what I mean."

He even dared to use his naughty boy smile. She could never figure out if it was an automatic reflex or if he thought it would stop her lecturing him when he became a parody of himself. Either way, it didn't work.

"Work! And you put down what I do in school!" She stepped closer to him, adrenalin overcoming any fear. "She was the one working. She seemed okay but that's not the point. It's prostitution without the money, isn't it?"

"I'm not even going to answer that." His face had set, his mouth slightly open in disbelief. She watched him walk slowly back upstairs, adjusting his jeans as he went.

13

"Oh, Jesus, I'm not going over there. Those skanky losers."

As she crossed the road, Becky looked behind her. Apart from Sarah, the others who had been waiting for the traffic to stop had resisted the appeal of MacBrumbies and slouched back into the college, delivering an unintended blow to the profits of junk food on the other side of the roundabout.

Why anyone would walk away, she could not imagine. The 'skanky losers' were so thin on the ground that she wondered if the march had been cancelled. The luminous yellow police presence was there, bunched in relaxed pockets, one of them talking to three older women who she hoped were going to be part of the protest. She had time to count: there were eighteen police, probably more waiting near County Hall, and only thirteen potential demonstrators.

"We should've started by now. Perhaps the rest are inside." Becky's voice was momentarily flat before she turned to see Ben crossing the road, on his own, behind them. She waved as Sarah, despite also turning, sought to restore a realistic pessimism.

"They won't be. Why start the protest by helping the profits of the very people you're protesting against?"

Ben had caught them up but barely stopped. "I'll catch you up later. I've just got to get some chips."

"Oh, shit - but get a move on." Reluctantly, Sarah smiled. "Hopes too high again."

She walked over to a woman in her early twenties who stopped unfurling a banner to pull out a large handful of fliers from a bin liner. Becky held back, self-conscious in the absence of a crowd but suddenly aware that a hand had tapped her on the shoulder.

"You ought to be working."

"What are you doing here?" Becky looked at her granddad, her anxiety tempered by relief at the company.

"Why not? I've had my run and thought I'd get some more exercise. What about you, then? I don't know what Dad would say."

"He'd approve of it in principle but still think I'd be better with my head in a book." A sudden gust of wind blew her hair across her face as Sarah returned.

"We're on the way now and -"

"You don't know my granddad, do you?"

"Oh, sorry. I thought -"

"Don't worry. Nice to meet you." Becky hoped his eyes were not too penetrating. "It's easy for someone of my age to be altruistic but we've got to do our bit, haven't we? You're still a bit isolated here, though, aren't you? Hardly a mass movement."

"Time to go." Becky tapped her granddad on the elbow. The woman Sarah had spoken to had started banging a small drum and was walking towards the main road, striking up a chant of "What do we want? No more cuts." Her voice was given a half-hearted response from the stragglers behind her.

"This is it, I suppose."

The policeman next to Becky smiled benignly. "You're not the decoy runners, then?"

She smiled back at him. He wasn't much older than her and the only good-looking one in the group who marshalled them on their way, at the front and the back. Better-looking, with his thick, carefully-cropped moustache, than the stooped man from the local paper, with a wispy beard that had never got beyond its infancy, who asked them to pose for a photo.

"Big chance, Becky. We'll be there with the entrants in the village fete, the horticultural shows."

"Oh, God, I hadn't thought of that."

"Don't worry about it - glib alliterative headline and then it'll be gone. That's all it is: today, a minor distraction to traffic; in the paper next week, another fragment of the county's life that doesn't disturb its equilibrium."

As the man wandered off, three cameras around his neck, checking the images on one of them, a woman, streaks of purple in her hair, briefly took his place, a single camera in her hand and no request for a group pose. Becky's eyes flinched at the flash, unnecessarily sharp against the blue sky, and then watched as the woman repeated the sudden but steady movement of her hand.

"Not her," Sarah had shouted to herself, covering her face and slashing her free hand through the air at the woman. For an instant, to Becky she seemed comical, a child blindfolded in a game, warding off imagined threats but otherwise rooted to the ground. Her grandfather, however, changed her mind in another instant: he had moved to the front and, despite an occasional glancing blow from Sarah's hand and repeated shots from the photographer, enough to fill an album, was calmly addressing what he could see of the woman's face behind the camera.

"You have no right to take these pictures."

No response as the clicking continued.

"You presumably have identification as a journalist."

No response again, no change in her behaviour as the policeman with the moustache stepped in beside her.

"You need to move on, sir, if you are part of the demonstration."

"That is precisely what I want to do but I do not, without my permission, want -"

The woman's camera was dashed to the ground, Ben's shoulder barging into her raised elbow, his foot then kicking the camera against the pavement kerb. When she ran to retrieve it, Sarah shook her head furiously at him.

"No, Ben."

He glanced back at her before kicking the camera onto the chippings under one of MacBrumbies' stunted but manicured shrubs and raising his fist towards the approaching policeman, a vain gesture as his arm was gripped from behind .

On another day, in another place, it would have been the catalyst for a riot. Not here, though, Becky thought. What passed for a protest had, a few seconds ago, seen the few who had bothered to turn up strung out along the road like runners, or loafers, in an enforced cross-country at school. Now they were reeled in on invisible string towards the raised voices behind them, slowly, haphazardly, unsure of what was happening or of whether it was worth the effort of backtracking.

The first of them watched, like Becky, as Ben struggled, for a few seconds, to free himself - before Sarah almost pressed her face into his.

"Look, idiot, stand still. This isn't one of your stupid gangster movies. Stand still and you'll be all right."

Her words - and his habitual response to her normally smiling abuse - did more to settle him than the restraining arm behind him. He watched, only an occasional twitch in his free shoulder, as the woman cleaned her camera with a tissue and scrolled through pictures she had already taken. There was in her no sign of agitation, no hint that anything was damaged, as she stepped back, poised to take a picture of Ben until the policeman placed his hand over the lens, with the muttered words, "Not yet", and gestured her away.

"You have no need to restrain him any more."

Becky watched her grandfather, reasoned, an unthreatening distance from the other officer, his words slow but not metronomic. He had stepped forward once more after recoiling initially, as everyone in the family would have done, from the sudden aggression.

"That, sir, isn't a decision for you."

"Clearly, it's not my decision but this young man can stand there without your holding him in an armlock."

"You aren't the one holding him. I can feel what he's like." The officer's eyes were not on her granddad, his words doubly dismissive as he glanced behind him and towards the road to his left.

"You first have to find out what's happened here." The officer continued to look away. "Our photographs have been taken without our permission by that young woman." He looked around but was unable to see her in the sparse crowd. "The woman whom your colleague prevented from photographing the young man you're holding at the moment."

Again, there was no response. Ben had visibly relaxed, his shoulders no longer tense, anaesthetised by the calmness of the old man's words. Not so for Sarah whose face was animated by an urge to intervene but who held back, perhaps sensing that a second voice would only fracture their moral ascendancy.

"I think you owe us an answer." The voice remained level, with no trace of irritation.

"We'll find out what happened." The officer's voice was equally level but heavy with boredom at what he had to do. He nodded as the policeman behind him whispered something, curt but apparently expected, after which he started to move away, pulling Ben with him.

"That is not an answer. You find out what happened before you cart someone off, not after."

"If you just leave it to us, sir." The policeman touched him reassuringly on the arm as a van braked sharply in front of them. The rear doors opened automatically and Ben was dragged inside, legs kicking, recoiling from the impact of his feet on the metal floor.

Sarah lunged through Becky's half-hearted restraint but failed to reach the van as her arms were pinned separately in the air. She swore over and over again, raging at their failure, probably at her own lapsing into the inarticulate, watching as the van turned in the car park and then sped out past them.

"What do we do now?" Becky's question was plaintive, answered only by her granddad's touch on her arm.

"Where's he been taken?"

"To the station, sir."

"You're telling me what I could have worked out for myself. Which station?"

"That, I'm afraid, is an operational matter."

"Is this the way the rest of this march is going to be policed?"

"If there are disturbances, it's our duty to respond. Now, I'd be grateful if you'd move on."

While he stared at the back of the retreating policeman, Sarah kicked the bollard in frustration.

"Have you got a car here?"

"Yes. It'll be a long walk, though, I'm afraid."

"Can we try the local station first?"

His nod was immediate - and she glanced at the others, none of whom she knew. "You lot carry on here. We can't let them win completely."

They seemed more interested in commiseration, in conducting their own wake, rather than the seemingly futile walk towards the city centre, but Sarah's glare decided them and away they shuffled, their voices briefly animated until they were drowned by the road noise.

14

"She's bloody well not." The glare in Sarah's eyes made Ben's head recoil, a stock gesture whose bland appearance of shock was undermined by a wariness in his eyes that he had overstepped the mark. "Anyway, she's my mother, for God's sake. And if she was a lesbian, what would it matter?"

"No, it wouldn't, it wouldn't." His words were barely audible.

"You need to wake up. Get real, whatever you'd call it. Stop pissing about all the time."

She walked on, in her annoyance trying to get in front of him but failing. Clinging on, he must have made them look like one of those married couples, walking, unspeaking, unloving. She grimaced: the comparison hurt.

As for him, he was incorrigible. The day before, they had got to the police station just when he emerged. He had not registered what they had told him. "Something about future conduct," was all he could manage, brushing it off as insignificant. Far more important for him had been the handcuffs they had put on him in the van, a tangible souvenir of his mistreatment. He had come up with no precise recollection of when they were removed: "the good-looking one did it in the interview room - that was what they called it."

Already she had seen that what should have been a new focus for a campaign, for letters to the local papers, was blurring in his imprecision. With a few prompts, she had dug out clearly enough what had happened at the start but, after that, where was the news interest in hearing that "a well hot officer" had asked "a load of questions"? He could joke about it, enhance his reputation, his modest notoriety - and that was it.

He had kept telling her not to take it so seriously, not to take anything so seriously, and her flaring up had, for him, no doubt justified his criticism of her - what he had described, in a rare clarity, as her self-righteousness.

"I'm going to see her, anyway. It's down here." She edged across the pavement, ready to turn left. "You're welcome to come." Her lifeless tone contradicted her words.

"No, I don't think so. I'm going down the park. Look, I'm sorry." His words were so gabbled that, at first, she missed the apology.

"Forget it. Just try not to say the same bloody thing on Monday." She half-smiled at him, like a tolerant teacher, and the glimmer of forgiveness was enough for him to walk away with a primary school skip and a rueful backward glance.

Her anger, though dissipated, left a residue of dissatisfaction coating the world around her. The granite buildings would once have been part of a striking, traditional country town, not elegant but stolid; now they were cheapened by the viral attacks of brash but fading paint, charity shops and worn signs offering cut-price baguettes and happy-hour beer.

Most of the people, most of the things in her life underwent the same corruption by perception. Although her mum said it was a form of depression, the bleakness did not cover everyone. If life tried to be a black-and-white film, Ben was one of the majority absorbed into its greyness, with the few like Becky still flashes of bold red and blue against the monochrome background.

She stood to one side to allow a woman, ten years older than her at most, to pass with her buggy, a double-decker or whatever it was called, in which two children slept. She knew that didn't have to be her lot - she would have fought it if it was - yet could see nothing in the woman beyond a humdrum routine of meeting expectations. A decade earlier, she must have had expectations of her own.

Ideas, ideals were a partial solace. Her mum, with a smile, called it escapism but always seemed proud, pleased - less so when Sarah had told her once, a wry smile in return, that her daughter was her own form of escapism. They had ended up, though, agreeing that defining reality was too difficult for either of them.

The street where her mum lived, however, would not have been a problem. Ideals were in short supply in the blue recycling boxes, their soggy, coloured cardboard and drinks cans overflowing across the tangled, square patches of grass and unkempt shrubbery. Not all of them, not her mum's, but enough to make your heart sink.

A familiar, brisk wave levered her out of her introspection: her mum was standing outside the alleyway that led to her flat. Sarah's step quickened towards her as she edged away, in a suppressed hurry.

"Come on, girl. I'll tell you why in a minute." She paused to hug her daughter, her eyes fixing her face, a cursory examination. "Can't go in, I'm sorry. Usual chaos - not there, but work. It's all going ahead - 'outsourcing' our jobs. What sort of language is that? I may not be as bright as you but I can still understand what they're trying to say."

She smiled to a couple they passed. "Much better, thanks. You're looking well too. Sorry I can't stop." She looked back over her shoulder. "They've moved in next door. Really nice but will talk all day. Anyway, we've been called to a meeting - or, as they put it, it's there if we want it - to find out what's going to happen. One of your father's mates is going to 'clarify' what their intentions are. What was that phrase one of your teachers used - 'the arrogance of power'?" Sarah nodded. "I can tell you now: pay will remain the same but only to start with - and our pensions, in effect, will go. Kevin wants us to turn out in force. Not that I needed telling but some of them do. Ginny - you know her, don't you? Brilliant nurse but doesn't have a clue what this is all about."

"It's the same at school." She thought of Ben, although the word 'brilliant' hardly applied to him, but said no more.

"It must be bad if you can't stir them up." A sudden grin on her face, she wrapped her arm around Sarah's shoulder, without slackening her stride. "How's your work going? Easy as ever?"

"It's all right. Be glad to get to college, though." She hesitated. "Can I come to the meeting with you?"

"Don't see why not. You won't be able to say anything - if you can manage that - but it'll boost numbers."

They had stopped at the pedestrian crossing. "You wouldn't have said yes if it had been -"

"No. If it'd been him speaking, no. All too exposed, I suppose."

As the cars stopped for them to cross, she raised her eyebrows, uncertain, apologetic, and then squeezed her daughter's arm.

The hotel seemed quiet as they entered, not that she had any way of judging. A receptionist, barely older than she was, offered to help them with the information board. It was not her assistance they needed but a code breaker's. Two meetings were scheduled in the conference rooms, one run by Questor Pierce, the other by ISH Holdings. Neither mentioned the hospital, care, the NHS; both were to start at 2.30.

Standing in front of the conference rooms, on opposite sides of a first floor landing, was no more helpful. Divided by floor to ceiling windows that looked out across fields, no doubt 'rolling gently' in the hotel brochure, two women, each dressed in black, each slim and in her mid-twenties, stood next to seemingly identical wooden tables laden with small, shining folders, pens, name badges - and a signing-in clipboard resting informally but neatly at the side.

They approached the woman on the right, the one with the marginally less-pronounced suntan. Her face showed a moment's confusion when Sarah's mum mentioned the hospital and then reset itself in its confidence.

"Well, you're welcome here if your aspiration is to invest in a private pension." She glanced at their coats. "If not, I think my colleague over there will be able to help you. Rebecca, these ladies are yours, I think."

And so they found their way in, each with a Questor Pierce pen and folder as well as a clip-on badge that gave name and role. Before Sarah was able to speak, her mum signed her in as a part-time cleaner. She laughed, part apology, part inverted snobbery, as soon as they were out of earshot.

"It's got to be plausible. They'll be on the lookout for intruders - they'll know you're too young to be a nurse. And forget your diet - that cake is too good to miss."

Coffee and cake in hand, they surveyed the room. Chairs, a

third of them already occupied, were arranged in concentric semi-circles in front of what normally would have been a varnished, wooden dance floor. Behind it, taut white curtains created a seamless screen onto which a slideshow of an uncluttered hospital, with nurses and doctors, male and female, of all ages and ethnic origins, was being projected.

A man beckoned them to sit next to him.

"This your little girl, then, Sue?"

"Is the badge that easy to see through?" Turning from him, her mother sat down, tugging at Sarah to do likewise, staring at her to say nothing.

"Sarah, this is Geoff."

He shook her hand, his slightly oily, the touch lingering. She pulled away as her mum leaned forward.

"Not many of ours here yet."

"What did you expect? Not like you to be naïve. Oh, I missed that. Keep my seat for me."

As he made his way behind them to get a matching piece of cake, Sarah glared knowingly at her mother.

"Not the noble man of the people, is he?"

"He's not as bad as he looks."

"It's not the look I'm on about."

She made no attempt to disguise what she had been talking about as he rejoined them. Around them, more people sat down but when the aural wallpaper changed from soothing chamber music to rousing - but not strident - Sibelius, there were still more seats empty than taken.

Two men and two women strode on to stand in front of the screen, the top half of which, above their heads, showed them against a pale blue background. As one woman stepped forward and the other three took seats that framed her, the projected image showed the woman from the waist up, strong and alone.

"Ladies and gentlemen, my name is Naomi Robbins and may I begin by thanking you for giving up your time to join us at the start of a new phase in the development of Questor Pierce. This is an exciting time for us and we're particularly pleased that so many of you are able to share it with us."

Her voice was unhurried, the pauses controlled, her eye contact measured in its direction and inclusive; her appearance, however, was not what Sarah had anticipated: she was in her forties, smart but not showy, with looks that would not have drawn Geoff's attention, a persona that implied she actually had worked for a living.

"Sitting alongside me are three people who can help illuminate what we're planning, with you, to do and what we've already achieved in a hospital broadly similar to yours. On my left is Paul Smith from Questor's Human Resources Department to whom you may wish to ask questions at the end. On my right are Sanjay Virdee and Maria Thomas, nurse and doctor respectively, from Ansborough Cottage Hospital in Dorset which we've now been running successfully for over three years. They, shortly, will give you their perspective on what it's like to work in an NHS hospital run by Questor Pierce.

"Let me begin, however, by filling in for you my own personal background. After completing my training, I worked as an NHS nurse for several years - as a staff nurse, in fact, for the last three. I then had a break while my two daughters were very young and it was during that period, when I had a little time on my hands, that a friend already working for Questor suggested that management and ICT training might equip me well for a slightly different return to work. The modules were completed in between feeds and nappy changing - you can imagine what it was like." She paused as a little laughter answered her self-deprecating smile. "After that, I resumed work outside the home in a junior management role with Questor and there I've stayed, in varying roles, ever since.

"I've only given you this personal background so that you can appreciate that we're not an alien financial group, imported from another planet, but that we're people whose background we share with you and who are equally passionate about meeting the needs of patients." Sarah nudged her mum and, flat against her thigh, stretched out one finger from her clenched fist. Her mum smiled, with a little shake of her chin. "We're equally committed to the well-being of our staff, as I hope my colleagues from Ansborough Cottage Hospital will confirm shortly.

"To now give you more specifics: when we take over the running of your hospital on June 2nd, your pay and conditions will remain as they are at this moment in time. Staff are our most valued resource and they have to be treated accordingly.

"On a day-to-day basis, I'll be responsible for the way the hospital operates. That will, of course, mean changes but these will be organic." She proceeded to outline a management hierarchy that, to Sarah, seemed impenetrable but which gave her an opportunity to look around. She assumed that everyone there worked at the hospital - it was hard to see why other outsiders like her should subject themselves to this public relations exercise. If they were all at the hospital, something was seriously wrong with recruitment or with the attitude of younger staff to union membership. There were, at most, three people under thirty-five.

Behind her, on a chair against the back wall, was the same bearded old man from the local rag, with his three cameras, one poised to take a picture that, redundant in its blandness, could have been replaced by a Questor Pierce press release. Seeing him, however, triggered associations from the day before and her eyes scanned for a second time the paltry audience. None of the three younger people could have been the woman photographer but, on the right, there was a darkened cubicle, its top half open at the front, from which one man, who had emerged once or twice before the speakers had begun their presentation, controlled the lighting. From the right half of the cubicle, however, an elbow protruded and part of a female profile, facing towards the audience, was just visible.

If it was her, nothing could have happened yet because there'd been no flash of a camera - and if the shots did come, it was hardly a revelation that would make the national news. Perhaps she was just suffering from what George Osborne, in his latest fundraising speech in the City of London, had called "the paranoia of the left."

"So we're as committed as you are to sustaining and then improving the quality of patient care. Like you, we do not feel that patients, once they've been admitted, should have to wait, in often cramped conditions, to be seen and/or treated. Our pledge is that by 2017 waiting times within the hospital will have been cut to a maximum of one hour."

Sarah nudged her mother and mouthed, "Which month?" They exchanged raised eyebrows, her mum's expression briefly indulgent but proud, before her attention returned to the speaker who was now winding up after two more pledges, her part of the electioneering complete.

After a suitable delay as if, despite everything, applause had been expected, the doctor and the nurse stood up together, a double act, relaxed, bouncing self-deprecating remarks off each other before the man grew serious and addressed his audience, head raised, hands outstretched. Sarah, reluctantly, had to admire

Questor Pierce for risking a speaker of Asian origin in an area that still thought of them as aliens - but, then, they had made sure he was good-looking.

"This is, as you know, too important a matter for it to be taken lightly." She could feel her concentration wandering immediately. "You naturally want to know if Questor have changed our working practice and the answer is, unequivocally, 'yes' - and for the better. I work in Outpatients and the scheduling of appointments -" she watched as the detail he gave seemed to earn grudging interest from some of the listeners. Her mum, too, seemed absorbed, her right hand clenched loosely against her mouth.

"Elsewhere in the hospital, rotas have been rearranged so that staff spend more time with a small group of patients and, so, really get to know them. Obviously, there are sometimes emergencies or serious staff illness when rotas have to be changed at short notice but, generally, that awful business of patients explaining their illness, their needs, repeatedly as each new nurse appears has disappeared. Come and see us at Ansborough and the patients, I am sure, would tell you how much better it is.

"Finally - and I may be speaking out of turn here - I imagine Questor will use with you a method that was very successful with us. When they took over, a member of the admin staff was twinned with a long-stay patient, recording every detail of her day - it was, in fact, a lovely woman, over eighty but who seemed twenty years younger - even down to the detail of what she chose for her meals, how long she was given to eat, how much assistance she was given, how many doctors and nurses she saw in a twenty-four hour period, and so on. It's from that investment of time that so many changes have been made to benefit the people we're all passionate about - the patients."

They sat down to a tentative smattering of applause, petering out in the face of questioning looks, in some cases dismissive glances. Sarah's outstretched two fingers were given a nod by her mother and then a despairing shake of the head.

"I'm sure you have questions." The woman, calmly on her feet again, was quick to maintain momentum. "To any of us, on anything you've heard."

There were immediately several hands raised but one voice behind her cut across them all, impatient, less, it seemed, from anger than from frustration at the predictability of what he had heard.

"Do you really expect us to believe that an organisation out to make profit is going to free up a member of staff for a whole day - and all night, apparently - to observe a single patient?"

"All I can do is assure you that the observation was exactly as I've described it. Not the same member of staff, obviously, for twenty-four hours," he smiled, "or sleep might have invalidated some of the observation!"

The humour had not worked on the man behind her. Turning, Sarah saw him grunt, kick his chair back and walk noisily out. The two men next to him followed suit, ostentatiously placing Questor Pierce's literature back on the chairs they had vacated.

"You are, of course, free to leave at any point but we'd much rather that you gave us the opportunity to address your concerns. Gentleman at the front."

"Our hospital's income has dropped by between six and seven percent over the last year. If that continues, how will you prevent a downward spiral in which services are closed, creating a further drop in income?"

She looked briefly towards her Human Resources man before answering. "You talk about a continuing drop in income but, with respect, I think that's a false premise. Our experience is the exact opposite: improved effectiveness as an organisation not only improves the way our staff function but also, therefore, attracts more income from the GP commissioning bodies."

"That's not the point." The interruption came from the front, from a man who must have been the 'gentleman's' friend. "The question was about shutting down services." From the improvised lighting box on the right, Sarah saw a single flash at the same time as the image projected on the screen was enlivened by a pulsing information bar at the bottom, its colours ever-changing and strident.

She waited. More flashes came but always when someone in the audience was speaking and always when the screen burst into hyperactivity.

"You said that our pay and conditions are safeguarded. What does 'our' mean? What about new staff?" Her mum's words - precise and seemingly neutral - drew her back to the discreet lighting of the hall. She felt the pride that a parent might feel at a school sports day but one that she rarely divulged for what it would reveal about her own tangled feelings, her admiration for her mother and how she had withstood the grotesque mistreatment that he had meted out. Not a word misplaced when you could have forgiven her if her whole world had been dislocated.

"I hope that you've seen this afternoon that 'our' is a term that covers all of us here, me, you," and she waved inclusively. "I hate to borrow a term that has unfortunately, to some extent, become devalued but we are, genuinely, all in this together." It was her first major mistake: derisive laughter and groaning broke out as several were on their feet, backs turned to the speaker.

It reminded her of school - not just of those lessons when McKinley lost control but also of what they had done in English on how context and background could sublimate or destroy the meaning of the simplest words.

School again was her cue - when moments of chaos like this were an opportunity to get away with something that would otherwise, in a formal setting, be impossible. As the meeting broke up, many making for the door, criss-crossing, uncertain where it was, while others formed small huddles and the speakers consoled themselves with gathering their papers, all magnified on the screen behind them, Sarah pushed her way apologetically towards the lighting box. Standing like a child in front of a Punch and Judy booth, she sought to adjust her eyes to the gloom, to find faces so that she could confirm and remember the woman's identity - but there was no-one there. Not the photographer but, sitting on a tripod on a ledge below the box's aperture, was her camera, temporarily abandoned in the confusion.

Sarah reached her arm through and, with a rushed jerk of her hand, released it from the tripod. It was lighter than she had expected but still too bulky for her to carry it unnoticed in her hand. Her mind shuddering at what she had done, the action of a second with all its potential consequences that could not be undone, she reached for her mother's bag sitting, sagging and open on her chair.

"Mum," she responded to her puzzled stare, "I need a tissue" - and the camera was gone, buried in her mother's debris. "I'm sorry, Mum," she cut across the condescension in Geoff's eyes, "I've got to have some fresh air. I'll take your bag."

"No, no, I'll -" but her mother's protests were too late and Sarah was gone, in the disgruntled straggle of hospital staff, past the cluttered tables, down the stairs, and, with a nervous glance at the empty reception desk, into the fresh air.

Her mother was next to her before she had time to find an inconspicuous place to wait.

"Whatever's the matter with you?"

"I'll tell you now." Her mother's concern was not allayed. "Just keep moving - and here's your bag, all zipped up for once. Oh, Christ," she muttered at Geoff's approach, "not him again. No, I'm fine, thanks."

And, with a tug on her mother's arm, they were gone.

15

Pollard watched the printer spewing out a fifth copy of her letter of application. The image of vomit was accurate: there was nothing smooth and flowing in the paper's emergence as it spluttered unevenly out in the lulls between the grinding sounds that something so small and electronic should not have been able to produce. It sat there, grey and malfunctioning, a million miles from the glossy manual with its alert faces and fashionable living rooms, the colours bright but decorously subdued in all the right places.

She looked around her living room. It too was a different species from the balanced, uncluttered advertisers' construct. Even if she had been tidy, there simply was not enough space. The room had squashed together dining table, two-piece suite, television, bookshelves, even a small refugee freezer that could not find a home in the tiny kitchen.

Most of the time, she wasn't old enough to bother. The pressure of marking, working out how to ditch the latest man who was getting too claustrophobic - they both took priority. But there were such things as prospects - or there should have been. Renting like this was not what she had expected, not what her parents still said they expected. It was the subtext for her application, an underlying motivation that was sure to be tested at interview.

She could see the questioning coming if she got that far. "Miss Pollard, why are you applying for a sideways move if it's not for more money?" The school in Hertfordshire was still under Local Authority control and in a wealthier part of the country: it would mean an extra £1,500 a year for doing what was fundamentally the same job. How would she deal with the question? She shunted it aside until it had to be answered.

She read through what she had amended and then tucked it into an envelope. She left it unsealed so that she could apply the advice she always gave the kids - and which they normally ignored - to run through it again in the morning when she, as a fresh reader, could assess its impact. 'Impact': perhaps it was just tiredness that made her mock her own seriousness - it was, a glance at her watch confirmed, after ten o'clock and the fiddling around with the application had left her with marking still to be done.

As she pushed the envelope carefully to one side and heaved the pile of books from the floor onto the dining table, she wondered if she was doing the right thing. She saw the name on the Year 9 book at the top, Jamie Pearce, no genius but bright enough and like a sponge in the way he absorbed everything they did in class. He was one of many and it was what made the job, for ninety percent of the time, so enjoyable. It had taken her three years to get to this point and she could be throwing it away for a place where, even after a further three years, she would be less happy.

The older ones like Sarah and Becky she would miss. In a few months, they would be gone anyway but there would be others, each year, growing into their shoes. You could see it at the Duke of Edinburgh meeting earlier that day. Some of the Year 10s had been losing momentum and, after school, Becky had stayed on to fire them up. As the teacher, she had just sat back and watched the listening on both sides, the friendly abuse, the continuity.

Afterwards she had told Becky that she might be leaving. Probably another stupid thing to do - she had not told Toad or any of her colleagues yet - but Becky's regret, not for herself but for the school, had stuck in her memory. She had been a bit over the top in her praise but the almost adult perception, the gentle, respectful smile, were potential building blocks for a lasting friendship.

Something else that she might be throwing away.

16

One or two fingers were drumming the table, a rarity when most of the people there could analyse body language and probably prescribe for it. The clock was approaching seven and still they waited.

From the car park, they heard a door shut. "That should be his last one."

"Oh, it is. There's no-one in reception."

"He'll be another ten minutes, though." Wry, patient smiles were exchanged.

"If we're lucky."

The estimates were right: pockets of conversation bubbled away for a quarter of an hour before the door opened and an apologetic Goldsmith walked in.

"Not like you, Colin."

He shrugged his shoulders and sat down. Maurice Allen made the introductions, principally for the man on his left. He identified each doctor in turn, urbane, unhurried, before turning his head.

"Most importantly for us tonight, I'd like to introduce Martin King. Now, you may grumble about changes in your role but, at least, you only ever need to introduce yourselves as doctors. Talking to Martin, his job title has changed four times in two years, I think I'm correct in saying, but he's now accurately designated as a Commissioning Implementation Adviser - or CIA to his friends."

"Yes - a little unfortunate. But thank you anyway, Maurice, and thank you all for sparing me the time after what I am sure will have been a very tiring day for you - even though none of you seem to be showing it. Most of this session is for you to ask questions that, fingers crossed, I may be able to help you with but, first, I'd like to fill you in on developments from on-high and what other commissioning bodies are doing.

"I know you're fed up with all the changes but, believe me, you haven't seen the half of it. Every day - and I mean every day - something new arrives by email or by post. They're the ones to watch out for - loads of signatures needed - and - "

He was getting no new smiles and, on one or two faces, a tightening of the lips was turning a welcoming reassurance into possible condescension. He pulled his shoulders back.

"Anyway, enough of me and my moans. As far as your position is concerned, I feel pretty clear about the progress you've made after talking to Maurice regularly. I gather, to use a sporting term, that you got off to a slow start with all these reforms but now you're hell-bent on catching up."

He spent ten minutes giving them a largely accurate summary of the practice's current situation. Goldsmith struggled to conceal his irritation: even if it had been wholly accurate, the summary would have been unnecessary; and he suppressed the urge to correct the minor inaccuracies which were, after all, only like misplaced commas in a policy document whose fundamentals were flawed. This man would love a discussion on those commas with which he could bury the ethics.

King coughed and reached for a glass of water.

"Going forward, however, you've got a couple of choices. One is the volume of business you're doing. The other is whether you change - how shall I put it? - the financial basis on which you're operating. Do I need to clarify those choices?"

"I think you do." Sheila Beckford's irritation was on the surface. "I'm not clear which aspect of our work you're referring to as a 'business'."

"All of it, really."

Goldsmith saw him looking at her, hair tied austerely back: a quick assessment of her weight, her age, probably, and of whether she was worth 'getting on side', as he, no doubt, would put it.

There was a silence, momentary, until he resumed. "Okay, I'm happy -"

Allen cut across him with a gentle tap on the table. "What I'd like to do is build up a list of all the issues we've got and then we can group them and work through them logically. I've made a note of the point you raised, Sheila."

"I don't know how, unless you're psychic, Maurice. I didn't get on to an issue."

"Rest assured on this, Sheila. Would I dare to put words into your mouth?" He smiled flirtatiously. "The point I've noted down is our modus operandi as a surgery. Just use it as a trigger for when we move on to discussion. I'm sure you won't forget what you intended. Now, other issues, please."

His list grew rapidly, with barely any repetition. Goldsmith sat, happy to hear his concerns raised by others, saving himself, if necessary, for the discussion. He watched King, initially reluctant to have control eased away from him but now enjoying a few moments' shelter. He was sitting back, with a light half-smile that combined with the quizzical tilt of his head to suggest an infuriating smugness.

"Fine." The points appeared to have dried up. "We seem to have a cluster of issues that have, at their heart, the number of patients that we're referring on for treatment. That would seem a logical starting point for us. Martin, can you lead off?"

"Before you start, Mr. King - all of this, Maurice, was supposed to have been outlawed by the Department of Health two years ago."

"No, no, Sheila, this isn't what was happening in Harrow. Please, if I could," he looked to her for silence, her assent of sorts, "return to Martin and his introduction?"

She nodded.

"Thank you, Maurice. Now, I've pored over your spreadsheets and, while I understand that patients' well-being is your main concern, the financial side is going to have to run it close in the years to come." He smiled apologetically. "In January, for example, twelve more patient referrals than the year before have pushed you from a reasonable underspend to a break-even position."

"Surely, the underspend is not 'reasonable'." Goldsmith pulled himself up in his chair. "I cannot think of anything more 'reasonable' for us than breaking even."

"Colin, I know your concerns but let's hear Martin out."

"Thank you. Sorry I used the wrong word - what I meant was 'quite substantial'. I didn't mean anything about how," as he hesitated, Goldsmith watched him ransacking his limited vocabulary for an alternative, "logical it was." His poise was fracturing as he detected the critical flickering of some eyes around the table. "The size of that possible underspend is in the same ballpark as several of the locality groups we work with elsewhere in the south-west. I can think of one - and, for obvious reasons, I can't name it although if I tell you it's also in Cornwall, you can probably work out who I'm talking about - which has come in with that sort of figure for five months in a row."

Goldsmith's eyes never moved from King's face and how it teetered back towards confidence, like an adolescent struggling to ingratiate himself with an older audience, searching for a fact - that the woman down the road was a 'goer' was probably typical of his repertoire - to gain him credibility.

"That is serious money which, you know as well as I do, opens up several possibilities. They've taken one approach - and it's not one size fits all - but -"

"What you're saying, I take it, is that we should aim to underspend so that we can line our own pockets."

"Sheila, I don't think anything as crude as that is being suggested."

"Oh, for heaven's sake, Ian, that is precisely what is being suggested. What Mr. King won't tell us is if he is on commission in all this. Nice irony, isn't it, how the word 'commission' can have such different meanings - or are they different?"

Allen held up his hands. "Let's not linger on semantics, Sheila. Look, it's getting late and we've given an initial airing, thanks to Martin, to key issues that are going to face us. What I propose -"

"We haven't touched on anything of clinical significance - for example, when we should ration treatment because there are, of course, some instances," Goldsmith placed an exaggerated emphasis on the word 'some', "when drug costs are exceptionally high; our criteria for referring patients to hospitals like Glenfine; our policy for deciding on the balance to be struck between those patients who are traditionally ours and those who are outside our practice area; when, if at all, we allow a patient from outside the practice area to move rapidly up the waiting list." He paused at the muttering around him. "The rumours are there - and not just in this room. Anyway, I could go on," he managed a smile. "I won't here because it's not the occasion - but, please, can we make sure there will be an occasion?"

"Rest assured, all those issues will be hammered out. What I would propose is that we work through them, one by one, at our coming monthly meetings and that, in the meantime, I, with Martin, draw up some financial illustrations based on the last few months' figures."

"Surely it's the wrong approach to have illustrations before we have criteria."

"Oh, no, Colin, the illustrations are no different from ones you get in the post - if you don't like them, you tear them up and start again. If that's okay then, I'd like to thank Martin on your behalf," King nodded quickly, not delaying the winding-up of the meeting, "and - I hate to remind you again - could I ask any of you who haven't contributed yet if, on your way out, you could pop something in the envelope in my drawer for Julie's leaving present?"

Goldsmith did not move, numbed by how ineffectual his words, no matter how well-chosen, were becoming. He watched as King left, deliberately on his own as Allen took far longer than necessary to gather up his papers, and Ian Johnson, head resting on one hand, attempted to mollify Sheila. As the others stood up, he sat, isolated, unmollified, a sign of impotence, not strength.

17

Liam would have nothing to say, Sarah knew that. Probably that was why she had asked him, why she had stood at his door, her arm pressing against the bag she had borrowed from her mum. The hurried hello - he had not seemed to react to the haste that she had felt was so out of character - and he'd just shrugged his assent when she asked if she could use his computer.

As he opened up the laptop, there was a brief glimmer of curiosity.

"Why didn't you use one of your dad's? I thought you said he had three."

"He has - but don't ask." She fixed him with a resigned look. "Too much hassle. And mum hasn't got one now" - but he lost interest as the computer sparked into life.

Once his mother had brought them in a cup of tea, he looked at the first photos as if they were a recently discovered family album, pointing with surprise at a picture of Sarah's mother but not asking about the darkened room or the adults on the chairs around her.

She sipped at the tea reluctantly - there was nowhere else she was ever offered it - but its warmth was soothing. The fact of her having taken the camera was like a grain of grit in her eye that would not allow her vision to clear, her mind to settle. Anything else she had done at school or at any of the protests she could not only justify by its context but also by those absolute ethical standards that she clung to as a reaction against her father.

Telling her mum had exposed that piety. She had been, at best, neutral. "I know the end justifies the means but you've never stolen anything in your life, have you? And it *is* stealing. But they're all doing worse things than stealing, I suppose." After those words and, under a barrage of questioning comments and looks, she had found herself a part of the world of relative morality.

The pictures flicked back slowly, as she worked her way through the questions asked in the hotel conference room. The photographer, assuming it was her, had seemed brisk and assertive outside the college but there was no evidence in the shots' sequence of an accompanying organisation. There were four pictures of Sarah's mother, all virtually identical. So it was with anyone who had spoken, each captured four or five times with facial expressions again seemingly identical, the only nuances being the slight shift between animation and irritation.

Her boredom was rising until the images' brightness changed suddenly and they saw MacBrumbies in the background. Confirmation then: it was that woman - and her memory card was chock full. Perhaps nothing had been saved elsewhere.

As they scrolled through the pictures - there was Becky's grandfather, one shot after another - the potential worth of the camera sank in. It might be the only record of the last few days that the stupid woman had, a woman who had seemed so inaccessible, so together, but who now would be furious at the loss. Quite where its significance lay was difficult to see but it was, nonetheless, a small revenge.

"Hang on."

At Liam's words, as he stirred from the torpor induced by seeing every subject so many times, each differentiated by a millisecond but by no perceptible change in expression, her finger scrolled back instantly to the scene, shambolic but reassuring now, outside the college.

"Hang on, that was your dad, wasn't it? Go back the other way."

He reached his hand across but she, ignoring the light touch of his fingers against hers, did herself what he had wanted - and there before her was her own tiny front garden, the half-open door and standing, central, his suit on but his shirt unbuttoned at the top, his tie loosened, was her father.

She steadied her finger, muttering once, despite Liam's silence, "I don't know." She clicked again but that was all - they were back in the darkened conference hall. One shot, that was all, the bloody woman. Without it, Sarah would have known nothing.

18

The restaurant was so much more cosmopolitan than at home. That was a real drawback - the only one that Goldsmith could put his finger on - of Cornish life: the village familiarity of people even if you were living in a town, the largely monochrome colour of those you passed in the street, the visitors who were so predictable in their ethnic mix and in their weight, the bloated junk food eaters in the main resorts, the lean walkers elsewhere.

Around him now were faces, some from northern Europe, some from south-east Asia, he could not place it exactly, where the skin colour of India began to merge with the bone structure of China, all overlaid with the gentle lilt of two Canadian voices. It would have suited him to sit alone, happy in anonymous silence, but Andrews would surely be joining him soon.

He had no idea why. All he had said on the phone was that it was a constituency matter but such a public pretext was often a prelude to a seemingly relaxed raising of a personal health problem. The venue in London was consistent with that possibility - public privacy was non-existent in Cornwall for a GP or an MP - and Andrews had seized on it, brushing aside Goldsmith's apologies for being out of Cornwall on a two day course and suggesting this Greek restaurant not far from Westminster.

Goldsmith looked at his watch. Time-keeping obviously was not one of Andrews' strengths. He looked again - ten minutes late - and then reminded himself that not everyone worked, flexibly or otherwise, to a precise timetable of patient appointments. Ten minutes did not matter - as he was often telling patients and was increasingly telling himself.

He looked across to the door and saw Andrews talking to the waitress, with an easy familiarity, the air of someone who was a regular there, someone who was as comfortable in restaurants as in his own home: the turn of the young woman's head, his discreet glance - and then his confident movement across the restaurant, slow and apologetic as he eased his way past other diners, towards their table.

Goldsmith stood at his approach, conscious of how stooped he seemed in comparison with the upright figure, perhaps three inches taller in reality but a seeming giant in his eyes. He steeled himself to take the initiative.

"Good evening, Tom, nice to see you." His words were no sooner uttered than he winced inwardly at the surgery manner he could not shuffle off.

"Indeed it is. Sorry I'm a little late - my own fault and then I had to catch up with Maria." His eyes moved back across the room. "Lovely girl, my brother taught her."

Goldsmith followed it up, feigned puzzlement at such a coincidence, knowing the initiative had gone.

Andrews, however, appeared to have no intention of rubbing it in. They talked of their families, of Becky and Kirsty in particular, the girls' plans for the future, and a balance was restored well before they ordered.

"And look Colin, before we go any further, this is on me. No, not on expenses." His self-conscious smile was a reaction to the look of surprise in Goldsmith's eyes. "Literally on me. It was my idea: I wanted to sound you out on a few things and you've been good enough to spare me the time." He did not wait for any agreement - and Goldsmith's nascent protest was swept aside.

After the waitress had taken their order, the conversation flowed smoothly from the girls' interests, to their possible career paths in medicine - both deemed it unlikely, as self-deprecating as Becky herself might have been, proud parents in the extent of their empathy - and onto developments at the surgery and beyond.

Why did Andrews time his mouthfuls so much more conveniently? He had asked Goldsmith, cogently and as if time were unlimited, how smoothly the surgery's commissioning had gone before spearing one of the biggest chunks of meat in his stifado; Goldsmith had responded - it must have been equally cogent, he hoped - but only after a rushed, apologetic swallowing and a cursory wiping of his lips.

"It's alien territory for us all." He hesitated for another swallow. "That's one reason for not taking it too quickly." His circumspection was probably overdone - he sensed, as Andrews' eyes turned towards the waitress, that commissioning was not the reason for arranging the meeting.

"I'm sure you're right." And so it had gone on: in anything - the pressures on the surgery, perceptions of the A&E service, the decision to press on with the closure of the cottage hospitals - just the slightest hint, never more than that, of where Andrews' sympathies lay.

It was a game of manoeuvring to which Goldsmith was not accustomed: for him, there was only a bland public persona at work or honesty at home; for Andrews - even though his veneer of cynicism might reflect a deeper questioning of what his government was doing - his job must entail an endless range of personae, each partially a product of his varying listeners, be they constituents or colleagues. Who was Goldsmith, at a first encounter, to accurately interpret the man in front of him?

"What about the age profile of your patients? It must slow your work down enormously."

Goldsmith answered his smile. "Not exactly. I know what you mean but it doesn't feel any different from what it's always been. You're going on the local demographics, presumably?"

"Yes, to some extent, but I was thinking more of the really serious cases, the ones who have to be referred into care."

"Well, that's not a huge issue for us. We're only on the fringe of what the hospital's doing."

Andrews was no longer concerned to top up his wine. "You may not know then but I've got constituents concerned about elderly relatives who have far more hurdles to clear if they're to qualify to have their care funded - and it seems far worse in Cornwall than elsewhere in the country."

"As I understand it - and don't quote me on it - that shouldn't be so. There are relatively new national criteria in place but nonetheless there are problems of interpretation in determining whether someone qualifies on health grounds for financial support. One complication is the number of agencies involved but not us, thankfully, in any significant role."

"Who is key, then?"

"Impossible to say. I simply don't have enough to do with it. I do know two people who've been through the process, had to sell their homes and who are convinced, obviously enough, that a shortage of money is the principal factor. No evidence, however, that I'm aware of."

Andrews looked hard at him, chewing on the last of his food. "What's your opinion on it?"

The shift from information-giving was sudden. "On the whole set-up, it's a mess – a market started by Thatcher. Much the same as what's happening to us now." He tugged himself back. "But on the problems people are experiencing, how can you be anything other than sympathetic? Despite that, though, you can't really get angry with the poor devils in the finance office - or with people like the district nurses each carrying out their separate fragments of the assessments. It's like phoning up a switchboard and being batted from one department to another. 'Small is beautiful', isn't it, if the decisions also get broken up and passed down the line?"

Andrews raised his eyebrows, smiling as his top teeth pulled at his bottom lip. "It's not just us or Thatcher, is it? Blair, he did it as well, didn't he?"

"Yes."

His pause was so long that Andrews interrupted. "But this is worse - that's what you're thinking - and it could be laid at a local door, couldn't it?"

19

It was a lunchtime, a hopeless time to talk about anything, kids in detention trying any tactic to avoid getting on with the work they had to complete, others coming in to drop off bags or pick up bits of their lunch - and in the midst of it all, Sarah appeared, impatient like a thwarted lover, almost demanding to be seen.

Her patience was no greater when she came back after school, pulling up a chair while Pollard was still clearing the debris of the day.

"I need your advice - because you're not a sixteen year old." There was no smile.

"I've got my uses then?" She carried on checking off the books to be marked until Sarah's scraping her chair made her look up.

"Go on, then," and she pushed the books to one side. Her intended glance at Sarah while she carried on clearing her desk became a fixed gaze at the girl's eyes which were bulging, animated, above an unsmiling mouth. Into the small space on the desk that the teacher had cleared, Sarah placed a camera, silver, a little scratched, larger than most of the newest digital ones she had seen.

"You've been trying to emulate those advertising shots?"

"Oh, God, no - this is for real." The girl's dismissive certainty broke Pollard's gaze, made her want to interrupt - but she checked herself. "It's not so much the camera as the memory card" - and she recounted everything that had happened: the theft itself, the pictures she had seen with Liam, what her mother had said, with only the single image of her father omitted.

"I don't know what to do with it all. I could return it, with or without the memory card. If I kept the card - or saved it all - I could just sit on it until some point in the future when it might be useful. Or I could use it locally, even nationally, to publicise what's going on. Or other options that I can't recall or haven't thought of."

Pollard said nothing at first. She watched the girl's fingers clicking one of the controls through ten degrees and back again.

"Are you comfortable with it? Because you don't look it."

"That's not the point. I so want to get it right. If I do, it could really expose what they're doing. That's why I look on edge, although there is the morality of what I've done. What you said about that guilt-ridden bloke in the play - a cloud over the sun." She touched the camera and recoiled.

"For starters, there's no reason whatsoever for you to hold on to the camera - but let me think." She tried to apply the contradictory advice that she had picked up piecemeal in her three years of teaching. In a nutshell, cracked but just intact, you were supposed to strive for that ideal mix of closeness and distance - closeness so that any student would confide in you the horrors of abuse at home but distance in knowing when to pass the problem on and how to avoid implicating yourself in what was only one person's view of the mess. It had all sounded fine in theory.

"But first things first. There may be things you tell me that I'll have to pass on to someone else."

"Bloody hell - it's a bit late now, isn't it? That includes what I've said already, does it? Great!"

"It's a procedure we have to follow."

Sarah stood up. "You sound like the fucking police - 'anything you say…'." The mimicry in her voice was too rushed, the stress too great.

"Sit down, Sarah, please. And I know it's difficult but watch your language. Look, I'll listen. Okay?"

The girl, tensed, blocking any agitation in her fingers, sat down and waited.

"I haven't heard anything yet that I would have to pass on but I'll flag it up if I do." She knew that for a while she would be thinking aloud. "As I said, the camera should be returned. How - that's another matter but we can leave it for a bit. There's no point in keeping the card either as, if you want to retain the pictures, you can copy them. As for their publicity value, I wouldn't have thought there was enough there to interest the national media." She held up her hand to stop Sarah from talking. "And I don't want to see them - that's not the point. Locally, perhaps, depending on what they show."

"You're making this all so theoretical." She rubbed her face in her hands. "If I wrote like that, you'd slate it for being waffle. I just want you to tell me what you think."

"How many people have you told?"

"Mum, you, four or five of them here."

"So, those four or five will already have passed it on to at least twenty more."

"Probably."

"Look, I think I've said all I've got to say. You've got

yourself into a difficult situation and the detail of it only you can sort out." She tried, in her softened, slower voice, to re-establish eye contact with the girl, who had turned her head away. "It's all to do with the individual taking responsibility."

"Oh, Christ." Sarah pushed her chair back. "I just wanted some help. I thought that was what it was all to do with as well. Some hope!"

"Hang on a minute!" Her call went unheeded as the girl flung the door open and left.

* * * * *

Sarah was trying to calm herself, making a drink and scrabbling in the fruit bowl for something that was relatively fresh when the door opened behind her. Her father's face had, tautened on it, that familiar impatience overlaid by an attempt at civility. She turned away, ignoring the half-hearted small talk that she knew even he was not convinced by.

As she opened the door to escape to her bedroom, she picked up his change of tone and glanced back.

"That Saturday. Harbour Sound Hotel. I need to know where the camera's gone."

"What are you on about?"

She tried initially to face him down, easy enough with the temper from school still coursing through her.

"The bloody daft meeting you went to."

"I don't know what you're talking about. The meeting wasn't bloody daft because it was all about Mum's job, in case you hadn't uncovered that trivial little detail. But the rest of it - I don't know what the fuck you're talking about. Am I supposed to have stolen something - or what?"

"A camera. A photographer's camera. CCTV picked you up lifting it. It wouldn't have been obvious to everyone but it was to me. Come on, Sarah - just be on the level. Where is it?"

His smile, sure that he had her trapped, enraged her.

"Why are you involved anyway?"

"I have connections." He checked momentarily. "You know I have connections but let's not get sidetracked. You've done something you shouldn't have done. We want to get it sorted - give me the camera and I'm sure I can smooth everything over."

Her hand clenched on the freezer door handle. "Connections. Such good connections that they'll help you wreck Mum's job. Lovely people you know."

"That's not fair and you know it. I know loads of people," his smile was threatening to emerge again, "but I'm just the middle man. I'm not making the decisions. It's just that here I can bail you out of a real mess. So will you -"

"Whatever it is, no. Yes, I did take the camera and no, you're not having it. It's not just me anyway. We're still working out what to do with it."

" 'We'?" He sat down, his pose of concentrated reflection tightening her grip on the freezer. "That makes it trickier to sort out. Look, you may as well sit down."

She jerked her head sideways, just the once, refusing.

"So who've you told?" The upwards tilt of his head accentuated his apparent concern.

At first, she said nothing but it was a silence she knew she would not win.

"Mum, Becky, several people in school, a few others. I told Miss Pollard as well but she just came up with the usual weak adult response."

"You told that woman! And you showed her the pictures?"

She released her hand. "Okay. I'll answer that but nothing else because you don't have the right." She sat down defiantly opposite him. "I showed her no pictures, especially not the one of you standing out there, grinning. Very cosy but just another connection, of course."

"Dead right." She could have hit him for the confidence with which he stared at her. "That's all she is, another connection. Couldn't have put it better myself. Nothing more than that."

"In the front garden! Or what passes for one. And the way you're standing: don't you think I can tell the difference between a business photo and a - oh God, you know what I mean - like a family picture, one for an album?"

"Of course it's not a family picture. How -"

"You know that's not what I wanted to say. Wrong word. That's all. Wrong word."

"Sounds unlikely for someone like you. Words are what you're supposed to be good at, aren't they?" She felt the hurt in her eyes, a sudden electrical spasm. "So." He hesitated, as if to pick his words. "Back to the point. What exactly did that bloody teacher of yours say?"

"I told you - you're not getting anything else out of me." She glared at him across the table. "Nothing whatsoever."

She held her stare, determined at first to outstay him, but after a few seconds she pushed her chair back and stood up.

"Silly male posturing," she muttered and walked up to her bedroom.

* * * * *

"Your father wants to see me. Has he said to you what it's about?"

"You must be joking."

It was the first time Pollard had seen her on her own since that fiasco. In the two intervening lessons, Sarah had said little, more perhaps out of boredom than anger. Now she was quiet - but how receptive was impossible to tell. Her arms were hanging loose by her sides, her fingers flicking backwards and forwards.

"Sorry about the other afternoon." Her words were blurted out. "I was well out of order." Pollard smiled, her hand fluttering to brush the apology aside. "But I know why he wants to see you - or I can guess."

Pollard sat forward to listen as the girl recounted what her father had said, seeming to spare him at points to protect her self-esteem, her eyes cast down by the time she finished. Pollard, still leaning forward, looked at the top of the girl's head, the hair slightly tousled by the rain, her nose just visible.

She clicked her fingers in front of Sarah's face to break the silence.

"It must've been awful for you."

"Well." The girl looked up, a fragile, relieved smile returning to her face. "It's not the first time. You get used to it."

"Has he spoken to you since?"

"No - and I certainly haven't. I can be a stroppy madam - isn't that what you said to my mum once? Well, it's true - and I've no trouble in keeping it up."

"I can imagine but at least it's not with everyone." She smiled back at the self-consciousness on Sarah's face. "Anyway, he now thinks I'm part of some conspiracy with you: is that the long and the short of it?"

"I guess so. He didn't like the idea that you'd been told, I could tell that. I don't know why - but if he thinks you're on my side, he'll find a way of getting back at you. Not what most girls say about their father, is it?"

"No, it's not the norm." She hoped her voice had the necessary detachment. "It could go back to last year."

She replayed her previous meetings with him - his rage at one, the ingratiation at the other that still made her back squirm.

"Well, I may find out soon enough."

She was looking at Sarah but her eyes were filmy, the words spoken to herself.

20

"Oh, shit." Sarah looked at the stain spreading across the rug. The table was still wobbling from her stumble, the glass somehow still intact. "Get me a cloth."

"Just fucking leave it. She's used to it."

She tugged at Ben's sleeve. "I don't care. Just get me one."

Reluctantly, he pushed his way to the cooker, grabbed a damp, scarred tea towel and flung it in her direction. Crouching, through feet, she retrieved it, dabbing with a repetitive aimlessness at the damp patch that was now lapping at her wrists.

To still her head, she sat up on her knees. Becky was leaning against the freezer. Liam was leaning against the freezer. Becky with her orange juice in her hand, her one lager to loosen her up now counter-balanced as everything in her bloody life was. She watched them talking and then, a jolt of self-consciousness penetrating the alcohol, put her head down again to rub away at the spill.

Ben's legs were over her head, his groin pressing down on her. "You'd be a much better slave than my mum." His hands were pawing at her back; her hands were her only support, her head succumbing downwards until her teeth asserted themselves and fastened on his ankle. His kick to release her helped her, brought her head up, recoiling, into his groin.

He shouted, stepped back and gave her a gentle push with his foot to leave her sprawling on the floor. "Emancipation - isn't that what you call it?" And there she lay, the dampness seeping, unnoticed, into her jeans.

21

Jackie from the office had knocked on the door, her normal tentative knock, and told her that Mr. King had arrived for his appointment. The images stuck in Pollard's head, like the slides she projected onto the classroom screen, as she walked down the corridor.

The seating area in the lobby was unoccupied but only because he was standing at the window, staring into the car park. As he turned, scanning her briefly from head to foot - curious, dismissive, she could not tell - before settling his eyes on her face, she tensed and shook his hand.

Walking back to the classroom, she tried to stay exactly level with him, fighting that nervous need to take the lead but not wanting him behind her, viewing her unseen.

She ushered him into the classroom, pulling up one of the kids' chairs for him and moving her own chair out. She sat down, her right elbow on the desk, a discreet distance from where he was now sitting - all as they were supposed to do, even down to its seeming spontaneous, not anxiously arranged in advance.

"Nice to see you again."

"And you. Good of you to fit me in."

If there was a hint of sarcasm in his voice, she ignored it. "How can I help you? I presume it's about Sarah."

"It is indeed. Luckily for everyone, probably, I haven't got anyone else." He paused. "You're too young to know what it's like to have a daughter of this age. You try to help and get rebuffed. You never get asked for advice. I know I'm not the only one but that doesn't make it any easier. All I ever try to do is help."

He looked at her, his implication that she would know what she had to say. She waited, unwilling to play his game.

"Okay - to cut to the point." With no table on which to rest or bang his hands, he stretched them behind his head, raising his eyes above her. "Sarah has stolen a camera. You know about it, apparently. I want you to tell me when you knew about it."

"A few days ago when she told me after school."

"After she did it, then?"

"Yes, but let's just pause a minute. I am here to help but not to be interrogated."

"Who said anything about interrogation? I just want the truth." He smiled. "Just because I don't fanny about, mincing my words like you lot here, doesn't make me a policeman."

She hesitated, unsure if speaking or remaining silent was handing him the initiative.

"Don't you think you should have told me straight off? Who else did you tell in the school?"

"I didn't contact you because you clearly knew. From -"

"If you thought I knew, you must just be taking Sarah's word as gospel. Bit naïve, isn't it?"

"Mr. King, we're talking about your daughter and I would trust completely what she says, even if you wouldn't."

"Are you criticising me?"

"No - I'm just responding to what you said. It's not my job to criticise."

He stood up and walked away from her, carefully pushing chairs under the desks to clear a way for himself. He turned against the far wall.

"Start again. Who else here have you told about what she's done? You must've done. I seem to remember you're not a great one for standing on your own feet."

She felt her back stiffen, her teeth clench. "No-one. It wasn't necessary."

"Not necessary! What sort of training do they give you lot? So you're now completely exposed on this?"

"Hang on, Mr. King. There's nothing to be exposed over. I was just listening - and that's a big part of my job. And I presumed you wanted to see me because you were interested in helping Sarah."

"Of course I am. But I can only do that if I know what role other people've been taking. People like you." His eyes moved down from her face. "You're in this group that Sarah tries to keep hidden from me, presumably?"

"I don't know which group you're referring to but I'm not a member of any group of which Sarah is also a member."

"So you know about the group."

"That's not what I've said."

"No? Why else would you come up with that politician's answer? I thought your subject was all about cutting through the crap that the pig ignorant rest of us speak? Same old bloody hypocrisy, isn't it?" His voice quickened in response to her rising to her feet - not in desperation, she was sure, but to heighten any anxiety he hoped he had stirred in her.

"I really don't think there is anything more to be said that can benefit Sarah. Perhaps, therefore, you would like to leave."

"Perhaps I will. Perhaps I won't. Is that how you enforce discipline? On a voluntary basis?"

"Mr. King, you're now just being rude." She scooped up her folders as if to restore them tidily to the shelves beside the door. "If you're not leaving, then I am. I'll leave you to find your own way out."

As she walked along the corridor, she heard "Fucking useless", the start of a sentence, its volume raised, before the door, delayed, closed automatically behind her.

22

Although the sun had emerged, in sheltered hollows the dunes were still damp from the night's rain. Becky watched Liam, child-like, leaping from one crest to another and turning to urge her to follow suit. Forcing an admiring smile onto her face, she tried to launch herself from where she stood and, missing her target by feet, sprawled in the sand below him.

The touch of his hand blanked out all the disappointment. He dragged her to her feet - but gently. "Come on," and the pressure of his hand increased as he pulled her up the slope. His hair, flopping, covered his collar but, each time he turned, she saw the brown, unbroken sheen of his neck below the line of his jaw that was close enough to touch.

Another stumble into a hollow and another clamber, her hand tightening on his, before she made herself lose her balance and he had to support her weight. That was when he kissed her, tentatively at first but, as they pulled each other down onto the sand, more slowly, almost languidly, his hand stroking her neck, his finger grazing her ear.

Her neck but no lower. She squirmed, her movements

conscious now but failing to draw his hand down from where it had settled. Only ever a repetitive caressing under her chin. Her hand edged down his jumper, ignoring a sound, a seagull on a roof if they had been inside, distant but coming closer.

She brushed his jeans and quivered at the hardness below the surface. Before her hand could linger, however, he had wriggled clear of her, cross-legged, peering over the marram grass, as the irregular thudding of feet pitching from dunes onto uneven sand came closer still. Hands and feet: her hands straying in her best pretence of arbitrary movement and finding not a hardness but a dampness in the denim, a softness below that could have been squeezed like a slug; and feet dislodging sand, an audible crumbling from their impact.

More than feet. A cough, healthy but habitual, that she recognised. She raised her head, only to lower it immediately.

"Oh, God, it's Granddad." She pushed Liam down into the sand and put her hand on his mouth, the moment gone, a mother to a child. He shifted his head back, a tremor - relief or irritation, she could not tell - in his eyes.

When the sound of each stride had receded into the distance, into inaudibility, she freed him from her hand and propped herself on her side.

"What's he doing up here?"

"Oh, he's always running. The sand, it helps his legs, he says." She paused, staring, still shielded by the largest dune from any unlikely backwards glance from her grandfather. "I bet he knows. No idea how he saw us. But with a bit of luck he won't tell Mum and Dad."

She looked down at him, surprised at what would have been, in any one else, condescension.

"You may think it's funny."

23

Toad called in to see her at the start of her most difficult class. Struggle enough to settle them down without an unwanted spectator. Part way through the register, Pollard wondered whether to press on in his brooding presence and introduce the new unit before leaving them in supposed silence while she spoke to him discreetly in the corridor. She opted instead for aborting the register and, the less risky option, asking them to talk quietly among themselves - where else were they supposed to talk? - until she got back.

Why he did not just issue an appointment card, she could never fathom. The request was terse enough - 11.15 in his room - with his passing reference to consulting her timetable the only nod in the direction of either conversation or consideration. The brevity suited her well enough, though, as she was back in the classroom before the mock-fights started.

11.15 was very different: outside Toad's room, apart from what seemed the remote ringing of his telephone, there was never a threat of sound, the peace almost monastic in its security, a sanctuary in an environment whose defining characteristic was noise, actual or suppressed. 11.15 she knew would be 11.17 or 11.18, the enforced wait to which everyone was subjected before the door opened and, smiling, he ushered her in.

In fairness to him, he was never like Ray - perhaps he knew he was too old and repulsive for even the lightest of accidental touches. She was offered a chair and had taken the middle one of three in which she sat blinking against the light from the window opposite while he adjusted his bulk behind his desk.

"Parents' evening - I'm sure you're ready for it."

She nodded, a redundant gesture as his eyes continued to look at the wall above her head.

"There are, of course, other points in the year when we see parents, many of them more important than tonight's set-piece. The ruck rather than the full-blown scrum."

She waited, a blend of boredom and anticipation, for the rugby analogy to develop as ponderously as the digger she could see trundling back and forth in the car park.

No more words, however, came immediately as his eyes briefly settled on her, his lips closed and swollen.

"You had one of those points recently with Martin King, I believe." She nodded unnecessarily as his eyes were again elsewhere. "It seems that his daughter - Sally, is it? - "

"Sarah."

"Ah, yes. It seems that Sarah has been involved in a serious theft. A shame because, looking at her records, she's a very bright girl. I believe you're aware of it."

"I am. Sarah came to see me."

"Well, Martin King came to see me. He was very concerned, understandably, about Sarah but also about the way in which he alleges you handled the matter."

"Was he making a complaint?"

"No, I wouldn't have described it as a complaint. My approach has always been to cultivate, wherever possible, close relationships with parents so that we never reach that stage. Certainly not with someone like Martin King who has been very helpful to us in the past and will continue to be so, I am sure, in the future. I don't want to get into all the detail but -"

"He was extremely rude to me." She was blurting out the words. "Aggressive at points. You know he's done it before."

"No tears, though, this time." His eyes were the only sharp point in that face where everything, chin, jowls, seemed to sag. "As I was saying, I don't want to get into all the detail but I do need to know who else you have told about what the girl has done. You know our procedures, of course, and know that a matter of this seriousness had to be passed on."

"I made the judgement, probably wrong again, that I should respect confidentiality. Sarah had -"

"It certainly was the wrong judgement." He paused. "So, despite all the Inset you've had, you and I are the only ones who know what she has done."

"I've told no-one else." She felt all her other possible words retracting, like the head of a snail sensing danger. Toad, tilting his face from side to side, seemed to be considering options that were as equally weighted as his cheeks.

"You are, with time, going to be an invaluable asset to the school, I'm sure. Please, however, spend some time refreshing your memory on what that says." He waved his right arm back and to his side, stretching towards a yellow and green folder, isolated on his lower shelf between primary school bookends. "You have your own copy. Common sense spelt out in inordinate detail but commonsense nonetheless. If you took it all in and applied it, it could save you from getting yourself - and the rest of us - into a mess like this again."

His words became as dispassionate as one of his assemblies, stripped of urgency, if not of condescension. She found herself resentful, passive like the kids sitting in the hall, waiting for the signal to leave, her mind shuttered against each consecutive insult.

Early warning of the signal came as he shifted awkwardly in his chair. "I won't keep you any more as I know you have a lot to do." He didn't even stand but gestured her towards the door.

She stood momentarily nonplussed before turning and, in her haste, barely heard his words over the noise of the door and the handle as she tried to push it - rather than pull it - open. "Just you and I know – that's correct?"

She nodded, firm enough to be unequivocal, brief enough to terminate the contact, and left.

* * * * *

She had never felt less like a parents' evening. Her normal stride - her mother would have called it sprightly - shortened, her stomach already cloyed at the prospect of cellophane-wrapped rolls and hardened shortbread that could break your teeth.

Ray managed his usual leer as he held the staffroom door open for her and then brushed against her, on his way out, as she hesitated over where to sit.

Everywhere earnestness in its different forms: her own departmental colleagues in their self-deprecating irony; or Jim Siddons calmly, obsessively, trying with Maths staff to resolve a problem in the evening's room arrangements; or Jean and David in their Olympian detachment loudly discussing a walk or a meal - it could have been either - planned as the highlight of the next in their series of smoothly running weekends.

At least Toad wasn't there. If he had been, she would not have walked out - she wouldn't give him that satisfaction - but he would have conditioned everything: where she sat, how much she said, where her eyes fell - and she hated herself for it.

As she sat down - Jim and his problem seemed the least obtrusive option - with her token nourishment unopened in her hand, she churned over her irritation. Toad had given her no reprimand; she had not lost her rag. The fifteen minutes - interview, meeting, she didn't know what to call it - had got nowhere. Humiliation for her; comical inadequacy on his part, once the whole episode had the comforting distance of history that could be shared.

"Do you need a pair of scissors to open that?" Siddons, solicitous, gentlemanly, pulled her from her reverie.

"No, thanks - just savouring the anticipation. Rooms not big enough for the thousands who are coming?" She pulled at the cellophane. Siddons, unthreatening, leaning on the chair next to her, seemed in no hurry.

"Something like that. Poor planning on my part - needed a younger brain on it."

"As long as you don't ask me. Sorry - scatty female stereotype again." She stood up, brushing a few crumbs into her hand. "I'd better eat this in my room. Annoy Karen! But books need sorting."

He followed her out. "You don't mind my asking, Emily, but you don't seem your normal self."

"I don't mind at all - but no, it's just a headache which Mrs. Emerton will no doubt ease when I see her."

She laughed and went her separate way down the corridor.

Mrs. Emerton lived up to her billing. She twice came earlier than the time of her appointment and, gentle, acquiescent, seemed equally surprised each time that she had to wait. When she returned a third time, carrying a cup of coffee and presumably after seeing other teachers of Susie's, she was, in fact, late.

She heard what Pollard had to say but listening was harder to ascertain. Her eyes flitted around the room and her whole body turned once as the door opened.

"Not like Ben, then?"

"I'd never compare -"

"I would. I don't know what to do with him. He's not a bad lad but he just doesn't think. He gets caught up in these protests and I keep saying about the cost of petrol. It's always £10 and I can't remember the last time I was able to fill up. That's what he needs to get protesting about, not this student stuff. And the cost of food - he's hardly ever in for meals but when he does come in, he eats like a horse and cleans the cupboards out. You must see it. Every time you go to Tesco's, something has gone up. Is that where you go?"

Pollard seized the pause that the question offered as a chance to reclaim the initiative.

"Mrs. Emerton, is there anything you'd like to ask about Susie?"

"Good God, no, she's no trouble. She was out with me the night he had that party. Round at my sister's. How they all got there in that time, I don't know. Course it would be one time we're late. After midnight. You should've seen the state the place was in. Rug ruined. Smell of smoke everywhere - and I'm not daft, it wasn't just cigarettes. Some of them'd been in my bed as well. You weren't there, were you?"

The woman's eyes had a sudden focus, a spinning top stilled.

"No, no, certainly not." The sudden resumption of

113

concentration had made her stammer, a slip that a sharper brain than Mrs. Emerton's could have interpreted as guilt. "Nothing like that out of school. Sorry, not that I do it in -"

"And he got himself arrested. He said that wasn't what it was but it sounded like it to me." She was off again, recounting, as if through shattered glass, the incident that Becky and Sarah had related to her - until her spinning settled briefly for a second time.

"What would you do? He thinks the world of you. Not like that, mind. But he's always talking about what you've said."

"In that area, I'm afraid, I've got much less experience than some of my colleagues. Why don't you -"

"Look, you've got a queue, just like Tesco's." She stood up clumsily, a sign in anyone else of temper. "Thank you very much. You've been most kind."

As another parent edged forward, unsure of her appointment time after such a delay, Pollard watched Mrs. Emerton meander her way out, talking arbitrarily, it seemed, to anyone in her way. Was this Pollard's only source of praise, the only counterweight to the criticism, the indifference of Toad? Small consolation.

24

"They're just a complete bunch of wankers."

"Look, Martin, I'm not being prudish," Marriott's face had hardened, his patrician lips pinched, "but that is the third time you've said the same thing. We need, as I gather they say nowadays, to move on."

"Okay but you're not on the front line. I've only given you half the fucking excuses they come up with for not making money."

"For that," Marriott grimaced, "I suppose, I should be grateful - but could you dispense with the military metaphors?"

"The school's better than the bloody doctors. You wouldn't believe -"

"I think I'm a fairly good judge of what I do and don't believe." He stood up, his fingers loosening a photograph from the pile of papers on his desk. "I don't believe in this either - this Big Society farrago - but at least you're paid good money for it. I'm sure he is as well."

He pushed the photograph towards King who glanced at it without turning it around.

"What's he got to do with it?"

"He's your way in. Plenty of experience, apparently, of this sort of thing. And you'd better look properly at the photo. That, I'm assured, is how he looks at the moment." He noticed the frown on King's face as he picked up the piece of paper. "Younger than you, isn't he?"

"He'll need to be."

"Not like my second deputation of the day. Long-standing party members with whom I fully sympathise. Old enough for you, let alone him, to be their son and they have steam coming out of their ears over this new housing development. The first lot went away a little calmer so perhaps my diplomacy will work again."

He tilted his head downwards, staring momentarily at King who had pushed the photograph back onto the desk.

"I suppose what I'm saying," he looked at his watch, "is that it's time for you to go."

25

"We all want to protest but there's no point in just doing the same old thing."

"Nobody's saying that."

Sarah looked around her. The anger in the voices was escalating, attracting brief interest from other tables in the college canteen.

"Hang on a minute, Lee. You've got a load of old biddies around the county picketing surgeries for weeks and what've we got here - eight, nine people? If everyone who's ever been to one of these meetings was here, that would be fourteen at most." He didn't wait for confirmation. "We're not pulling anyone else in."

"So what do you want to do - advertise? Join the enemy?"

"Don't be so fucking stupid. It's what we make the issue - make it more appealing. We're only here for two years, most of us. Sorry, not all of us," and he nodded apologetically to the small group from the school, "but what happens in the college, to us even, is asking for too much altruism."

"You're still saying the same thing, Adam: tart up what we're doing, find some kind of gimmick. What we do has got to stand or fall on its merits."

"Oh, Christ." He turned to Sarah. "Why did that bloke - the one who got himself arrested - what made him turn up?"

"Probably because he thought there was going to be a bit of trouble. I don't know him that well. Different sets all the time. I don't think he could've told you why we were there."

"And that's just what we don't want. A load of yobs drawn in because there's a chance of a fight."

"No-one's saying that. All right, he was a bad example. But what about the way we make our point? You know, as well as I do, that we're seen by that lot as a bunch of weirdos, people to avoid, no fun to be with."

"All image again, isn't it? That's all you keep coming back to, Mr.Chairman."

The sarcasm brought a momentary pause.

"Look, Lee, it's not my bloody show. I'm just trying to get us to make some progress."

"We were talking on the way here, Adam." Lisa, prompted by Sarah, was earnest but uncertain. "About Uncut. They've probably got the issues right but it's their humour that gets people with them and it's not threatening." She nudged Richie.

"That's right. If it's a laugh, we ought to get a lot more to turn up and as long as it's something worth fighting over, what's the problem?"

Self-conscious at being the focus of eyes turned on him, he looked down.

"You can't argue with that then, can you, Lee?"

"No." He shook his head irritably. "Give it a go. See what happens."

26

The rain showed no sign of relenting. The trees which, in arching over the road like a cathedral roof, normally kept the tarmac damp at worst in heavy rain, had failed totally to repel the deluge. Jonathan Oliver, with the road clear in front of him, straddled the white line to avoid the flooding on either side, his speed unusually cautious, purely in the hope that the rain would ease by the time he got to work.

His deliberate delay achieved nothing. When he squeezed in, once again, to the tiny parking area, the rain was still pouring down. In case anyone should be looking out of the downstairs windows, he sat in the car for a minute or two, examining his empty diary, willing the sky to clear. All in vain - and so he headed off towards the back door, tiptoeing through the enclosed courtyard that was already flooded.

Hanging up his coat soaked the small patch of carpet between the door and the window. He scooped up the mail from a brown chair, threadbare and institutionalised, and added it to the desk, alongside the four or five piles of paper, discrete but seemingly unattended to in his absence - and probably not discreet.

A holiday, if that was what you called it, made no difference. The pinboard on the wall had the same clutter: one or two synopses of government guidelines for residential homes; a reminder in red, indelible pen that Philip Skewes must have his new cream applied four times a day; a gaudy, multi-coloured, hand-written request for home-made cakes for the following week's fundraising cream tea; and a grey, fluffy glove puppet, with pins stuck in it. He felt a tremor of pride: whatever else he paid heed to, it was not the pervasive public sector mantra, fostered by successive governments, that display maketh the organisation.

His eyes were caught by the lights of another car pulling up. Through the net curtains, he watched the driver, obscured by the rain on the windscreen, check his pockets, draw his collar up and smooth his hair before heading for the front door, not pausing to check the locking of his car.

The door must not have responded to his push. Oliver, flicking through the mail, smiled at the three stabs at the bell: it was one of those rare days when someone had remembered the guidelines. The bell rang twice more before he heard Maria's footsteps and the door open after the usual dropping of the keys.

An unfamiliar voice echoed down the corridor.

"Excuse me a moment." A delay, perhaps to remove his coat, perhaps to shake the rain off onto the mat. "I've come to see Jonathan Oliver. At nine o'clock but I'm afraid the rain's held me up."

"Ah, Mr. Oliver - come this way, please. Mr. ... ?"

"Andrews. Tom Andrews."

Oliver glanced, bemused, at the empty page in his diary and opened his door to see Maria followed by the MP, straightened to his full height and smiling broadly.

"Mr. Andrews - good to see you."

Maria stepped away from them both, deferential but self-contained, and back out into the corridor. Her closing the door, however, was followed, immediately, by an insistent knocking.

"Sorry. With you in a moment."

His attempt at delay failed. He shook his head gently at Betty as she squeezed him back into the room, nudging Andrews against the window, her voice strident.

He took a pack of bird seed from his desk drawer. "You can give them some now but that's it for today." He pointed at the calendar and she nodded, grabbing the seed and scuttling back out into the corridor.

"She's a character. Never any niggle. Everything's an excuse to laugh." He watched her go, craning his neck to the left. "Taken the right door, as well. God moves in mysterious ways. I'm sorry." He lowered his shoulder blades, his one application for the day of what his physio was always telling him. "Sorry not to give you a proper welcome."

"Not at all. This is your real work."

Despite Oliver's best efforts, a stubborn six inch gap in their height remained - before he bent to scoop a paper from one of the piles on his desk. "Another missive from one of your mates." He waved the document at the MP. "New criteria we have to apply if we wish to appoint someone like Maria who is not a British national."

"Is she Malay, Filipino -?"

"Hurdle after hurdle - and the first is making sense of all this. Jargon's the kindest word you can use for it. They categorise everyone from anywhere in the world - at least the bloody yarpies only had whites, coloureds and blacks and it was within one country. Still, probably not your doing. Look, do sit down." He paused. "How can I help?"

"More of the same, please. I got your letter and, as I said in my reply, I wanted to get a closer feel for the issues that are affecting you here."

"You'd need as long as it takes me to plough through that bumpf - and more." He had stood again and was scrabbling through a tray on top of the filing cabinet above Andrews' head. "Let me make you a cup of coffee - or tea?"

The MP shrugged. "Tea of preference but it doesn't matter. I don't want to take up too much of your time - I can see what it's like." An alarm, impatient, staccato, had sounded for a second time. "In your letter, what appeared to be your major concerns were these immigrant quotas - and how the Local Authority decides the level of financial support they give to some of the very ill people you have here."

Oliver muttered something that Andrews, even though he turned his head, obviously did not catch. "Sorry, dropped the bloody teabag down the back. Never mind. Should be strong enough." Stretching, he grunted and then abandoned his token effort. "We don't just deal with ill people, as I'm sure you realise." He passed Andrews his tea and, sitting down, assumed his best diplomatic smile.

"Indeed I do - and I'm interested in every type of resident but it was you, in your letter, who raised the financial support issue."

"I dare say I did. It's just these things change daily. Yes, Jenny?" A slim, heavy-eyed woman, not waiting for a response from him, came in and, with a wordless apology to Andrews, gesticulated towards a cupboard on the wall. He nodded and, while she removed from it a small box of tablets, he continued, an orator who has had a brief interruption from a heckler.

"Where does the deterioration of old age become illness? This is a case in point." He called back the woman who was closing the door behind her. "Jenny, are those for Joan Bennett? I guessed so. No, that's fine."

He turned again to Andrews. "Joan's been here for six months or so. Healthy in many ways. Eats as much as I do but she's had a couple of TIAs since she's been here and at least one stroke in the past. Hence the medication - and that's only one of three different forms of treatment that people here are having for conditions that fall broadly, in layman's terms, into the stroke category. All a continuum. And everything, everyone here falls into one continuum or another." He hesitated, a grin spreading across his face. "Should it be continuums or continua? You must have had a public school education, I suppose?"

"I didn't actually. Local school." Oliver watched him trying to free his calves from his sodden trouser legs.

"Oh, same as me - not around here of course. Never mind, anyway. The fact there are no distinct categories means a dividing line, arbitrary some would say, has to be drawn somewhere. And that dividing line has shifted."

"You have -"

"Look, I'm probably being too abstract - too good an opportunity to miss, having someone like you here."

He turned his eyes from the opposite wall to the man in front of him.

"Jenny, the others, they're paid for their practical skills, not analysis. Shouldn't be any other way." He paused. " Look, why don't I show you one or two of our residents? Make it all concrete?"

Andrews nodded.

"Very little I can say as we go around, for obvious reasons. Just remember the names."

At the end of the corridor, they turned into a spacious lounge, perhaps two rooms in its nineteenth century beginnings. All the chairs, each of them pressed back against the wall, were occupied but only in one pocket to their left was there the sound of intermittent conversation.

"Come on, John, wake them up for me." A man, head tilted back, eyes shadowed by glasses that looked like broken bottle tops, smiled calmly but said nothing.

"Now, Irene, why've you still got that orange there? Come on, you like it." He offered a segment to her lips and a piece disappeared, not bitten off, but more by natural erosion. He crouched beside her, feeding her for three or four minutes, her eyes like glass, no visible reaction to the orange, much less to the unfamiliar visitor beside him.

He rose and stroked her hand. "See you later."

He walked across the room, a teacher centre-stage before a tranquil and undemanding class. "What about you, Joan? Lovely to see you down here." Looking sideways at him, her eyes lit up, her fingers, two of them clawed, stretching towards his arm.

"Hang on a minute, let's straighten you up." The woman had an array of cushions, in theory keeping her upright, in practice only supporting the angle at which she had keeled over. "Cor, you're a weight." He pulled her forwards, rearranged the cushions and settled her back, upright and visibly grateful.

"You're interested in politics, aren't you, Joan? This is Mr. Andrews, our local MP." She looked at them both and, bright-eyed, made some sounds, an occasional word, only the falling intonation at the end hinting at the close of a sentence. "Yes, I thought you voted for him."

"Thank you very much." Andrews had stepped forward, gently to shake her hand. "I hope you'll do the same the next time." As he struggled to extricate his hand from the sudden rigidity in hers, she smiled, a mixture of self-deprecation and resignation.

"Don't be daft, Joan, you've got enough elections left in you to see the Tories consigned to the scrapheap but only if you let Mr. Andrews go." He prised her fingers open and her smile remained unchanged, as if her fingers were nothing to do with her. "I'll see you later."

He glanced around the room before putting his hand on Andrews' arm and guiding him back to the corridor. "I'd hoped you could see Dennis. Sometimes, though, he opts not to come down. He would've been a better contrast with Joan - but that's just a rare neatness on my part. Irene is probably the best example here of what we were talking about."

He ushered Andrews back into the office and closed the door. "Joan's the resident I was telling you about. You saw some of the problems she has. Add to those very poor mobility - she cannot move, unaided, from her chair - and a range of worrying skin conditions, plus a host of other issues I won't bore you with, and yet when her assessment was done, she didn't come within a million miles of receiving financial support. And, to be honest, that was the outcome we expected.

"Irene, however, is another matter altogether. She was the resident I helped with the orange."

Andrews nodded.

"If I list all the health problems she has, you'll get an idea of what we're talking about. Type 2 diabetes, Parkinson's Disease, cognition problems (she gets confused about time and where she is), severe short term memory loss, osteoarthritis that's much the same as Joan's, peripheral vascular disease and heart failure. That's probably not all of them. Oh, and paranoia - I was surprised she allowed me to feed her that orange.

"I won't go into all the medical detail but she's someone I would have expected to be funded. Six months ago she was assessed and turned down. As a result, her son's had to put her house on the market."

"That won't be quick."

"No, although the authorities are very good in that respect. They make bridging finance available. But I mentioned her son - he's an example of a key difficulty in the way it's always set up. He's a nice bloke but, putting it bluntly, as he's not very bright and acutely shy, he can't be the advocate for his mum that someone like her desperately needs. And without an advocate, I'm not saying they steamroller it but the case doesn't have the balance it should."

"Can't you act as her advocate?"

"To some extent but we're compromised by relative judgements - how Irene compares with other people in the home. Someone in the family is not compromised like that. He'd be able to fight his corner, if he was up to it."

Andrews brushed his hand through his hair, his eyes trained on Oliver's hand that was waving in support of what he was saying. "But it's not cut-and-dried that she's been badly treated?"

"No, it never is. It's what I was saying about these continuums - or whatever we agreed to call them. Everything Irene's got wrong with her can be argued over. I might call a condition 'severe' but that doesn't automatically fit it into a slot determined by the criteria. And, in fairness, there's got to be flexibility."

There was a knock at the door. Andrews moved his hands forwards onto his knees and looked straight at him. "Please, I won't take any more of your time."

Oliver opened the door. "Is it urgent?"

There were no words in reply.

"Okay, I won't be long."

"Don't bother to shut the door." Andrews was standing. "Seriously." He nodded in agreement with his own words. "I'll be off but what you've said has been invaluable, especially Irene's case. Would your secretary -"

He laughed. "Different world here, I'm afraid. Maggie does the secretarial bits, some cleaning - and some care work when we're short. She'd love to be called my secretary. But, anyway, you were saying?"

"Could Maggie give me any information that doesn't breach confidentiality? Date of birth, National Insurance number -"

"Look, I've probably overstepped the mark in what I've said already." Oliver leaned against the door to close it. "I'm sure you mean well but I'd better speak to her son before I go any further."

"I quite understand." Andrews had stood, straightened again to a height that dwarfed Oliver. "But if you could - I'm sure we'd be able to help."

27

It was surprisingly casual of Toad, walking into Pollard's room in the late afternoon calm, a letter in his hand. He stood, though, a little awkwardly as if the room was as unfamiliar to him as to a parent who saw it only once a year.

"I've had a phone call from Mrs. Hayes. In passing, she said how pleased she was with Jessica's progress since she moved up. Start of the year, was it?"

"No, January."

"All the better, then, to get such a reaction in a short period of time. Well done."

"Thanks."

She felt like one of the kids facing her down. If Toad had expected more of a response from her, he was not going to get it. She glanced briefly at her desk but then looked back up at him. She could not take the resentment any further.

He raised his hand with the letter.

"I've received a request for a reference from a Venton Grange School in Hertfordshire. I hate to be pernickety but, again, you should have let me know about it at the point of application."

She raised her eyebrows. "Sorry."

"It doesn't matter now but bear it in mind in future. Not that I would expect there to be any applications in the immediate future." He folded the letter twice - and then a further time so that it was barely visible in his hand. "You see, the business with Martin King's daughter -"

"Sarah."

"Young Sarah, yes. It's been decided to take the matter no further. I believe there was a photographer involved. She doesn't want to press charges and the police, thankfully for the young girl, will not be pursuing the theft as the camera has been returned and as they, anyway, have more than enough on their plates at the moment. Less pleasantly for her, I am sure her father will be dealing with it at home, using all the severity it warrants. That, I think, is more or less it as far as the world outside this school is concerned."

His hesitation was unnecessary. In a public context like an assembly, Toad could never structure a speech to maximise its impact yet, in a private context like this, he could weight his sentences with such precision that it made any additional forewarning of a threat redundant.

"As for the school itself, I also will be taking the matter no further. For the girl, that would always have been the case as the incident did not occur on school premises or in school time - and it's not part of a pattern of behaviour that we here have any record of. For you, the matter is also closed as I have said everything I need to say but," and he looked down at his clenched fist edged in crumpled white, "I have to advise against any applications like this. There is no point." His face, heavy and inflexible, attempted an avuncular smile. "I have to write an honest reference and I could not exclude comment on this recent incident. In two or three years, it might be different. You've got a career to rebuild and, with your talents, you could well be successful. But not now. You must see that."

He stared at her, awaiting a response.

"Two or three years." She tried to stifle her reaction. "It's the spirit of the age, isn't it? One strike and you're out - or, in this case, in."

Powerless to leave her own room, for a few seconds she froze until he, after scanning the room and returning his eyes to brief scrutiny of her face, reached behind him for the door handle and left.

28

It was a balmy Sunday, the first of the summer. From the window, Goldsmith could see the trees motionless, until, each time Mary carried something else across the gravel, sparrows darted from their cover to set the leaves quivering. Within a minute, once she was back in the house, they had returned, unsettling the branches like a stone in water until each leaf, picture-book and in place, was calm again.

The rhythm was not unlike the cycle of appointments on a working day. He was tempted to time her - she was emerging at regular intervals - but his watch would only have given him a reminder of how late it already was.

To his right, supposedly in his line of vision, the computer screen accelerated, unwatched, through its repertoire of news headlines, offers and update alerts. Only the rapidly changing colours impinged on his consciousness as his eyes stared out into the garden. For a second time, he lifted to his mouth the coffee cup that was long since empty.

His father was examining the plates, the cutlery, the glasses that were accumulating on the table. He moved each pile carefully before replacing it, purposeful, curious. From his vantage point in the house, behind the glass of the window, behind the table, Goldsmith watched his father, like a child absorbed in the marionette actions of a character in a computer game, each action more fragmented by the metal squares of the latticed window through which he stared.

His father had turned now to the barbecue, lifting the lid, shutting it, tilting the whole contraption to look underneath it and scratching his head. He replaced something in his pocket before walking back towards the house, towards the window behind which Goldsmith was sitting.

He dropped his eyes to the screen, to the latest update waiting to be installed.

There was a tap on the window. "Sorry to bother you, Colin. Do you know where the tongs are?"

Looking up through filmy eyes whose distraction he hoped would be mistaken for broken concentration, he shook his head. "Sorry, Dad, don't know but Mary's in the kitchen."

His father moved beyond the range of his eyes that were raised again. The neighbours' cat rubbed its back against the table leg. Mary's voice, a bang of a saucepan lid, and he fled into the bushes. Mary was organising everything, his father on the barbecue, Becky who had just got up, him sitting at the computer but downstairs.

She knew him too well, better than he deserved. The way she had said, "You can't even look me in the eye, can you?" - before reassuring him, sitting him down. "You'll be fine. Just stay inside until the food's ready." He looked at the hand that she had rubbed repeatedly and plugged the memory stick in. He loaded the data but turned again to the window.

Becky was holding the lid of the barbecue while her

grandfather arranged the firelighters. Whatever he was saying made her laugh, as it always did. He had probably been the same at that demonstration both of them had been caught up in - coincidentally, they had said.

They were that close. Perhaps the start of it all had been his mother's death. After the initial shock, his dad had seemed encased in a shell which everyday problems could not penetrate. He ran four or five times a week despite severe arthritis in his knees. He listened to Becky - was listening to her now - as if the listening only needed to be one way, as if no difficulty of his own was worth sharing.

Becky was retrieving two of the firelighters that had dropped on the grass. Probably a combination of arthritic fingers and failing eyesight that he would never discuss, brushing off any enquiry, even the relatively well-informed ones from his son.

Never a complaint. Not even like mild Mr. Jenkins who had made an appointment two days earlier and who had every reason to complain. He had been to see him only two weeks previously, worried about what seemed like small spiders in his eye and flashing lights when he went out at night. He remembered the amused, apologetic, uncertain look on his face as he said it. Perhaps the man, like his dad, had been too self-deprecating. Perhaps that was why he had made the mistake.

He had told him that it could be a retinal problem and that if there was any deterioration, he should go straight into A&E. Why had he not taken the usual safety-first option?

Through glazed eyes, he watched Becky raise her arms in the air like a cheer leader as, presumably, the barbecue was underway.

The inevitable then had happened: his symptoms did deteriorate, he went into the hospital and, on the same day, had surgery to repair a tear in the retina. "Ten days longer and I would have lost the sight in my eye." He, in fairness, had said it only once and had been very rational about it. "You've been very good to our family. I'm not here to make a song-and-dance about it. I just wanted to make sure that you knew the facts. It might help in future."

It was another tunnel, another burrowing beneath him. He was the one to give advice. He had been.

Outside, Becky lowered her arms and, stepping back, bowed in mock-obeisance to her grandfather.

There was a knock at the door. Mary's hand on his shoulder.

"You really must come out now."

29

Kirsty ran a few paces and then decided that shouting was more of a strength of hers. Liam turned and waited. She could not believe her luck: he was on his own and it was a quarter of a mile, ten minutes the way she walked, before they reached the club hut.

"What you doing today?"

He seemed to like the implicit admiration. "Probably take a ski out if they don't talk too long."

She walked a fraction behind him, showing that she could keep up but not enough to quicken their pace.

"Can't see Sarah being here." Unresponsive, he was staring across her, out to sea. "You know she's supposed to have nicked a camera?"

"She wouldn't have done that."

"She said she did." At least, it didn't seem to have impressed him. "Looked quite proud of it. All gone quiet now."

He shrugged his shoulders.

"You like girls with a bit of meat on them?"

He turned to look at her. "What you mean?"

"Not like all these lettuce and muesli eaters." Her words were quickening, her place in the physical pecking order gnawing at her confidence. "Someone who gives you something to grab hold of."

His eyebrows were raised.

"Someone like me."

A half-smile eased onto his face as he grasped the drift of her words.

"I know this probably isn't the way you think a chat-up should go." She tried to stifle a tremor of alarm: was it not just the incongruity of the way she had spoken that had caused the smile? "I just thought there was no point in beating about the bush. Well, no, you'd be more than welcome to beat about the bush." She could see that her words had lost him. "A bird in the hand. Two hands needed and preferred. And they say proverbs have gone out of the English language. What a load of bollocks." The flurry of words, his lack of comprehension, was the best outcome to be grabbed at.

"Oi."

What she would have dreaded only a minute earlier was now a relief, a distraction, a way out as long as he said nothing, wordless, she hoped, in his bemusement. They stood and waited, with him looking at her as if nothing had been said, while the trickle of people behind them coalesced before enveloping them.

They were among the last to arrive. The boards and the skis were outside the hut in haphazard readiness - but with no-one starting to pull them down to the water.

Once inside the crowded hut, they joined a huddle, only half of them changed.

"What's going -"

"Oh, God, Sarah's dad's here. That'll go down well."

Through the crush, Kirsty could see Martin King's head at the other end of the room, scanning those there, briefly gazing in their direction. Malcolm stood next to him, looking at his watch and the clock on the wall.

"Is she here? She's not done something again, has she?"

"He wouldn't be here to get her - not standing like that alongside Malcolm. Anyway, she's not."

"Bit of hush, please." Malcolm had banged on the wall behind him. "You'll be off out in a couple of minutes but I wanted you to hear a few things Martin King - Sarah's dad, poor fella - has to say. Then I'm going to be showing him around for half an hour or so. Duncan's got the pleasure of organising you lot until I get out there."

He waved his hands to subdue the muttering and the cheering.

"You can see how bloody popular I am. Martin, over to you."

"Oh, Christ, here we go again." Liam raised his hand behind him, in front of her face, only for her to grab and bite it. He turned, his other hand tightening on her neck until, after the longest possible delay, she loosened the grip of her teeth and stood smiling, preoccupied, at the back of his head that was turned away from her again.

"A couple of minutes is all I need. Most of you know me so I won't waste time on introductions. What I want to get across to you is an idea that has been kicking around for a few years - and show what it can mean for you. The Big Society - you're doing it already, helping yourselves, helping others, which is what it's all about, and all the government is doing is putting in more help so that you can do the job you're already doing so brilliantly even better.

"The main sign of that is standing right next to me. Andy Kew - he's a volunteer like you but he's got a degree in something I don't understand" - the man on his left, tall, in his mid-twenties, shifted awkwardly at his introduction – "has all the knowledge, all the contacts with other agencies, to help make your work more effective. He'll be with you on club night evenings and at weekends."

The front row was quiet, only an occasional glance breaking their appearance of attentiveness, but behind them heads were turning, muttering had resumed although, for some of the girls, staring at the new man was a rare instance of silent concentration. For Kirsty, Liam was temporarily forgotten - perhaps permanently as she daydreamed.

"I've said enough, anyway. Andy will be out with you in a minute. All I can say is keep up the good work." King stepped back against the wall.

"Outside, then, with Duncan. Get a move on." Malcolm's voice had more than its usual edge of impatience. "And you, you've missed what your father had to say."

Sarah kept her head down. Standing silent with Becky behind Ben, they momentarily obstructed the outward tide of those desperate for some activity.

"Christ, he's gorgeous." Kirsty prodded her.

"Oh, God, give it a rest."

"Not your dad - I'm not that desperate. Sorry, I didn't mean it like that. But him, the one in the grey jumper." She pointed her thumb, close against her body, her attempt at discretion.

"As long as it keeps you happy." Sarah allowed herself to be swept back out. "Why the hell did I bother to come tonight?" Her words were for Becky, for anyone.

30

"Nothing's going to happen about it." Sarah stirred her coffee. "Not as far as the police are concerned. Plenty already has at home." The spoon barely moved, the tiny eddying on the surface of the cup almost imperceptible but holding the staring of her eyes. "I just want to be normal." Her finger flicked at the corner of her eye as if she had just woken. "You never thought you'd hear me say that, did you?"

Becky put her arm around her. "What's your mum said?" Three Year 10s glanced across from the table in the corner, nudging each other.

"She wants me to move out. Go and live with her, even if it is on the floor. But that's not feasible, not until later in the summer anyway because I've still got to get to school. I just don't know what to do."

"Is it bearable at - with your dad?" Becky's voice, quiet at the best of times, was a whisper.

"Probably. He'll go on the way he always does but the worst with me is past. He blew his top over the bloody camera as if he was so squeaky clean. Ranted at 'all the strings' he'd had to pull to 'put a lid on the affair'." Her smile was not forced. "He really does speak in clichés like that all the time but God knows what the strings are that he's pulling."

"Did he want to know why you'd done it?" Her arm tightened. "I would."

Sarah eased herself gently away. "In your different ways, neither of you understands. I've told you already that I can rationalise it by saying I wanted to get back at that woman for the photos she took of Ben - and your granddad - but it was more like that Yeats poem, 'a lonely impulse of delight'." Becky looked blankly at her, pupil to teacher. "As for him, no, it wasn't that kind of conversation."

"I don't know what to say." She stared beyond Sarah to the rain outside.

"It doesn't matter if you don't. It won't stop the rain." Across her face, a small tremor pursed her lips. "On more important matters - that's what Polly would say, isn't it? - how are you and Liam?"

"No idea. You'd better ask him." Her voice, conscious that the need for reassurance had not passed, was subdued, her eyes returning to the umbrellas on the pavement. "Anyway, you know I told you about Polly leaving?"

"What?" Her face had tensed.

"At Ben's party - or whatever you want to call it."

"Oh." She looked away disdainfully. "You're not joking, are you?"

"No - she's trying for another job."

"You can't ... Oh, it doesn't matter. Why did she tell you?"

"It just slipped out. D of E meeting a few weeks ago. I suppose it mightn't come to anything and she didn't seem absolutely sure about it."

Sarah sighed, thrown back into introspection. "She's taken a load of crap from my father but she'll always listen to me - well, nearly always unless I'm having a bad day." She sighed again. "I guess it doesn't really affect us. They can't leave immediately, can they? But I'd just thought -"

"Oh, God, I wish I hadn't -"

"Forget it - it doesn't matter. I've got you. Who could possibly need more?" Her eyes, back in the world again, scanned the room and fixed the table in the corner. "What's the matter, children? Nothing worth talking about?"

She stood and, taking Becky's arm, strode out of the café, in the best approximation of a stately departure that a sixteen year old could achieve.

31

The rain had driven everyone into the college canteen, the grass banks outside visible through the long glass panels and deserted. They sat, more compressed into their corner than usual.

"Is this it, then?"

"For us, yes. Lisa couldn't make it because she's got an oral exam tomorrow."

"Okay, anyone who wants to - get a coffee and then we'll start."

While they waited, just five of them still seated, they split into their separate conversations: Sarah and Richie, tall and compensating with a barrage of theories for his self-consciousness, at one; three second years at another, their time at college almost spent, their thoughts on university only dragged back to the present by duty.

Lee and the others nudged their way slowly through the tables, pastry in one hand, coffee in the other.

"You haven't been listening, have you?" Richie stemmed his flow as he raised his eyes nervously towards Sarah.

"Sorry, I have. Honestly. But what's he doing here?" With

Lee were three unfamiliar faces - and one she was sure she recognised.

"We've whipped up more interest in five minutes than you lot have managed in six months."

At the back was the man from the club that Kirsty had obsessed about, the same heavy grey jumper, fraying at the edges. He stood, reticent perhaps from being visibly so much older than the rest, while the tables were pushed apart and more chairs pulled up.

"Am I okay here?" He sat down on a new chair, next to Sarah of all people. "I heard them talking at the till. Sounds more interesting than my course."

"Right, let's get on with it. Saturday's fine for everyone?"

There were nods but not everywhere. "Sorry, I'll fill you in later if you're still interested. I've forgotten your names."

"Louis."

"Andy."

"Susie."

"Everything's been bought. Enough to cover all the dicks in Whitcross for a night. I'll need a fiver from each of you, though. None of them are going out in advance. They're going to have to turn up to get them. We've got a couple of women who've done face-painting - they say it'll stay on unless there's heavy rain."

Adam worked his way through the arrangements, his shorthand confusing the recent additions to the group, his staccato delivery glazing the eyes of the regulars - apart from Sarah. She had planted her feet on the ground, her hands clasped on her waist, her face set, the tension in her body ratcheted up by the relaxation of the man next to her. His back had slid down slightly despite the plastic rigidity of the chair, his arms flopped, monkey-like, by his sides.

At one point, she had sensed him turn briefly towards her. It might have been to her; it might have been to Richie next to her. She kept her face firmly, to the end, on Adam, as tense herself as his final words: "Should be good, get at least fifty there."

"It is going to be a laugh, is it?"

Lee's question was to no-one as the coffee cups were pushed into the middle of the tables and Adam, picking up his battered folder, walked away.

"What's the matter with him?"

"So much for filling us in." Kew was talking to her as he stood up. "I know it's against these NHS reforms and it's this Saturday but -"

"You were at the life-saving club, weren't you? To promote this Big Society crap."

"I was. Don't remember you, though." Irritation flashed across her face. "Look, I'm not doing that because I want to. All the placements in voluntary work have dried up and something like that is all there is."

She made no response.

"Look. Let me start again. My course - Diploma in Social Work, part-time - is supposed to take me out of here most of the time on placements. But they're not there -"

"Because Government funding of charities has been hacked away." She looked straight in front of her, her voice angry but impersonal.

"Probably right. But what am I supposed to do? I've done jobs, here and there, bits and pieces, since I got my degree. Saved enough for this course. It's something I want to do but the woman organising it is hopeless. Finding a placement is voluntary as well." Sarah's eyes did not move. "What do I do? Give it up? Or take the chance that came up with this Big Society thing?"

"But it's bollocks!"

"I wouldn't argue with you but it doesn't actually harm anyone. Not like the NHS or welfare. There's nothing wrong in encouraging people to get involved even if," her face tightened, "okay, it's trying to plug gaps they've created elsewhere."

He sat silent, looking straight ahead, before rubbing his face with both hands.

"It's not ideal, I know. I don't like the set-up, the bloke who drives it locally, not someone I'd trust -"

"You're talking about my father." Still her eyes did not shift from the advert, a new, cut-price breakfast offer, on the glass panel opposite her.

"Oh, Christ, I'm sorry. I'm just going from bad to worse, aren't I?"

"No, that's not how I'd put it."

"But what they're doing to the NHS, it's intolerable. Calling it reforms is a joke." She looked at him with resignation. "I think I'd better go." He nudged his chair back. "If you could not tell your father, I'd be -"

"You haven't got a clue, have you?"

Before he could answer, she was on her feet and gone.

32

"Yes, I am just talking about the hoops you have to go through."

"Teaching a seal the tricks to perform that the audience expects."

"Yes, again, but it's only this last couple of weeks." Pollard looked at them, patient, amused. "If you're not interested, why are you here?"

"Rhetorical question, Miss. Which type of writing are we supposed to use lots of them in?"

"If you know to ask that question, you'll know the answer. Now, is this it, do you think?"

Sarah and Becky - no-one else. A quarter to four, two weeks before the first English exam, and the only two to turn up for the revision session were the ones who needed it least. She should have known it: what she had planned was too straightforward, guaranteed to see work fragment into friendly but aimless chat.

"Okay. Planning for the poetry question. Ten minutes is the most you can allow yourselves. Title on the board. Look at the method in your books if you can't remember it. One minute to choose the four poems that'll give you most to say."

She watched the two girls thumbing through their anthologies, intent, enjoying the time limit, the problem-solving. The writing would be another matter.

"Minute up. What've you got, Sarah?"

" 'Salome' -"

"Remember you're looking for the poems that give you most to say on the question. Where's the 'change' in 'Salome'?"

"Well, he's had his head cut off. You can't have much more of a change than that."

"But you don't see him before he's had his head -" She stopped, aware that a serious counter-argument was unnecessary. "All right, let's have the ones you've really put down."

"Change is an interesting concept, Miss. We're about to change - or, at least," she put on her best imitation of Fletcher's voice, "our circumstances are. We will not, in September, be here any more -"

"Sarah, I know this is voluntary, but we have to crack on. Becky, you look as though your brain's in gear, what've you got?"

"Three I'm definite about. One I'm not so sure -"

"But you will, Miss. Or I thought you would be until I heard a rumour about you trying to get another job."

Pollard glanced at Becky and smiled reassuringly when she saw the apprehension in the girl's eyes.

"It's all right." She turned to face Sarah. "That was the idea a few weeks ago but not any more. Change of plan. Exactly what you need to do by the look of it. Next stage: two minutes to list as many points of comparison as you can. Similarities or differences, it doesn't matter. Off you go."

Nothing happened: no pages were turned, no pens started scribbling.

"If you're not being interviewed on Saturday, then why don't you come and join us? All against what they're doing to the NHS. Should be a laugh. Nothing nasty. Nothing to compromise you."

Pollard held up her hand.

"Look. Leave that for now. I'll give you the two minutes again. Come on - let's get a bit of focus."

33

Goldsmith checked his patients for the morning: several for whom it was unnecessary to consult their recent records, so familiar was he with the pattern of their health; two - a married couple who had just appeared on their lists - were probably, one at a time, doing little more than outlining their medical histories; and Amy Goddard.

For her, he did pore over the records. The publicity in the village was remarkably accurate - they had not distorted her symptoms in any way. Ian's explanation to her that she would not be able to have Herceptin was there, followed by three appointments in the intervening weeks, each with a different doctor, where the same view had been adhered to. Her last appointment had been the longest by far but with the same outcome.

He could not blame her for the fact that it was now, after Sheila, his turn. If anything, he thought it would have come sooner. His own reputation for thoroughness would have pointed that way, particularly with his growing vulnerability that some patients would sense as clearly as he did.

He was late seeing her - a minor irritant alongside everything else she had to deal with, but an irritant nonetheless. She was fourth on his list but the young girl, pregnant and in the same year as Becky, had taken twice her notional time allocation. He could have referred her on to Alison but it had taken five minutes to get her to relax sufficiently to open up with her worries - and she would only have had to repeat the thawing-out process with the nurse.

As he led Amy through to his consulting room and apologised, he took in her appearance, walking beside him. Her head was wrapped in a scarf, her eyes a little more protuberant than he remembered them as being in the photograph pushed through his door. She glanced across at him, upright, an almost jaunty smile in brushing aside his regret at the delay.

The door closed gently behind them.

"How are you feeling now?"

"It seems to be levelling out. It was one of the things I was going to ask you - how long it would stay settled down. But, day by day, I can put up with this."

"I'll come back to your question but in what sense is it levelling out?"

"The nausea's more or less gone." Her eyes fixed him. "Look, Dr. Goldsmith, I suppose you need to check my symptoms but that's not really why I'm here. I've said the same thing, over and over, to so many people -"

"And you're getting fed up with it."

"Yes. I just want to get everything done that can be done - and I don't feel that's what's happening. The other doctors've been very nice but -"

He did not interrupt. Instead he waited and then, when her eyes dropped, an acknowledgement that she may have been out of her depth in achieving that delicate balance of tact and firmness, he spoke.

"I understand and I'll try not to put you through exactly the same dreary set of questions. I will, however, have to ask you some. Tell me first what you hope I can do for you."

"I've seen on the internet there's a drug that could really help me. My understanding is that the way I am now is as good as it will get. Sooner or later, there's only one way it can go. No, no, I'm all right." She brushed aside his reassurances. "But this Herceptin could be a game changer."

"Not much of a game, is it?"

"No, definitely not. But they won't give it to me and I don't know why."

"Okay, we'll come back to that in a minute." He concentrated on the screen. "You've finished the chemotherapy?"

"Yes."

"And you've another hospital appointment next week?"

"Yes, on Wednesday."

"And you haven't had one since the chemotherapy was completed?"

"No."

"And your symptoms - I'll keep them to a minimum. You mentioned nausea but that seems better now?"

"Yes - it's only occasional, now, and I might be imagining it."

"Did you actually vomit when it was at its worst?"

"Yes."

"Has your weight dropped?"

"It did but it's picking up again. They told me to eat smaller meals and more of them and it seems to work."

"How tired are you feeling?"

"That's better as well. I've just got this cough I can't get rid of. Wakes me up at night and then sometimes I can't get back off. Waiting for the next cough even if it doesn't come. That's the only time - middle of the night - when it gets on top of me. Not normally, though."

"I can see that."

In looking at her, he felt guilt - not at his treatment of her because she had not been to see him since she was a child, but at his own frailty, his own struggling with sleep. For her, what she could not escape at one o'clock in the morning could be proven medically even if it must seem an elusive presence in her body. It was fact - unlike his anxiety, whose source he could identify but not isolate. As he, hopefully methodical and unhurried, questioned her, instances of his insomnia remained below the surface, a chaotic but recurrent motif.

"If you're stable at the moment, there's no action we should take until you've been back into hospital. They'll give us a fuller picture than anything I could work out today. The same applies to the question you asked earlier: how long you remain stable is impossible to predict. A key factor is your resilience - mind over matter, you could call it - and you've got plenty of that."

The envy that briefly joined the undercurrent of emotions beneath his words must have eluded her. "And the -"

"Herceptin?"

"Yes."

"First of all, it's not a wonder drug. It's been successful in the treatment of breast cancer at particular stages but isn't suitable for patients with certain conditions - for example, any heart problems. I'm not saying that's the case with you but it would be an aspect of detailed analysis that we'd have to carry out.

"Second, it is exceptionally expensive. That, obviously, is not a concern for you but it's been an issue, since it was developed, for whoever's had to pay for it."

"But I know of two people in the Whitcross area who are getting it. Not just silly rumour - I picked it up on my course."

"I can't comment on that - it may well be the case - but without boring you with the detail of all the changes of organisation the NHS has undergone and that you've probably had to go through in as much detail as I have, the decision-making process has now altered. That's why it's possible that you could have two people with a similar condition, not many miles apart, receiving different treatment. It may not -"

"So if I don't get it, it's down to you lot here."

He swivelled his body, not his eyes, to change screens. "The key decision is still the hospital's but the CCG - you know what I mean, the Commissioning Group - has an important involvement."

"So your answer is yes."

He placed his hands in front of him, separate, fingers curving but not clenched. "We're talking about a hypothetical situation -"

"It doesn't feel very hypothetical."

"No, of course not, but we still don't know what you'll be told next Wednesday. What I suggest you do is make a provisional appointment, anyway, for the beginning of the following week when I should have your results through from the hospital."

"So then it won't be hypothetical?" Her mouth, small, had set.

"I'm sorry to say it may still be but it'll have moved on - and, looking at you, definitely for the better."

He stopped, a light questioning smile on his face. She looked back at him but did not take up the tacit invitation to ask anything else.

"I'll see you, then, not one of the others?"

"That's entirely your choice."

"Oh, I think I will."

Her words he would normally have interpreted as a vote of confidence. Her hint of a smile as she left his room was not so easily read.

34

"I'll go and get what you need. Was it just root ginger?"

Andrews nodded. "And a couple more leeks, if they've got them. If not, I can manage."

Kirsty smiled as her mother left: so predictable of her to find a pretext to leave the two of them together when it was one of his rare weekends at home.

"And one of those lemon cakes." The door closed, with no reply. "What do you eat when you're not here?" He was searching methodically through the drawer next to the sink. "It can't be like this. You wouldn't have the time, would you?"

"No - on both counts." He was replacing the contents of the drawer. "Do you know where Mum keeps that short black knife with the serrated edge? No, I thought not - it doesn't matter. What - oh yes. No - too many meals out. Salads when I'm in, however, to balance out the excess. Quick but healthy."

Over his shoulder, he gave her a wry glance.

"Do you think if I was a public figure, it would keep me slim?" She was talking to his back. "Being a princess might be pushing it. I think I'd jump straight to being Queen. Scope for the odd cake."

"Is that the careers advice you're getting? More ammunition for Mr. Gove even if he wouldn't use it against your school."

"Why's that? Oh, yes - see, I am learning." She scooped up the scraps of mushroom and onion. "These are finished with, are they?"

He nodded. "What other giant strides have you made in your political education?"

"Not a lot. I'm still only top of the second set. Waiting to make my push into the top set."

"And what are the top set saying?"

"You're sure you want to know?"

He was searching again, a cupboard this time. "Where's that gone now? The smallest saucepan, the one of Nana's. It was always down here." He rubbed his face. "No, go on - you tell me. I am listening."

"Nothing very complimentary. Not about you personally - they're always very careful there. But on your lot in general, they've got nothing good to say."

"I'm going to have to leave this until Mum gets back. The other one's not the right size."

She raised her eyebrows. "Two millimetres - I can add that at one sitting."

His smile, after a struggle, was restored. "What were you saying about the bad press we're getting?"

"Well, it's all black and white, not shades of grey in the middle ground. Like everything is a big conspiracy, with 'a coat of gloss over the top'. Sarah's words, not mine."

"Everything? What stands out, though?"

"Oh, the NHS - even I can work that out."

"Look, we can get this cleared up, anyway." He threw a tea-towel at her. "So it's fairly predictable stuff?"

"I don't know. You'd be able to tell if you were there but you wouldn't be," she stretched her arms wide, the tea-towel dropping to the floor, "because you're way too old."

She grinned but, getting only a partial smile in return, decided to pick up the tea-towel.

"One thing they think is that it's a way of helping 'a bunch of con-men' - Sarah's words again - make money out of people who are ill."

"Does anyone else say anything?" As he placed a glass mixing bowl carefully on the draining rack, he looked across at her.

"Oh, we say our bit but we're only on the fringes of things. Sarah comes back from meetings with loads in her head. A bit like you - several steps ahead because of who you know and people are bound to listen. No, I didn't mean that: not just because of who you know," she had winced at the firmness with which he had rammed the remnants of packaging into the bin, "but like a prophet." She grinned again. "Oh, Christ, you don't like the Biblical stuff, either, do you?"

"And what do Sarah and her inner circle plan to do next?"

"Don't really know." She opened the cupboard on the wall behind him. "Is this where this goes?"

He nodded. "Have a guess, though, even if you're not sure."

She busied herself, making space in the cupboard. "I think they're talking about some sort of protest on Saturday. It's meant to be a laugh, more like street theatre, getting through to more people, people like me, than a stodgy old march."

She shut the cupboard door at the silence behind her. "I'm not sure that I'll go ... "

"You've got to make your own mind up." His back was

157

talking to hers. "The problem with anything like this is you don't know the people that are behind it - apart from Sarah. You don't know what their motives are."

"No, no, I don't think I'll go."

"It's your decision but there are trouble-makers - I wouldn't call them anarchists because they're too well-organised - who take over whatever's been planned."

"Good laugh, though." He had turned to her and grimaced at her words. "I don't think I'll go. Keep up with it by text."

"Well, that may -"

"All done?" Her mother had come in through the back door. "Not much done here." She smiled at the hob. "Too much talking?"

35

The mist had cleared in time. At first glance, the cathedral seemed afflicted by boils in shades of red and pink; a longer glance brought even an uninterested onlooker nearer the truth. These were no boils as they eddied upwards and sideways in the gentle breeze.

The black lines - seven or eight at most - stood out, a contrasting colour against the surface of the balloons. Few they may have been but the face was unmistakeable. The swelling of the rubber puffed out the cheeks of a likeness that would have been instantly recognisable even on a piece of paper. It could only be Cameron.

The perimeter of the square was dotted by students, in ones and twos, coats unbuttoned as the first patches of blue appeared in the sky above. They stood at each road that funnelled Saturday morning shoppers through the square, accosting them, clumsily, counterproductively, with balloons that few, mainly young children, took with any enthusiasm.

In the centre of the square, beside a table laden with leaflets and pens, stood a group of women in nurses' uniforms, most in their forties, two much younger, talking intently to a man earnestly securing copies of petitions to clipboards, the sustained hum of their exchanges a counterpoint to the bursts, loud like sudden fireworks, of younger voices.

"A bit public for you, isn't it?"

Kew looked up from the table. "Why shouldn't - yes, if you could put the address in full. It seems to carry more weight." He turned back to Sarah. "It is, I suppose, but I'm not owned by them, any more than you're determined by what your parents think."

The softness in his words, the implication of a connection between them, had no effect on her.

"You haven't met my mother."

The woman had finished signing the petition but lingered, intrigued by what she had heard.

"You're welcome to any of the leaflets." He uncovered some from beneath Sarah's bag. "No, I haven't - but you know I meant your father. Anyway, I just wanted to help."

"That's what the Big Society is all about, isn't it? People getting involved? I'd have thought you'd have brought some others with you."

"Look." He tried to secure her eyes. "I'm pushing my luck enough as far as your father is concerned - I had to keep it low-key. But at least -"

"What do you want me to sign, then? I can't interrupt my shopping for long." Pollard was smiling over his shoulder at Sarah, her hair swept back in a way she rarely unleashed in school. "Don't look so surprised. Just because I'm in my twenties doesn't make me part of the establishment."

"You can do more than sign if you want."

"And blow up balloons, I hope. I'm sorry to be so rude, talking across you."

He looked around reluctantly. "No problem. I'm Andy, just helping here."

"I'm Emily, just Sarah's teacher, although that doesn't deserve the word 'just'. Hard work sometimes, isn't it? Not averse to telling me what I should do on occasions. Tries to sort out what I think, as well."

Sarah pulled her away, resenting the sharing of intimacy in her voice. "Come over here, Miss. You can do some of the talking if you want. We've got several points around the square where we're explaining, answering questions -"

"You've done all right for yourself, haven't you? Bit of a lapdog. How long's that been going on?"

Sarah's look, the pressing of her thumb to her lower lip, was answer enough.

"All right, got the message. I thought the age gap was a bit wide. No, no." She held her hands up at the incipient signs of protest. "Where do you want me to help, then?"

"Oh, Christ, no - Ben's going to fuck it up again."

Pollard followed the girl's eyes to the far corner of the square. Seven, eight, nine figures - she found it difficult to count - had been stopped by the police.

"That's what he said he wanted the whole event to be. Not just balloons but 'something to liven the day up'. He somehow saw the film of that novel and just pinched the idea."

As they edged closer - not close enough to be involved but enough for Pollard to pick out the pinkish shapes the police had stopped - she let out a laugh.

"I wouldn't have thought he read 'The Guardian', though. It's the bloke on the back page, isn't it?"

The giant condoms covered them from head, including the bubble of air at the top, to the tops of their thighs, with pink tights down to their shoeless feet. The only additions to the cartoonist's creation were skimpy white shirts flapping well above the waist, open at the neck, with sleeves rolled tightly up over rubbery arms.

"That's brilliant - and it's not just pinched. Look at those shirts - they're dead right."

"Miss Pollard." The voice was unfamiliar, older than she had expected. "I hope you're not involved in this."

She turned to see Martin Goldie's wife, head tilted, confident in her vision of the world. Her first name would not come but anonymity suited her better. They had sat on the other side of the table at parents' evening, the mother silent, brooding, while her husband, methodical, articulate, now a governor, raised his concerns. Pollard had always pictured them at home, roles reversed as he was fed grievances by her intensity that he could turn into polite but probing questioning.

"I've only just got here but isn't it marvellous to see young people involving themselves in what's going on in the world?" Guilt flickered inside her at the concessions her words had made to the woman's intolerance.

" 'Marvellous' is not a word I would use for people who obstruct us from shopping and who indulge in this public display of obscenity." Her hand pointed in the direction of the giant condom wearers, her face averted in distaste.

"In fairness, I think it's only an attempt at humour. Whether it succeeds or not is always going to vary."

"I'm not in one of your classes, Miss Pollard, and something very different is required to make me laugh."

Glaring, she moved away, heading for the opposite corner of the square from the police. Pollard was tempted to point out how few of the city's shops were in that direction but bit her lip.

Behind her, the police had corralled the condoms in front of the theatre, the only building not open for business that early in the morning and the only one that might have sympathised with this gesture at street theatre. Instead, its granite façade provided an impassive backdrop.

Around the table, there was empty space apart from three distracted bystanders whose eyes were drawn away by the police activity. Leaving the table to their colleagues, two of the nurses moved across to Sarah.

"Look, love, if it was later and your mum was here, we'd tell her but, sorry, you'll have to do. We didn't come here for this. We wanted to make a point, not muck about."

"Please, it's only part of it, a small part, and ... We - they wanted to inject more energy, get more publicity ... " Her voice trailed away. "But I guess it's not working."

"The one in the middle is dressed up in drag. It's so childish. Can't you see?" Gently, by the sleeve, they pulled her towards the theatre.

"No, no, you haven't got the point. They -"

"It's what my son might do at home and he's only ten - stuff bits of padding down his shirt front, in a bra he's nicked from my drawer. Anywhere else, it'd be good but not here."

"Oi, Miss."

The police turned in their direction.

"Oh, no," Pollard muttered to herself, "that woman trotting back to her husband was bad enough."

One of the policemen, red-faced, a little overweight, walked towards them. "Is the one on the right anything to do with you?"

"I teach him but not at weekends."

"So you haven't brought him here?"

"No."

"Put him up to this?"

163

"No."

"Helped organise it in any way?"

"No."

"So you wash your hands of it? I thought you were like us and these girls in blue: work wasn't just nine to five, you're never off duty. We've all heard the arguments."

"I wasn't saying that. I will, of course, help in any way I can."

"Then persuade him and his mates to leave quietly - not just this square but the city itself."

Reflecting, she looked past the policeman at a distant point on the wall, as she had done so many times in front of a class. "I understand what you're asking but there are one or two things I'd like to clarify." Her mind scanned options while her words bought her time. "The principal one is what they've done which has created a problem. At the moment, they seem to be standing quite innocuously but I know I may only be getting a partial view of it. A second point is that I think Ben Emerton is the only one from our school although it's hard to tell in those outfits."

She felt her mind clear.

"So – what's he done?"

"They've created an obstruction for several people who are just trying to do their normal, relaxing Saturday shopping. We've had several complaints from people who are offended by their appearance. Your young gentleman was arrested two months ago in a violent disturbance and warned as to his future conduct. I think that's enough for anyone."

His arms were crossed in front of him, his eyes tilted downwards, the look of someone who had seen this so many times before. She felt her own experience was under attack but sensed that their stand-off, extended by her playing for time, had become more of an attraction for the onlookers than Ben and his followers, if that, unlikely as it seemed, was what they were.

"All right. I'll talk to him but it needs to be on his own."

"I can't -"

"You're asking me to use my influence. I can only do that as I would in school. I wouldn't deal with a problem in front of an audience."

"Okay, so long as it's quick."

She decided not to prolong the power struggle, not that this officer would have recognised the phrase.

"Ben, over here a minute."

He edged his way a little sheepishly through the police towards her.

"What's your version, then, of what's been happening?"

"Well, we just thought we'd do this as a laugh. No-one minded on the bus but this old couple started having a right go at us -"

"Hang on a minute. You came over twenty miles on a bus, dressed like that?"

"Yes and no-one could care less. But then this old bloke and his wife started on at us -"

"Not on the bus?"

"No, after we'd got here. Twenty minutes ago. John just told them to fuck off, that was all."

"He used those words?"

At his nod, she grimaced. "He's not at our school, is he?"

"No."

"And that's all you've done? You haven't blocked any roads?"

"What? All eight of us?"

"No - or pavements?"

"No, not really."

She ignored the policeman's voice behind her, the one minute warning.

"What does that mean?"

"Well, just once we whipped our bras off, all synchronised. Look."

Despite her protests, he unfastened himself to reveal perfectly inflated pink breasts, with protuberant blue nipples.

"You wouldn't believe the air would stay so long where you wanted it to be."

"Okay, look, cover yourself up." She suppressed a smile sufficiently, she was sure, for the policeman not to notice. "Do you feel you've done enough that you ought now go home?"

"No, I haven't done anything."

"You must have seen enough now." As he broke in, she knew the policeman had been listening. "Are they going to break all of this up of their own accord?"

She stuck, as a supposed commentator, to recountable fact. "No, I don't think so."

"And you're not going to do anything about it?"

"I've spoken to him, asked him about going home and he says no."

"And you leave it at that?"

"It's the limit of my influence and, to be perfectly honest, I don't see the problem with a few plastic breasts and condoms. It's quite witty - not brilliant - and it's Cameron to a tee."

"Oh, Christ, is it any wonder we're in the state we're in. Well, we'll just keep them penned here. Bloody teachers who think the Prime Minister's got tits."

He shepherded Ben back to the others, raising his eyes as he went. The nurses dropped away, shaking their heads, leaving only Sarah looking uncertainly at her teacher.

166

36

"And we just stood there for three hours. Couldn't even have a piss."

No-one interrupted: it was the same account, a little more embellished each time, that Ben had given to anyone who would listen in the shop, across the beach and now by the fire.

"Then they got us on the bus and two of them sat with us all the way home. Woke them up when I stuck a pin in Damien's tit. Went off with a fucking awesome bang." He opened another can. "She's after you, Liam."

All he got in response was an uncertain smile.

"You'll need a compass and all the other orienteering crap that Shagger gives us in P.E. Otherwise, you'll get lost up her thighs."

"Oh, God, Ben, give it a rest." He looked across at where Becky and Sarah had just left the fire and then at his feet. He kicked at the sand before gazing at the fire again.

"Here we go," Ben shouted as two arms reached around Liam's waist.

"I want to practise that carry we did the other night." Kirsty had slid her arms up under his, clasping his shoulder blades as if he were a drowning man. His feet were dragged back through the sand until she stopped, coughing violently from the exertion but retightening her grip on his waist when he slid himself back into a near-standing position.

"Oh, shit."

Her mouth clamped to his neck, until she belched.

"Sorry," and her hand slid down and squeezed him between his legs. "You can't move, can you?" He was tensed against the intermittent, forgetful strengthening of her grip until she overbalanced, toppling with him onto the sand. His unchanged rigidity went unnoticed as she thrust his hand down her unzipped jeans, chafing herself against his fingers.

"I'm not too heavy." She moaned. "Not too heavy, am I?" A glimmer of consciousness tried to interpret his silence and moved her off him onto the sand. She started to force her jeans down to her knees.

"Oh, fuck, fuck, fuck." Her voice was getting louder. "Too fucking tight. No!" She pawed at the empty air between Liam and the sand beside her. "Where you fucking going?" She switched from trying to pull her jeans off to tugging them back up while he briefly bent down to scoop up some sand to rub across his fingers.

As he moved swiftly back towards the fire, she slumped back, her jeans stranded halfway up her thighs, her fist clenched against her bare waist.

"Oh, fuck." She raised her head from the seaweed that she had fallen back onto, shaking herself to clear the smell, watching the figures by the fire, seeing one grow in height as it came closer.

"Look at the state of you. Come on. Get up."
She pulled down on his outstretched hand.
"Ben, finish me off, will you? No-one else will."

37

The first sign had been the police, two of them, walking towards reception, spotted by Pollard out of the corner of her eye. She had, she was sure, allowed no hesitation in her voice but to no avail. Three of the kids closest to the window had seen the man and the woman striding purposefully down the drive - and the nudges, the glances over the shoulder, had rapidly spread.

The second had been the same officers, twenty minutes later, walking back out of school towards the car park. Not time enough for the normal process: for information to be gleaned from Toad or one of the deputies, for someone to be fetched from his class or hers - more likely with the current lot - and for a course of action to be agreed.

There had to be a different reason for the visit and no paranoia was needed, she reassured herself, to guess at it, especially when Ben Emerton was called out ten minutes before the end of her next lesson. The class was over before he returned and his bag was carried away reluctantly, disparagingly, by the only girl in the group who was also going to Food Tech.

It was, therefore, no great surprise when Toad appeared at her door, with the sound of the buses still pulling out from the car park - but slightly unusual that he had not left it a little longer to heighten her anxiety.

The appearance was brief because he was through it without a knock, his only delay the turning of his head to wait for the door to ease itself laboriously towards its metallic, closing click. He stood against the glass panel, to block the eyes of potential witnesses, to spare himself close contact with her and, she presumed, any possible cross-contamination.

"You're incapable of listening, aren't you? I bail you out of one problem and you land us straight back into a new one. New ones." His voice reverberated on the last two words, exasperated at his own lapse into understatement. "I have our new status to protect. I haven't got County Hall to fall back on any more. If people like you destroy all our hard work, all the positive publicity, that's it - smaller intake next year, less money, fewer jobs for people like you. A certain justice in that but it doesn't stop there.

"What good could that demonstration, protest, call it what you like, on Saturday possibly do the school? Madeleine Goldie would not have been the only one in Whitcross on a day like that. Why give her more ammunition to prime her husband with? He's already had 'a quiet word' with me on the phone before he brings it up at the governors' meeting next week - and I'll have to defend you again."

"Again?"

"But that all pales beside a failure to cooperate with the police." In vain, she opened her mouth to protest. "They're just doing outside the school what we try and do inside it. Yes, I know there's a dividing line," momentarily, he seemed to respond to her facial expression, "but most of the time it's invisible. The important thing is helping each other out. They're in here all the time. It's the least we can do to return the compliment. If you can't manage it, you shouldn't put yourself in a spot like that in public."

He looked in exasperation at her face that had set, expressionless.

"Not even ushering that idiot Emerton out of harm's way."

"How was -"

"Unbelievable. So forget what I said at the last of our only too regular meetings. Go ahead and apply for any job you see. I don't care what it is. I'll draw a veil over this and the business with whatshername King. I'll find some good things to say about you and, with their meetings schedule, I'll keep the governors off your back until the autumn. After that - well, you can imagine … "

He attempted to interpret the tension in her face, the tremor in her eyelids.

"Have I made myself clear?"

He read her grimace at the cliché with which he sealed his threat-laden tirade as a smirk.

"That's what I mean. I don't know why I give you any time, any stay of execution. Just go. No. Your room. I'll go - and not a moment too soon."

As the door shut behind him, she caught fragments of Jackie's question and his words. Someone was "welcome to her." Someone else to see, now if he could, was the gist of Jackie's request after she knocked on the door and opened it apologetically. "I could ask him to come back another day if you'd rather," and she touched Pollard's hand, as it gripped the back of her chair.

"No, no, just give me a couple of minutes before you send him along." Jackie's eyes were raised, questioning. "Oh, yes - who is it?"

"I didn't recognise him as a parent. Too young for that. Mr. Kew. Andy Kew, I think."

38

Goldsmith's records had confirmed it: it was now ten days later than he had expected her to be seeing him. The most recent letter from the hospital was hopelessly, perhaps inevitably, out-of-date, telling him nothing that he had not learned from Amy three weeks earlier.

She was his final visit, the one closest to the surgery but also the one whose duration was the least predictable. His window down, he felt the breeze intermittently between thickets of trees. It helped him shrug off the accumulated heat, the burden of the first intensity of summer. Becky had been quieter than usual. Mary, alert to his sensitivity, had implied that it was not just with him. It was perfectly possible - he remembered the uncertainty of his own adolescence - but if there was something serious on her mind, he was not the one, in his current self-absorption, to whom she would open up.

How different, because of him, she had been a few years earlier. Dejected at school, moved down a set in English because of a scattiness in her spelling and punctuation that her teacher had not bothered to set in the context of all her contrasting strengths, on the receiving end of another girl's thoughtless words, she had cried to him, not Mary, her head burrowing into his shoulder. His mind had been so agile, his feelings so fresh that within half an hour he had seen her eyes brighten, like a limp plant revived by water.

What she now was fretting about he could not grasp. At home, when he sat on his own to focus on her, any insight was temporary, swamped by self-analysis that was inextricable from his struggle to understand what was happening at work - and even the threads in his thinking that had led to that glimmer of insight could not be unravelled.

Certainly not in the car where the most banal of stimuli - the roofs of the council houses, the village sign that he passed, the children pushing and shoving on their way home from school, so unthinking that one of them could overbalance into the road, under the front wheels of a car, no matter how slowly it was being driven - piled up in his mind until it seemed full.

Too full for Amy as he turned off the main road and into the estate. Why exactly it was a home visit - the receptionist had done the usual checks but it still did not quite add up - for someone who was such a fighter entangled itself with a sudden juddering of the car as he changed gear. The car's symptoms, if not the cause, cleared as quickly as they had come, taking with them any tentative conclusions that he had been inching towards about Amy.

He was walking up her drive when, for the tenth time that day, he retraced his steps to check the car was locked. As he turned back towards the house, Amy's mother had already opened the door.

"I thought you weren't coming." She stood like an animal being restrained on a leash of her own making. "I phoned the surgery to check."

"Yes, I'm sorry you've had to wait."

"Not right, not right at all. None of their stuff is making any difference." She was talking as they walked upstairs. "Not a scrap of difference." She held her finger to her lips as they reached the landing and an open door to their right. "In fact, just the -"

"Mum, please don't go on like that."

The voice was encouragingly strong. Walking into the room, however, swept away his optimism. Her scarf was ill-fitting, perhaps hurriedly wrapped around her head moments earlier; her skin, the absence of make-up accentuating its pallor, drew any remaining vitality from her eyes which moved jerkily from him, to her mother, to the window.

"Mum, we're all right now."

"No. You bloody need someone -"

"I don't. I know exactly what I want to say." Her mother showed no sign of moving. "Please, Mum. I don't have the energy for all this."

"Well, that's why you need me here."

"Please." The one extended syllable was long enough for her voice to break from a forced depth to a barely audible crackle.

Her mother left, her backward steps reluctant. Amy gestured towards the door which Goldsmith closed quietly.

"I'd expected you to see me sooner than this."

He pulled up a stool beside her.

"Cock up. I went in for the first appointment and they couldn't do anything. They said it was a breakdown in the equipment. Got me in a week later - six days. Felt worse day by day, and ever since."

"In what way do you feel worse?"

"No energy. I get up but when I do, I only feel like sitting down again. Too much effort to cut myself a piece of cake. When I

175

do, it's got no taste. Like paper, cardboard, even the icing."

"And what did they tell you in the hospital?"

"Not a lot. I had to work it out for myself. The bloke I saw was Indian." Her voice was fading, lifting, dipping again like a defective radio. "I told him the chemotherapy hadn't worked. He didn't disagree." She was retelling quickly what happened, her eyes fixed on the fraying edge of her blanket, as if she was bored by recounting again a minor frustration in a trip to the shops.

Suddenly, though, she had lifted her head, to fix her eyes on his. "Not much of a game, is it?"

He paused. "Nothing much wrong with your memory, or your sense of humour, is there?"

Involuntarily, he closed his hand on hers. While her head recoiled away from him, her hand stayed limp under his. Her voice came faint as if from another room.

"It's too late, isn't it?"

39

These three nurses," Marriott waved the newspaper at King, "hardly look as though they merit your usual epithet. 'Bunch of wankers' indeed. The sort of women my mother would want as ward matrons. Even she wouldn't argue with them. What they're saying isn't 'adolescent drivel' either."

King raised his eyes, resigned.

"You weren't there, were you?" After a brief glance, he continued. "No, I thought not - but you know the detail of what went on?" A cursory nod of assent was all he got. "How could I doubt your competence? You must fill me in later but from the perspective of the average newspaper reader, they've got exactly the publicity they were after."

"One photo. Pricks dressed as pricks. No quotes. That's it."

"But look at the contrast. Just the one picture of them but a bigger one of those nurses, put through someone's sympathetic filter, and a string of paragraphs on them, all quotes from the horse's mouth, no balancing comment anywhere in sight. Might as well have been a press release."

King had eased his watch over his narrowed hand and was

adjusting the time. "That's what you like about the bloody paper. What's it you say about Cameron - can't have it both ways?"

"If he can, so can I. There is, however, for once, an element of sense in what you say so I shall return to my original theme. That lot have won this particular battle. If what you say is correct - and I've no reason to doubt it because what they've done previously has been strikingly unsuccessful - their sole aim was to generate more publicity. For themselves and for their 'cause', whatever that happened to be on Saturday. Through their buggering about, they have put these splendidly stolid nurses on the front page."

He stopped to glare at King's forensic examination of the back of his hand, the culprit the metal watch strap that had been tugged back onto his wrist.

"You are following what I'm saying?"

"Would I dare not to?"

"You seem to overlook the fact that it's more your problem than mine. If she'd been anyone other than your daughter, the courts would have dealt with her - and, according to you, she's the only brain they've got. If we'd taken her out of the equation - that's the sort of business speak I'm supposed to use, I presume - by now the whole group would have been rudderless. However," he sighed, his long pause a large rhetorical flourish for an audience of one, "they're not."

"They're just a shambles. Completely hit and miss."

"True but what if they manage to be on target when the Prince and his wife are visiting Cornwall?" He picked up the paper again. "The problem should not be beyond us and the resources at our disposal. What about this young man, the star of the show as far as the police are concerned?"

"Ben Emerton. Complete birdbrain."

"He should, therefore, be easy to deal with. Not one of their ideologues, then?"

King snorted.

"If it's so obvious, why haven't you used your common sense? No flash of genius required. Let him be a birdbrain with us." For the first time, King was reflecting. "Give him the chance. Tell him there'll be lots of company. Not you personally, of course."

40

Sarah even wanted to get the post mortem out of the way. They sat in the quad at midday after the exam, in full sunshine, with the rest of the school penned in classrooms, a perk they had envied a year earlier. Picking over the bones of their answers, of their question selection, seemed to her - but not to Becky - a sterile routine.

Polly had sensed it after the History exam, saying all of the right things, most of them probably true: how only the bright ones felt self-critical afterwards, how the release of adrenalin in the run-up to an exam was likely to leave you deflated later. Yet the explanations didn't quite explain her mood. Although some of it was specific to that morning - like reducing English to a couple of answers under ludicrous time constraints - more of it seemed to do with Becky and what she represented.

She felt ashamed of that formulation of the jumbled sensations in her head but what, in Becky, had once been a source of envy was now a reason for irritation: the perfect home life, the absorption in the here and now that flowed from it - and Liam. She obviously was not happy with whatever wasn't happening between them but you knew that in a few months it would be an episode contained in its timeframe, not spilling over. Even here, a few minutes earlier, she had beckoned him to their table, flicked the hair out of his eyes as he listened to her questions about his grandmother and, finally, waved him goodbye, with only a slight pursing of her lips as a legacy of his presence.

Perhaps her mum was right - "Sarah, you're too old for your years." She looked at Becky walking towards the door into B block. Even such meandering had to her, from forty yards away, a purposeful air. If people watched her in the same way - and she dreaded anything so voyeuristic - they would detect either nothing or an aura of uncertainty.

Someone had, however, been watching her, must have waited for the opportunity that came with Becky's leaving: Steph, who sat on the opposite side of the room from her in tutor time, who did none of the same subjects as her, who was always friendly without ever really talking, who was going to be a hairdresser, who was already doing that for all Sarah knew.

She stood before sitting down. "You don't mind, do you?"

"No." Sarah shuffled back in her seat as if she were about to leave. "It's all yours."

"I wanted to ask you something. You're good at organising, aren't you?"

Sarah smiled, resettling herself in her seat. "No, it's not you." The girl had looked almost frightened. "It's just that in the English exam I couldn't even organise myself."

"But these protests - you do those, don't you?"

"Well, I'm one of them."

The girl dealt in certainties. Any qualification in Sarah's words was ignored in her rush to carry out what someone else had obviously asked her to do.

"You know my cousin, Amy?"

"I've heard of her."

"She's got cancer. They think it's gone too far to be stopped now."

Sarah listened to her account of Amy Goddard's deterioration, wincing at her own anticipation of more melodramatic revelations. As they came, she restricted herself to sympathetic nodding, waiting for the words to stop, trying not to appear as if approaching death was barely different from her own preoccupations.

"She doesn't want anything for herself. She says she's gone past that. She wants us to do what the," she waved the fingers of her hand loosely, "adults - you know what I mean - are doing. Just the ones our age. Show up what the surgery is doing because it's all their fault."

"I don't know. I don't think I can. I've just over-committed myself recently." The girl looked at her blankly. "I'm doing too much and not doing anything properly."

"But just as a favour. I can't do it. Not me."

"No, I'm sorry. Normally I would but not now." She quailed before the girl's incomprehension. "No, the answer's got to be no."

She was like someone who could not tear herself away from an illicit relationship. Before finding herself standing silent in Becky's hall, she had walked out of school as briskly as the preservation of her image would permit, through the back lanes to minimise the risk of any contact with Steph, her friends, any of them, who would be on their way to the beach, talking furiously, confirming each other's opinions uncritically.

She had chosen to cut across the park as the route the others were less likely to take on their way to the beach - and there had been Becky sitting on the grass, unzipping her bag and waving

Sarah across to her. She had lost her mobile - temporarily, only as long as it took her to empty the contents in front of her, another rapidly solved problem.

It had, however, been a prop, the offer of coffee impossible to turn down, and so - fifteen minutes after they had said goodbye in the quad - she walked through Becky's open front door, unusual, even in such heat, and heard the voices.

" - local control and all we get is something more insidious. I don't know exactly what the structure is behind him."

"Probably like al-Qaida." Becky's grandfather's voice, just audible, retained its humour. "He's an isolated cell so that if we interrogate him, he's got nothing to reveal."

There was a kindly impatience in Goldsmith's voice as he continued, the light-heartedness brushed aside. "It must be either the party itself or a government agency. The trouble is they're so difficult to trace. All the rhetoric about cutting costs, getting rid of quangos, means they have to conceal it all, probably just short of illegality. Contracting out, competitive tendering - you know the business jargon as well as I do."

Sarah pulled at Becky's sleeve, gesturing towards the front door. The discomfort on her face drew only an irritated grimace from Becky, a shake of the head.

"He's got his own website but that's no use. Normally, someone like that would play up any contract or connection with the government. Must be good for business but there's not a trace of it. Previous work he's done is there - commodity trading, meat, grain, I can't remember what the specific combination was -"

"Pictures of starving villages, as well?"

A light laugh, probably accompanied by Goldsmith raising his eyes.

"Personal profile as well. All carefully crafted to make him

183

appear a well-rooted family man. What his daughter would think of the way it's written, I can't imagine. Too bright to have gone along with -"

Becky's hands were shooing Sarah back out through the open door, her shoulder catching the door frame, the dull vibration ignored.

"Come on." She had turned the corner in a trice, red-faced in her agitation. "I'm sorry. I'm so stupid. I didn't realise who they were talking about. I wouldn't have stayed there but I wanted to find out what's been getting Dad down. Oh Christ, I am sorry."

"Forget it. There was nothing I didn't know. In fact, what your dad said made me feel better." She smiled.

"You being serious?"

"Oh yes. He obviously doesn't think I'm an idiot." She drew back into herself. "And he's not asking me to do anything."

41

"Why am I so bloody useless? Nobody's interested. And I'm not that ugly, not that fat, am I?"

Kirsty was in full flow, the questions aimed at Becky but rhetorical.

"What am I supposed to do? Fucking lose weight but everyone says we're not judged on that. Mum means it but what's the use of that? You don't want to get laid by your mother, do you? As for this place," she waved her arm behind her at the exam hall, "it's a fucking cocoon. No-one's a bloody racist in PSHE, no-one's sexist, no-one's ageist, no-one's fattist - and then you get out of the classroom and off it all goes."

"It's not -"

"It's all right for you." She stopped, sensing the edge in her voice. "Sorry. What I meant is you've got to be one of the targets to know what it's like. And I've got the fat. It was like he couldn't even bear to touch it. I could feel it."

"Kirsty -"

"I was doing it all for him. Well, no, you can't do it all, can you? And I could feel him all stiff against me."

"Who are you talking about?"

"Liam. Who else would it be? And the only bit that wasn't stiff was his cock. It just leaves you with people like Ben. He was all right but it's like scrabbling in the bins for food."

She seemed to have finished, the storm blown out. Becky wrapped her arms around her, more sympathetic than she would have believed possible five seconds earlier.

"Nothing's that bad." She switched to remoter, neutral ground. "You take older people. I've seen - I've seen some of them, in what we've done in Food Tech, who are really well looked after."

"Oh, yeah, I know - and my dad is working on something to do with that, I think. But that's not much use to me, is it? Fat and old is what I'll be. Perhaps I should blacken my face as well."

42

The meeting - and it was a delusion to give it such a title - was a shambles. Sarah had told them the canteen was a lousy idea, that people would drift in and out, that the noise would be a pain ... The guy from the college with the shaven head who had never liked her for being too young, for not always sitting quietly and serving her apprenticeship, had said flexibility of attendance was a good thing, that the noise would give them cover for what they were saying. Anything to oppose what she said.

To rub it in, he turned to Kew.

"You're older than most of us -"

"All of you, probably."

"How did we look to you? Did we help or fuck it up? Come on, be honest. You don't say much."

"I thought it was good. We're not a company aiming at consistent PR so it's bound to be a bit rough at the edges. One thing - and I hope you don't mind me mentioning it," he looked across at Ben who was sitting down with a plateful of pastries, "I thought the tits and bras were overdone. Great joke, brilliant props but the message got a bit lost."

As Ben carried on eating, Sarah found herself defending him.

"What was it that got us the press coverage, then? Not the crowds of people there. That was the usual joke."

A ripple of nods from around the table, a shout of "Go, the tit man" from behind him encouraged Ben to stop between mouthfuls.

"I just thought it was a good laugh and what I thought we could do next -"

"Look, don't we need to finish reviewing what we -"

"No, Lee, give him a chance."

"Well." He stood up and reached behind him for his bag. "These royal wankers who are coming down here in a couple of weeks." He produced a toilet roll and placed it proudly in front of him. "Looks normal, doesn't it? God, I feel like one of those magicians. But, you guessed right, it's not."

He began to unroll it. "Anyone need some? These bits are just cover," the paper spooled away onto the floor, "but look, as it all comes off, there are dark patches showing through and they're not my turds."

With a flourish, he tore off a final few sheets and held up the single piece on which two faces could be clearly seen.

"It looks like them, doesn't it, especially him? Kate whatsherface, the Page 3 girl, isn't quite so clear but we can sort that out. Probably a bit ambitious to go for two faces. Most of them'll have just one. You've got a good range too - the Queen, Philip, Harry, the whole lot. Andrew's my favourite - we've got his head twice its normal size. Give you a good target."

"But how do we use -"

"On the day they come down here, we'll set up a stall flogging the whole range. The great British public can take their pick of who they want to crap on."

"Eh?"

"Flop it down there below you before you start. Then take aim. Really rub it in when you've finished."

"But what are we trying to achieve? The people who come and wave their flags aren't going to buy that."

"So what?" Sarah bit back at Kew. "It's the same argument again, isn't it? Doesn't matter if they don't buy any. Look at the publicity."

For a few seconds, nothing more was said over the laughing as the toilet roll was passed around. Laughing that was decisive.

"So we go for it then?"

Sarah, looking straight ahead, only sensed the nods that passed for a vote.

"You'd better get the production line going then." A grin at Ben did not mask the nervousness of his hands. "Further ahead," Adam was searching for his words, "there's some sort of protest planned at old folk's homes."

"That's not what you're meant to call them."

"Oh, God."

Some scraped their chairs back; some, in irritation, drifted away; a few laughed as Ben spread out more of the toilet rolls for inspection.

43

"Another success, Tom. They've reported what you said in the House on Monday." Lewis pushed the paper across the desk. "Timing just right again for Thursday publication."

"Nothing national?"

"That's not the point, is it? Although you might get there if these other MPs want to get in on the act." He pointed to the computer screen. "Age UK and The Alzheimer's Society now added to the list. Letters to you and the press. No, don't bother to look at that one. I'll find you the best one. Even read you the highlights. Save you that trouble as well."

He opened the new file.

"Don't know how they managed to email it but never mind. Joint signatures, clearly retired - they refer to themselves as lifelong Liberal voters. You know the type. 'Grave concern' at the formation of the coalition, how their Liberal voting had started out of an 'intense loathing' of the Tories, blah, blah, blah. This is the best bit, though. 'Your independence in fighting the injustice suffered by Irene Croft - and many others - has restored a little of the trust we once had in your party.' A shopping list of other issues on which you should make a stand, mind you, but -"

"That can wait for another day."

Lewis followed Andrews' glance out of the window.

"No sign of her?"

"No - she's never late but she's not one to be early, either. She wouldn't be today - Kirsty's got an afternoon exam and that's really hard work. Rather her than me."

Lost in the imagined scene at home, he was late in reacting to the ringing of the phone.

"Ah, sorry, I thought it was going to be someone else." He shooed Lewis out of the room. "And how are you? Which of your many pies is your finger in today? And there is no innuendo intended in 'pies', I can assure you."

The door opened behind him: Amanda nodded as he pointed, shrugging, at the phone.

"Sorry to cut in. Someone's just arrived. Can I give you a ring later on?" He scanned his diary. "Yes - after four would be ideal."

She had propped herself, with a sigh, against the desk before he put the phone down.

"Good timing - that would've been a long one."

"Glad 'someone' has her uses. You're ready, are you?"

"For what your mother used to call 'being taken out for lunch'?" As he searched his pockets, she smiled. With a flourish, he waved them at her. "That expression of yours is almost condescending."

"Not at the keys, no. And I don't think condescension is the right word. I just wonder what some of your attitudes are under all the irony. Anyway, my mother's expression hasn't been passed on through the generations."

"As if I didn't know."

"Fine. Yours is the last word on it but we need to get a move on. I haven't got your flexibility - I need to be back at work by 1.30."

The waiter broke her flow briefly.

"She's not right. And, no, it's not a typical teenage crisis."

The impatience in her eyes blocked the interruption he was about to make.

"And it's not just the eating, the weight, although I agree with you it's a factor in her self-esteem." She looked at him as he swallowed. "You know what's coming, don't you? Your hardly ever being at home - it seems to eat away at her sometimes. At other times, it doesn't matter and I'm certainly not saying it's the main cause -"

"You don't need to labour the point. It's like child poverty. Universal Credit doesn't cause it but -"

"Kirsty is not a victim of child poverty."

"Just an analogy, or it would've been."

She glared at him. "The politics is part of the problem. She doesn't know where she is with it, with you, any of it. All these protests - the royal visit, what they seem to be planning at St. Budoc's, that condom business, you name it - she's completely torn. She wants to do what you'd want her to do but she's just as likely to do something to kick at you."

He shook his head with suppressed annoyance.

"She's better out of all that but okay. Kirsty. You've obviously thought it through - let's hear it."

44

"So they've gone all right?"

"Which one?"

"No, in general. You can't expect each one you take to go perfectly."

"But which one did I have this morning?"

Sarah carried on transferring the contents of the fridge to the bin.

"Hey, hold on. I can eat that."

She passed him the remains of a block of cheese, from which a cloud of mould was starting to rise.

"Just cut off the green bits." She turned back to look at him, holding the cheese, and bit her tongue - his words hadn't been a command to her.

"So which exam was it?"

"Look, girl, aren't you going to make any sort of effort? It must be more than two months now. I had a go at you but I'm not the only parent in the world who has to do that."

"As a matter of fact - oh, for God's sake, put that revolting thing down - it's nine weeks and four days. And why should anyone speak to me the way you did?"

She turned away from him again and began trimming the tomatoes and cucumber.

"I can't answer that, Sarah. I can't. I'm -"

"- doing my best."

"Well, I bloody well am. Just because your brain's in a different class from mine doesn't mean I'm not trying. I know other people, like that English teacher of yours, understand you better than I do but they don't have as many balls to keep in the air as I do."

His eyes showed a flicker of pride at the accidental double entendre. She guessed that with his cronies it would have released a flood of sexual innuendo. With her, he knew better, just.

"Becky understands me well enough and she's got plenty of her own to deal with." She threw a chunk of tomato at the bin and missed.

"She's only sixteen. What problems is she supposed to have? Unless her father is too much of a straitjacket. Pompous prick."

"You, you haven't - what you know of him -" She screwed up her face in frustration at the anger that had made her inarticulate before him. His seemingly patient smile was a final goad to her. "What you're doing to that surgery is indefensible but they're on to you, they'll work you out, all those lovely strings you pull."

"What are you talking about?" His words had slowed.

"They're not there yet but they'll find out who you're working for, where your money comes from."

"He's told you this?"

"No. He wouldn't be so unprofessional."

"So it's just your superior intuition, is it?"

Both her hands clenched the edge of the work surface. "No, it's not. I come back in this house and all I hear is you shagging

194

your latest hook-up; Becky comes in and hears people talking. We overheard him talking to her granddad - that's how I know."

"So where's what's left over of your famed integrity in that?"

"Don't you dare lecture me on that. We shouldn't have done it but Becky's worried sick. And she ushered me out after a minute or so." She put her hand over her closed eyelids and grimaced at her own defensiveness.

"So they - a geriatric and that neurotic doctor - are 'on to me'. How clever of them, how very clever - especially as there's nothing to find out."

On his way to the door, she watched him bend to scoop up the piece of tomato on the floor, sniff it and, after a calculated delay, place it carefully in the bin.

45

"I thought you said you were getting a move on."

Pollard looked up from checking the bus timetable. Kew was meticulously checking each dish that must already have been dry from a night in the draining rack.

"Perhaps I don't want to get a move on. Why rush to leave the scene of the crime?" He smiled back at her. "Great, that's ideal. Ten past ten." The timetable, half-dropped, half-thrown, slid off the work surface. "Oh, no."

He had left the dishes and his hands were gripping and kneading the back of her neck. She shut her eyes and sighed. "No, no, no - come on, we'll never get there." She eased his hands away and turned to him. "It's the only appointment I could get. And I hadn't anticipated that you'd be getting in the way. Look - grab your coat."

There was just enough time for them not to run, time for them to walk side by side to the bus stop. She was relieved that he had not tried to put his arm through hers. Even if now she wasn't going to be there long, she did not want the eyes of kids from school - or their parents - fastening on her.

"Have you never had a car?"

"No, apart from using my mum's when I was learning."

The queue was filtering onto the bus and they fell silent. Two girls smiled knowingly at her as she sat down next to him.

"Won't it feel like learning again when you do get one?"

"Might do." She unzipped her bag. "Deal with that when it happens. What are you going to do while I'm in the hairdresser's? Oh God, shut me up, will you? I don't know why I asked. I couldn't care less what you do."

She stared out of the window, feeling his shoulder against hers and not attempting to withdraw from the pressure. To maintain the contact, he pointed with his left arm at the boards, at ten yard intervals, that normally advertised a pub quiz or stock car racing.

"There they are. The whole world's protesting now." The boards had ended at two or three hundred people, all over fifty, all impeccably dressed, observing, not picketing, at the entrance to a small copse next to a field where excavators were churning the even grass into piles of mud. "Look at them - you won't get your kids there with their condoms even though they should be."

The National Trust banners receded into the distance.

"They were doing the same thing on the other side of St. Gerent when we went to the theatre last week."

"They'll be everywhere - they've got the time. And they'll probably be successful because they're Dave's natural constituency."

"Not like us." Self-deprecating, he smiled. "No, not you. Us as teachers. He doesn't give a damn about our votes. He probably wins more by antagonising us than he loses. But we're going to do it anyway."

He eased himself away from her. "You're incredibly coy

about all this."

"What's there to be coy about? You know the action the union is planning."

"Yes, but that's not all, is it?"

"All right then. See if you can guess. They're trying to drive us down into the local economy. Regional pay, performance pay – whatever it is now. So what would be the most ironic form of protest?" She looked over her shoulder, reassured by the empty seats behind.

"No idea. Irony didn't figure much in my education."

"Poor dear. All the more reason to start learning now." She patted him on the hand. "Local action. Leaflets to parents. 'Should Toad be paid £90,000, three times more than Bridget Martin?' Taking someone who's been at the school for years and who the parents think is brilliant."

"You could be sacked for that."

She shrugged her shoulders and laughed as the kids in her classes regularly did, proud of her latent adolescence.

"I'm going anyway. Toad's told me. So what've I got to lose?"

"You know you've got your figures right?"

"Near enough. The management in four Cornish academies have had a huge salary boost. Quite a modest estimate really."

"What about the woman you mentioned?"

"Average pay in the county is supposed to be twenty percent below London levels." She seemed proud of her figures. "That's where we got Bridget's salary from. Anyway, we've got the tenses right - all 'should' and 'may' in the rhetorical questions. But that's something else your education would've missed out, isn't it?"

He said nothing but nodded at her. Aware of the people now sitting behind her, she squeezed his arm and changed the subject.

46

"I know you, don't I?"

The girl with the tight skirt and welcoming smile put the CD with Cheryl Cole's hair tumbling, cascading, into a bag.

"We used to live next door to you, when I was still living with Mum and Dad. Nicola."

"Lovely name. She's great, isn't she? Did you see her last night? What a comeback!" King pointed to the bag.

"God, yeah - and she was so right about that woman, like my gran, who could yodel."

"Dead right - and it all comes back to me, now. You can't blame me for being slow, though - look at the change in you."

She handed him his card and receipt.

"Well, you haven't changed a bit. You ought to tell my dad how you do it." Her voice rose at the end of each sentence.

"And you ought to tell my Sarah how you do this."

"Oh, God, not me. Is she still the brainbox?"

"So I'm told - not that I can tell. Doing really well. Like you."

She smiled and, with a fluttering wave of her fingers, moved on to her next customer.

He hesitated at the bookstand by the door, glancing back between stares at the cut-price titles, before stepping slowly out into the street. He dropped a pound in the Big Issue man's bag and waved away the offer of a magazine.

"Big Society in action - you're a walking advertisement for your wares." Marriott prodded him in the heel with his umbrella. "No need to stop. It's not one of those days, not that I've had one this decade."

The outdoor ego of the man who halted and faltered over a computer screen was military in bearing and pace. He stepped off the pavement and back, confident in his rights and reactions against the oncoming cars; King was left in his wake, his own momentary briskness stalled behind an old woman and the mini-suitcase she was pulling.

"Come on. Chop, chop. I told you that you could use my room for the morning and I meant it. I didn't expect to see you here," he looked at his watch, "at 10.00 when my senior and better - and my younger - is arriving to see you at 10.30."

Struggling for breath, King tried to regain his jauntiness.

"I didn't know there were so many."

"Singular tense. Didn't they teach you that at school? He might, however, feel like the plural. Most of these types do. They've no intention of ever melting into the background. Otherwise, they'd never complete the smooth transition to MP five years after leaving university."

Fortunately well ahead of King, he waved his umbrella on a steep diagonal.

"Why've you got that on a day like this?"

"Aids the gait and, I am assured, it conveys an impression of power." He had waited for King to catch him up, unwilling to shout back in response.

"You'd come out to look for me, hadn't you?"

The amusement in his voice drew a reluctant smile from Marriott.

"I think you could say that. Equally, I couldn't settle to work with your appointment in the offing so some vigorous exercise on a lovely day seemed a good idea." He had reached the steps leading to his office. "Yes, much better idea. We must get a light in there. No good for passing trade. That's how you'd look at it, isn't it? Go on, up you go. Hannah's there. She'll make you coffee when Younger arrives."

The umbrella waved uncomfortably close to his face before Marriott strode off in the opposite direction, leaving him to labour up the steps.

"All this," he muttered to himself. "Bloody Royal Family."

He gathered his breath at the top, pulled his shoulders back and opened the door. It was like a transition from autumn to summer, from damp dinginess to warmth and light - and there she was, stretching over the desk, her skirt taut over her hips, glancing back at him.

"Oh, I am sorry, Martin." She straightened herself and smoothed her skirt. "I wasn't sure when you were coming."

"No need to apologise, no need at all." The repetition and his accompanying, smiling stare had more success than in the past: Hannah returned his smile, albeit briefly, before showing him through to Marriott's room.

He barely had time to consider the relative potential of Marriott's massive, cleared desk or the expanse of outdated but plush carpet in front of the window before she had gone to answer the phone.

"No, that's it - you're here. Just straight up the steps." She paused. "No, I know it's not brilliant."

He walked back out as Younger arrived: no knock and a slight downward tilt of his head. His navy-blue jacket, the precisely-creased trousers, the discreetly-striped tie, everything down to his shoes, polished but not gleaming, were casual, made him seem casual, but marked him out nonetheless. On racecourses, his type would have been seen a thousand times in hospitality suites, separated physically by only a few yards from the grandstand where people like King cheered on their losers - but socially by a chasm. On one side, the confidence of entitlement; on the other, mere ebullience.

"What a lovely view you have here?" He walked across to the window. "Is that a church or a school in the distance?" He was talking to neither King nor Hannah. "Simple but striking structure."

"Yes, it is."

Despite Younger's paying her no compliments, either spoken or by fixing his eyes on her, Hannah had fallen quiet, suddenly more passive.

"Would you like -"

"I do apologise. I haven't even introduced myself yet. Simon Younger and -"

He looked between them, the scales even, with him on one side and them on the other.

"Martin King - pleased to meet you. And this is the lovely Hannah that you spoke to on the phone a moment ago. Could you get us coffee?" He touched Hannah on the elbow and waved Younger into Marriott's room.

"Not at all bad. I remember my father dealing with a solicitor in Shrewsbury who had a room and a view just like this. A throwback to gentler times, I'm sure James would agree. What about you? You don't look the nostalgic type."

"No, not really, I just go with the flow. You're new to this area, then?"

"Yes, relatively." He picked up an alabaster paperweight from the window sill and rolled it in his hand. "And how are things flowing?"

"Well for me - and for us. The commissioning arrangements are making good progress and -"

"Why don't we sit down?"

As King responded, Younger moved across the room.

"I'm just closing the door for a moment. No, no biscuits for me, thank you."

He returned to the small conference table, saying nothing before slowly seating himself and leaning back, the gaze of his eyes at right-angles to King.

"It's all a matter of priorities really. I'm sure you see it the same way but it's worth having the discussion all the same. What are your own priorities?"

King looked across at him but still there was no eye contact as if all both needed to do was focus on a wall, white and blank apart from the picture of the Queen, and on which some powerpoint images would shortly be projected as an aid to King's thinking.

"All the NHS stuff, I suppose. As I said, the commissioning is well in hand and -"

"Yes, that's fine," he smoothed his hand in small circles over the immaculately polished table, "but I have to see where everything else falls in the pecking order. We have to prioritise resources; you have to prioritise your no doubt prodigious energies. We have a royal visit in the offing, a full house of key players, and we have to use it."

"The planning reforms, the Big Society, they're all well up the list -"

"Precise priorities, for Christ's sake. Think of it as a row of women." He pointed at the wall as if it housed a picture gallery. "Eight or nine of them. You'd like to fuck them all but which would be first choice, which second? All the way down which, I imagine from the way you looked at young Hannah, is the way you'd like to go."

The door opened after a gentle knock and she brought in the coffees on a small metal tray. King looked away as she walked softly back out and closed the door again.

"I can't say I blame you, though." There was a brief, conspiratorial smile. "The NHS is Hannah. Who's next?"

"Probably the academy reforms, the Big Society, then planning although -"

"Look, let's not take it any further. And we're not back at school, after all, I suppose, are we? But 'probably' is no good - we've all got to sharpen up our act. In places like this, planning has got to be the reserve fuck. You can forget the Big Society - it's a better bet than trying to flog 'the global race' around here but it's still a dead duck. The academies don't matter that much. The locals have no real choice because of transport but this urban wheeze has to be introduced across the country in line with our fairness agenda. Planning, however, is a very different matter, one that we have to make sure features positively in this royal visit."

King's nods were like the unnoticed disappearing feet of Icarus in Breughel's painting.

"As well as the immediate PR, we've got to nudge the developers towards the few brown bits you've got down here. It's a rural area: if we're seen to wreck the countryside, we also wreck our chances of ever wresting this seat away from our apparent colleague, our high-minded friend. Someone brighter than you might even tell me that it's in the coalition agreement -" he had caught a clenching of King's hands, a shifting of his neck as though he had a sudden cramp - "but that's irrelevant. We still have to work doubly hard to make sure we don't take more than our inevitable share of the flak."

"But I thought -"

"The link you've set up, the work we've done with him, all of it can only make anything else easier."

King's body had stilled, his eyes blank.

"Do you want me to tell you what to do?"

47

The school was quieter than ever at four o'clock. The exam season was dribbling to a conclusion, with only a few staying behind in the heat. It was a chore that Becky could have done without. She had anticipated that giving up her role as deputy head girl would be tainted by instant nostalgia. Quite the reverse: helping the Year 10s who were taking over, guiding them through their first duties, with Mr. Siddons fussing gently at her side, had been a statement of the self-evident, like explaining how to hold a pen to a six year old.

They had asked her to print out the list Siddons had given her a year ago and had not been able to find. She pushed open the door into the computer room and sat down. One more job and then home.

"Not talking today, then." Liam's voice came from behind the computers in the starkly lit room that she had assumed to be empty.

"Didn't see you there. You don't see what you don't expect, do you?"

He looked at her blankly.

"What are you doing in here?"

"I had to redo my front page for Mr. Williams. It's too late really but he said it was all right."

"He would. What's that? That's not a front page."

"No. It's meant to be a poster. They said it was easy if you had a computer. I don't know why I agreed."

"That's where your gran is, isn't it? Where I went with you?"

She looked at his border, the display impeccable if it had been for a children's party, and the two lines of writing, with already two misplaced apostrophes.

"That was only three or four months ago, wasn't it?"

He kept his eyes on the screen, his only acknowledgement a tiny shrug of his shoulders.

"It wouldn't -" She stopped herself, the trigger about to be pulled but the finger not moving, and changed tack. " Do you want me to help you with it?"

He swivelled the palms of his hands outwards and looked blank, afraid to ask, uncertain of any obligation he might be creating.

"I don't mind at all," and she sat down beside him. "So it's over the money that people like your gran get, is it?" She pointed at the screen. "This. These 'criteria for funding care'. You're going to need something a lot clearer than that if you want people to turn up. What's it mean?"

"I don't know." He grinned. "They told it me. I just got them to write down the words."

"Right." She scratched her head. "So who's the poster aimed at?"

"Anyone who's got a relative there, I think."

"And what about someone like me who's not a family member? Could someone like that come?"

"I suppose so."

"Could I come for real?"

"I suppose so."

"Oh, God." She looked at the curtain of hair obscuring his reactions and twitched her shoulders in frustration. "You did understand, didn't you? I really liked her. Whatever it is, I'd like to help, like to be there. Anyway ... "

She turned from his silence and began typing.

48

Getting drunk always ended like this. It was a game of musical chairs as everyone spun around and the numbers shrank, one by one. Occasionally by two - and each departure tugged Kirsty a notch closer to sobriety. Five of them left, then four, then three. The steps now were always the smallest ones possible.

Why did school never teach that? An immutable law of physical attraction that produced, as the left-overs of its operation, an assortment of waifs and strays. Life as the games of netball that her mum used to tell her about, that political correctness had now banned, where the uncoordinated, the fat, the useless, were left unselected at the start of a lesson and added arbitrarily, as an afterthought, to the teams that were already making their way out to play.

She sat on the wall and churned over what to do. She was well over an hour later than she had said she'd be home. Her mum would want her to phone - that wasn't the problem - but poking through the alcoholic mist was annoyance with herself at failing to stick to the most straightforward of the guidelines they had agreed as 'the way forward'. She wasn't far from her dad's office but even if he was still there and not in a hotel bar, he would not want her to turn up in this state. The buses would have stopped running - that option too was gone.

She looked up and realised the other two had disappeared, as if the breeze had blown them away. Another immutable law of physics: accepting defeat. Was there one that defined inertia? Sitting on the wall was uncomfortable, with a fragment of brick pressing into her; standing up and walking would go nowhere, might even end up on another brick wall, with her bulk hanging over into someone's front garden.

At first, she thought the voice had come from the house behind her but then she realised it was off to her right, towards the town centre, not that far away, in fact quite close to her.

"Are you all right?"

Seeing him, she shuffled herself forward to redistribute her weight.

"I'm fine, thank you. I am fine, thank you, thank you." She reached out for his arm to pull herself up. "I know I shouldn't say this but what a stroke of luck. I was thinking what you said at the club was brilliant - how we and you and all that -" She needed to sit down again but steadied herself on his arm. "Will you hold me?"

Kew put his free arm on her shoulder.

"No, not like that." She flopped her head against his neck. "Like this." She relaxed her weight against him and felt him dragging her with him.

"No, no, no," as he eased her onto a bench, sloping back and away from her legs, making it impossible for her to stand up.

"You're Tom Andrews' daughter, aren't you?" She said nothing. "The MP's daughter."

Her face was drooping, unable to see his scratching his head at the prolonged silence.

"I'm Kirsty, if that's what you mean. My father is a great man, the great man, an inspiration to us all. Will you fuck me?"

He closed his eyes. "Wouldn't it be an idea to phone him to get you home?"

"Just once. I wouldn't mind. As many times as you wanted. Oh God, please."

"He would want you to, wouldn't he? Ring him," he added, as she pawed at his leg. "It's too late to be out, especially when you're like this."

"Oh, Christ, you fucking sound like him," and she lolled back on the bench, staring at him. "You are fucking gorgeous, you know. Gorgeous fucking too - and do you know where my mobile is?" She patted her leg and pushed the contents of her pocket onto her inner thigh. "Somewhere safe and warm - unless you're let in. That's got you, hasn't it?" and her eyes closed, her head falling back, the smile fixed.

She might have dozed off momentarily, long enough not to savour his hand tightening on her mobile and pulling it from her pocket, short enough for the disappointment to linger like a tear in the skin.

"No, don't do that, please," as he scrolled through her numbers and lifted the phone to his ear. "Please not yet. Not yet." She glowered at him as he started to talk. "Not yet, I said," and slumped back, defeated.

49

"Oh, no, not again." Beckford's voice was raised as the first bar chart, its blocks as solid as the coloured bricks in a child's trailer, lit up the wall. "We've had these, month after month. Illustrations are supposed to illustrate, Maurice."

"And they do, Sheila. I've started each meeting with an updated version of our financial situation so that we can see how seemingly minor actions which we take can have a significant impact on our overall position. If we look back to May" - the previous month's chart, its colours pallid, was added for contrast - "you can see the difference -"

"Why is the past so weak in comparison? It's as if it's embarrassed to be there. No, no," she raised her arms to stop Allen, "I'm not talking about the mechanics of your infernal powerpoint. If you tried to display the data from three years ago, it would be so ghostly as to be almost invisible."

"Sheila, you imply a belief in the supernatural which is most uncharacteristic of you. All this shows is fact, an area in which you always operate brilliantly. Our referral rate on to hospitals - and the plural is deliberate - has shrunk by a further percentage point and I suspect that if the Spirit of Christmas Past - or, more accurately as you suggest, the spirit of midsummer 2011 - were summoned, we would see a far more significant decline."

"Presumably, you're going to give us the normal breakdown of those figures to show referrals by each individual practitioner?"

"Not at the moment, unfortunately, no. The system, as you know, has gone into naughty child mode again."

"Strange." She stared past King again, his thumbnail flicking his front tooth, as invisible as a minuting secretary. "I couldn't give you precise figures but I'm not aware of my referrals dropping at all." She looked across at Goldsmith who nodded his agreement.

"I can assure you they're accurate."

"I'm not suggesting that your image on the wall is being economical with the truth but one is left to speculate on the origins of the decline. A little 'tweak' - that's the appropriate language, I think - would surely have corrected the computer's behaviour?"

"If only it were that easy, Sheila. Tweaks cost money and - for reasons of which I am sure you would approve - we don't think it right to increase I.T. spending at a time when our budget is under strain from a number of other pressures."

"Yet, as I raised at our last meeting, we have enough money in our budget to upgrade our telephone set-up. That 0844 number is still being used - I tried it last night and, while I waited on the line, replenishing that selfsame budget by the minute, I was assailed by adverts from vitamin retailers, local supermarkets -"

"Sheila," he held up his hand in her direction, "as that issue appears later on the agenda, can we move on? The bar charts I displayed are not the main reason for tonight's meeting for which we have agendad our policy on taking patients outside our practice area. It was, as I recall, one of the issues that you raised originally,

Colin?"

"It was indeed." He glanced in Allen's direction before proceeding. "I've prepared a paper which looks at the issue in some detail," he passed the stapled sheets to his left, "but as it's probably better to consider it in full at our next meeting, for tonight I'd just like to highlight one or two points." He paused as the sheets completed their lap of the table. "If you look at the table on side two, you'll see a breakdown in hours and minutes, a little subjective, I suppose, but it's based on how Sheila and I spend our time at work. If you look at the fourth column, you'll see a figure for the time spent seeing patients who are not registered with us. I know it's the summer and the figure is far greater than the January figure would be because of the influx of holidaymakers but we all know, as do the protesters at our gates, the pressure that seeing those patients places on the speed with which we can arrange routine appointments for our local patients.

"We therefore have to think through the consequences of opening our doors to anyone from elsewhere in Cornwall and, who knows, perhaps from further afield."

"But we don't have a choice, Colin. It's in the agreement we've signed."

"I know that, Ian, and much as I dislike it, I'm not going to revisit that. I have, however, looked closely at the agreement and nowhere is there a limit set."

"That's because the point of the legislation is that there should be no limit - and, in any case, the patients you mention don't register with us."

"Of course I'm aware of that, Ian, but we're still the people who have to manage the situation. Part of that has to be setting a limit or we descend into chaos, particularly as the number of registered patients from outside our practice area is also steadily increasing. Let me give you an example at the uncomplicated end of the spectrum. I've just seen a young woman. Very routine appointment - blood pressure check and so on. As it was her first appointment with us, you can imagine how long it took." He looked across at Mark Stanley. "Yes, I know I'm seen by some as slow but a similar problem is bound to affect all of you - and then, of course, there's the administrative work that comes in the wake of the appointment. All of this could become unmanageable if we don't establish clear arrangements for -"

"Colin." Allen's smile of firm apology checked him. "As you yourself said in your preamble, I think we need time to absorb the detail of your paper and therefore this discussion is better left to our next meeting."

Goldsmith shrugged. "That's fair enough, as long as we do get the chance to thrash it out in full."

"You know that'll be the case, Colin." Johnson's reassuring expression had not altered. "But having run my eyes over your paper, it looks to me as though one omission is the financial effect of the way we implement this aspect of the legislation. We need to see a cost benefit analysis of taking on such patients."

"I quite agree." Allen had turned away from the agitation in Goldsmith's hands and, with a nod, drew King into the discussion. "You could do that for next time, I presume, Martin?"

"No problem, no problem at all. In fact, I could do you a back-of-the-envelope calculation in a couple of minutes."

Allen sighed. "No, that's not really -"

"One second, Maurice. Now you're once more allowed to talk, Mr. King," he shifted under Beckford's gaze, "could I ask if there's anything you know about health that can't be written on the back of an envelope?"

"Come on now, please, I think that's overstepping the mark.

Martin is merely here to help us."

"It does, however, go to the heart of the problem we've got at the moment." Goldsmith had settled his hands by clenching the table. "There's nothing personal in this, Mr. King, but should we be ceding control of our service from people with years of experience to people with virtually none?"

There was a brief silence. King's head swivelled around the room, uncertain if the question were for him to answer, visibly relieved when Allen spoke.

"That again is a matter of national policy over which we have no influence." He paused. "I'd like to suggest to the meeting, if it is agreeable, that we pick up one or two minor points of business before we return to the major items facing us. I've received, only today, a letter from the family of Amy Goddard."

"Maurice, this is hardly 'minor'."

"Apologies, Sheila. You're quite right. I only meant that it was not an item on the agenda. The letter is an understandably emotional complaint about Amy's death which we will, of course, investigate thoroughly. For the moment, until I have copied it to you, I think all we should minute is the fact that the letter has been received."

There was a trace of a smile on his face. "I can, however, divulge that there are the inevitable compliments for you, Colin - despite the fact that, notwithstanding your reservations about our new policy on hospital referrals, you did not contest, quite rightly I'm sure, the decision not to prescribe Herceptin for Amy."

"Maurice!" He looked away from Goldsmith in boyish surprise. "Until we've all seen the letter, none of us should be making any comment."

"You are, as ever, right, Sheila. In my defence, I was merely trying to support Colin in what may prove to be difficult times ahead." He held up his hand again in anticipation of her retort. "Sorry, you have no need to. I will say no more on the topic. So, on to another document received today -"

"One moment, Maurice. You asked if the meeting is 'agreeable' to this and I, for one, am not. As we have an agenda, we should adhere to it."

Allen's reply went unheard by Goldsmith, his fingers released from the table and tilting a pen lid over and over in front of his downturned eyes.

50

The streets were busier than Sarah had seen them. Busier but almost static: most of the flag-waving hordes had taken root, accepting, however remote they were from the square, that it was the best vantage point they were going to get. She had never before been in such a fixed crowd. Pushing through was so much harder than when, as she got off the bus, everyone had at least been moving. What had been waves in a sea were now densely packed statues.

She looked at her watch. She was still a quarter of a mile away and, at best, would just get there on time; how late some of the others would be, she dreaded to think. Ben was not the worst - four of them who lived in Whitcross, who had the shortest distance to travel, had not just been late but had missed the last demonstration altogether.

The weakest point was the occasional clump of primary school children, supervised at front and back but, like an army, most vulnerable in its underbelly. The flags, the banners carrying woven images of William and Katherine - she winced at the Daily Mail familiarity of 'Kate' fluttering above the heads of three seven year old girls - gave her a soft-limbed target through which to push her way on to the square. No doubt the banners had been made in whatever primary schools called D and T, in time which that hideous little man had said should always, even for such a young age, have a clear vocational relevance. Perhaps in the minds of the teachers, and unconsciously in the minds of the children, it was, like the chimera of X Factor success, a genuine life 'aspiration'. Those tacky documentaries had charted the woman's rise from sentimentally humble Northern origins to 'one of the highest positions in the land'. If she could do it, why not them?

Her irritation sharpened the elbows with which, head raised in disdain, she barged her way forward.

"Sarah, Sarah."

The bright, innocent face of the girl who lived on her street, with two other equally bright and innocent faces, stared up at her.

"Georgie. Sorry, didn't realise it was you. Didn't hurt, did it?" At least it was someone so young, someone who would not notice the tracks being covered. "Are you enjoying your day out?"

"Yes - and Miss is going to get us all a signed sticker to put on our flags. They're coming -"

"Georgie, can you keep over here, please?"

A formidable woman, only in her thirties, overweight and with a fixed smile, was sizing her up, her jeans, the untucked shirt.

"It's all right. We're neighbours." The smile must have been ironed on. "Honestly. Have a nice day. You too, Georgie. See you soon."

How an abduction was supposed to happen on such a crowded street, she could not imagine, as her own independent movement was almost impossible - to say nothing of the total lack of anonymity. Seeing a seven year old was one thing; being waved at by Mrs. Emerton who had no idea what her son had planned and who would assume Ben's 'nice young friend' was an equally enthusiastic bystander, was far worse.

She looked at her watch again. Eleven o'clock exactly as she nudged her way onto the corner of the square where, a month earlier, only a few uninterested people had been dotted, uncomfortable in the space, uneasy at the company they were keeping. Now, the swathes of colour, the faces painted in the Union flag, blurred identity exactly as the organisers would have wished but made it impossible for her to pick out the rest of her group.

"This is hopeless."

She turned to recognise Gary behind her.

"You here on time for once?"

"Might as well not have bothered. We're never going to sell anything here."

Her eyes followed his: how naïve, how utterly stupid to think they could set up a stand. The police cordon protected a circular, central area, fifty metres in diameter, its centre a dais surrounded by red carpet. There was no other space, nothing - even if the gently swaying crowd concealed someone who was not a tabloid-reading monarchist.

"Sarah said - oh, sorry, you're Sarah, aren't you? - one of the others from school said that she was going back to the park-and-ride like the rest of them to set up there. At least there'd be space."

"So I've just pushed my way through all those bloody people and now I'm going to do it all over again. All those morons - and the worst of it's the ones I know." She glared past him. "Not much option, is there? I'll tag along behind you. You're bigger than me."

Walking back, even with Gary as the advance guard, was worse than the walk into the centre. It was not just that they were going against the grain of the optimists heading for the square; the pavements had tightened as if the security barriers were applying a tourniquet.

Half an hour to squeeze their way a quarter of a mile. Half an hour to avoid the hand that she sensed he was constantly about to stretch back towards her, to press into her palm and tow her forwards.

Too late she realised that heading back as they were was like swimming against a current and that it would have been far quicker, infinitely kinder on the sanity, to set out in the opposite direction and double back to the park-and-ride through the outskirts of the city.

Too late as the crowd around them craned forward and set itself in concrete. The royal procession was approaching and there was nowhere for them to go, backwards, forwards, sideways. The four horses pulled the sort of carriage she had seen on television. Through the perspiring heads and arms, she saw another arm waving through the carriage window - and an ear, a hint of a cheekbone, probably female.

And that, it seemed, was trigger enough for hysteria. Women her mother's age were beaming, screaming, waving in a frenzy they would have ridiculed in a younger generation at a rock concert.

Even those on foot behind the carriage were greeted with rapture. The chameleon and the boy wonder were not there but two cabinet ministers, both of equivalent seniority and equally free of charisma, one from each party, walked amicably side by side. After them was a retinue of MPs - Kirsty's father, needless to say, was there - and local dignitaries: one the Mayor, to judge by the chain mail he had around his neck, the others councillors, businessmen - who could tell?

To most of the crowd, the day was apolitical - and that was

what they were cashing in on. Events like this would immediately be worth a couple of points in the local opinion polls but in the longer term, at the next election, would provide all the right photos of apparent royal endorsement.

Photographers were everywhere. It was no surprise to see the woman whose camera had been so easy to steal taking angled pictures of everyone in the train of hangers-on that snaked its way for over a hundred yards: the same certainty, the same energy but now the faintest trace of a smile.

Of course she would be there: her presence was as inevitable as the flags waving in the direction of the cortege. So, seemingly, was the grey hotch-potch of men bringing up the rear, the greyness broken only by a gesture of flamboyance in the colours of the ties, the colours, the colours of one which she recognised, which she recalled from the mid-mornings when his head would be thrown back and that same tie would encircle that mottled neck.

Her father's walk was more upright than she ever remembered it being. He could have been an old soldier in a Remembrance Day parade, earned dignity implicit in his every step. The only point where his coaching broke down was the darting of his eyes from side to side, as he hoped to catch, in the serried ranks on the pavements, the face of someone he knew, someone who could spread his fame.

Was she that person? There was a stalling in his movement, a surveillance camera rebounding in its scanning - and then he was past her. Probably not, probably just her anxiety, but she pushed Gary on anyway. They inched their way towards clearer streets.

"Where's Ben then?"

The two trestle tables were bare. The first bus spilled out returning shoppers, spectators - she didn't know what to call them -

who walked past with curious glances that failed to interrupt their conversation.

"We should at least have had a banner or something."

Silence settled on them, the gloom deepened, not broken, by Sarah's words.

"This was never going to work. There was no room for bloody tables, the police would've stopped us - and we'd nothing to put on them anyway."

"He might still make it."

"Yeah but I know him. You don't bet everything on someone like Ben. Give him five minutes more and I'm off. What the rest of you do - that's up to you."

She turned her back on them and, even though she was the youngest, no-one dared to break her separation from them.

She heard another bus arrive, the feet, the blurred rustling and talking - and then two voices behind her, distinct.

"He's wearing a jacket and tie."

"I didn't recognise him at first - you know when you see someone out of context."

"Giving leaflets out. As if he'd done it all his life. Silly grin on his face."

"What leaflets?"

"All the treats they'd organised for the rest of the day. Food fayre, bouncy castle - they couldn't think of an Olde English spelling for that - loads of crap, you name it."

"And Ben was handing that out?"

She didn't wait for the confirmation but raised her head, closed her eyes - and walked away, against the flow of people returning to their cars.

* * * * *

"I'll sleep on the floor." Sarah anticipated her mother's objections. "School's not an issue. If I'm late getting over there, it doesn't matter. I've only got to get my leaver's form signed - and I've got ages for that."

"You sure about that because I've got one of these marathon early shifts they've brought in. I'll be off a long time before you're up so you'll have to get yourself moving."

"No, it's not a problem - I'll hear you stumbling around."

Her smile did not elicit the normal warmth in response from her mother who was kneeling in front of the opened fridge.

"I don't know what we're going to eat." Sarah watched the tomatoes, the vegetables, all calculated as sufficient for a single person, being placed carefully on the work surface.

"How many eggs are in that box?"

"Hasn't been opened yet."

"Give them to me, then. I'll do an omelette."

Again the protest came but half-heartedly.

"Look, Mum, just sit down. It'll do you good - and it'll do me good to use my hands to do something. That's what you always say. While I do it, give yourself a laugh and watch the news."

Her mother was unusually acquiescent and turned on the television. As Sarah reached for the chopping board, she watched her mother clearing the table before she sat down, an automatic, busy reflex in supposed relaxation.

"Are you sure you're right to do so many A Levels?" She was staring beyond the television.

"It's not just me, Mum."

"Yes but organisation and you don't get on." She was suddenly back in the room with Sarah and smiling. "And that little fool," she pointed at the television and Gove, earnest of face, certain of his ideas, "has changed it all so the teachers'll be struggling to make it work."

"I'll be fine. Miss Pollard says I need something to stretch me so perhaps I ought to do more." Her mother was rearranging the papers again on the table. "Look, why don't you have a whiskey? There's nothing that's got to be done."

"Take your word for it. This is it, isn't it?" She pointed at the television. "They might even show you trying to escape." She glanced at her watch. "Oh, Christ, it's on instead of the sports news. How kind of them to agree that local people should have affordable homes. Like his mother with her bloody charity work."

They watched as applause rang out and flags were waved, with her father - thankfully not visible - somewhere in the background.

51

The light was strong enough through the flimsy curtains to pick out the marks on the carpet, one from spilt coffee a week earlier, the others a permanent feature.

"You said you needed to be getting up." Kew stroked her hair, dishevelled, and gently touched the smooth, unblemished skin of her shoulder, a contradiction. "It's just after seven."

Pollard grunted but did not move. He swung his legs out of the bed, leaving the quilt thrown over to her side, the coolness of the air on her back, and busied himself noisily in the kitchen with the kettle. Taking the coffee from the cupboard, he tilted, with the tips of his fingers, two jars, one of marmalade, one of honey, both encrusted, the labels obscured.

As he put her coffee on the stool that served as a bedside table, there was no reaction.

"Nearly ten past."

"No Year 11s now. Not the same rush."

There was only a slight movement of her head on the pillow. He propped himself up beside her and pulled the quilt over himself again.

"I bet you Trotsky didn't need to be goaded into life in the morning."

"He wasn't a woman."

"Rosa Luxemburg then."

She rolled to face him. "I don't suffer from delusions."

"No." He laughed. "What's on today's agenda, then? Are you sending a detachment to this protest at the old people's home?"

"I told you I don't suffer from delusions." She reached for her coffee. "There are a few I think, going from school but nothing to do with me."

"Makes a change. So what about these leaflets you were talking about?"

"Oh, not again."

"But I'm worried and you don't stand to gain anything."

Sitting up in bed, she stared back at him. "Who's 'you'?"

"All of you. You in particular. Any way you want to take it." He stroked her face, conciliatory.

"Anyone would think you'd worked in schools all your life the way you speak."

He settled back, a resigned expression on his face.

"Sorry if that's the way it seems. You know more about schools, your school, however you want to put it, than I ever will. But that's beside the point. It's about organisations, the way they work."

"Oh, Christ." She lay down, resting her head on his shoulder, before turning her eyes on his chin, his jaw line, set in concentration. "Toad's standing with parents isn't brilliant, we've chosen Bridget - I've said all this before, haven't I?"

"Yeah, you have but you're ignoring people's sense of loyalty. You send out a leaflet like that and a lot of parents will automatically turn against you. I bet you the school's next step will be to wheel out two or three of the governors, the ones who've got a bit of clout in the area, to turn the tide against you. Perhaps a public meeting, perhaps more indirect. And then there's what's done inside the school - the governors could be used, they'll try and create a majority -"

"You sound like the Sociology lecturer I had at college." She slid her hand down his chest and under the sheets.

"Okay. I'm sorry - but am I right?"

"Probably." Her fingers drew a figure of eight pattern on his skin. "I'm no expert." Her tongue brushed his neck and traced a line along his shoulder.

"But if it's right, what are you going to do about it?" His hand gripped her neck, his fingers kneading and pushing her closer.

"All right, all right, I'll pull out, as long as you don't." She shifted herself onto him. "Is that a deal? Can't speak for the others. Perhaps you ought to work on them as well."

52

Goldsmith heard her moving around and turned away from his reading to listen for her footsteps on the stairs. None came. He picked out the kettle in the kitchen and then no other sound: no television - he would not have expected that - but no radio either. He would go down in a minute - it would do him good - but there was the letter to finish first.

It was probably the mother's own work. She had obviously been talking to the others, the campaign group that had developed so quickly, but the wording - 'those of you over there' - sounded like the woman who had confronted him on the stairs on that visit to see Amy.

'She had no help when she really needed it. In those last weeks, when she wasn't up to it, I was the only one pushing. The hospital was no good, couldn't get their own equipment to work and have got doctors who can't use English properly. Dr. Goldsmith was very good, as I said, but we got to him too late.

'So what I want to know is why - '

The door opened behind him.

"I'm sorry, Dad. I made a coffee and didn't think about you.

Do you want one?"

"No thanks - I've still got half a cup here."

"I did wonder. The kettle was still warm."

Becky said nothing more but stood suspended in the doorway.

"What is it? Really."

"No, you're busy. I'll talk to you later."

Still she didn't move, despite the phone ringing. He put the letter down and swivelled his chair around, stretching across the desk.

"Never too busy." He waved her in, pointing to the phone, implying a brief silence.

"Fine, thanks." He nodded involuntarily at the politeness. "No, no gardening this morning."

His face set as he listened.

"Give me her name again. She's one of the new ones, isn't she?"

Becky balanced herself on the edge of the chair.

"You can check the records but I'm sure I've only seen her once. Yes, I did."

She stood again, hovering, before taking a step towards the door.

"So who did she report me to?"

He waved her back, his head shaking.

"Okay, I'll get in early to see Maurice. Yes, that's more than enough time to give it."

He sighed, gently rubbing his chin.

"Are you sure it's all right?"

"It's not you." He reached out and touched her cheek. "It never is. Just a complaint logged against me. It happens all the time now - but not normally to me."

"That's -"

"It's not even worth talking about. I'll get it cleared up when I go in. Now, more importantly, what's on your mind?"

"This is like being one of your patients, isn't it?" She looked nervously at him as she settled herself into the chair.

"Go on, then."

"I think I'm going along with Liam to St. Budoc's - the one I went to with him before, where his gran's a resident - on Thursday because they've organised a protest. But," her smile was wry, self-conscious, "I don't really understand what it's about - though Granddad said it was a good idea."

"He would, wouldn't he? He's getting the taste for it."

She relaxed into a broader smile. "And he said it was the sort of place he'll be needing soon."

"What - the first marathon runner in residence? So: you think you're going to go," he tilted his head gently, quizzically, "despite the fact you don't know what it's about. I think there may be an ulterior motive."

"That's just possible but I do want to know before I commit myself."

"Well, I can guess." He put his hand around his coffee cup. "You must have picked up something - you're not that daft."

"All Liam wanted to put on the poster was 'criteria for funding care'. The date and the place, of course, and that was about it."

"In that case," he leaned back, "I imagine it's about the fact that people with sufficiently serious medical conditions get, in effect, free care. Otherwise, you have to pay if you have savings or your own house. There's been a lot of concern about which medical conditions qualify - and how you assess them."

"What do you think?"

"It's like almost everything else in life, nothing black and white - yet I can understand the concern."

"So I'll go then." The statement was weakened by the intonation of a question.

He raised his eyebrows and opened his hands in front of his face, familiar signals to her.

"Right, I'll get this poster finished."

"Just make sure there's nothing libellous."

In her face, he saw the mercury of confidence drop.

"I'll have a look at it if you want."

He watched as she, restored, walked out of the room with a smile, a backwards glance over her shoulder.

He rubbed the tiredness in his eyes. It would be an earlier start at the surgery than he had anticipated and the letter, with its grievance, its certainty, was still there to be finished. He picked it up, resigned, unmoved by the compliment to his professionalism. At least, Becky was doing something concrete.

53

Early morning, for her but not for the world that worked. None of the cars acknowledged her existence, the drivers' eyes set rigidly in front of them, until one pulled up in front of her. She ran but only when she saw a woman's head turning back towards her. It was no more than forty yards but, in the morning warmth, that was enough to make her out of breath. Her lack of fitness had never bothered her but her appearance did - she guessed, from the stickiness of her back, at a reddened face, strands of hair stuck to her forehead - and she slowed before she reached the car.

"It is Sarah, isn't it?"

She looked blankly at the driver.

"Kirsty's mum. Kirsty Andrews. I'm going to Trelay if that's any use."

"Anywhere there'd be great." She settled in the passenger seat with a flick of her head and her hand brushing through her hair. "I missed the bus. Don't usually do this."

"No, no, I can quite understand that. Are you all finished now like Kirsty?"

"Yes. Not as finished as I thought I'd be. It wasn't as bad as everyone said it would be."

"And it's A Levels for you presumably. At Whitcross?"

As she answered, Sarah took in the detail of Mrs. Andrews' suit, the light material, the colour dark but not oppressive, formal but comfortable, worn for a day or two until the weather necessitated a change into something equally comfortable.

"I hope you don't mind my asking but do you know if Kirsty's particularly friendly with anyone now? You don't see as much of her, I think, as you used to. Not a criticism, of course," she looked away from the road, her full smile tinged with apprehension, "but I can't quite put my finger on something with her at the moment. You probably think it's none of my business, I expect."

"No." She shrugged. "Whose business should it be?" She thought of the volatility, the swearing, but it probably was not despair as far as she could tell - and generation loyalty took over. "I guess she's like the rest of us. As Miss Pollard tells us repeatedly, if we can't be up and down now, we never will. You ought to see me sometimes."

There was a brief silence.

"I hope she's right. She's leaving, isn't she?"

"I don't know. I heard a rumour."

"A real shame for the school if she did - but then she is young."

The silence deepened.

"Where would you like me to drop you off?" They were on the hill that wound its way towards Trelay. "At home? But you'll have to direct me."

"No, school's fine - I've got a few things to clear up. I'm going around to my father's later."

"If you're sure." She waved through her open window to an

234

elderly couple who had stopped to stare at the passing car. "Tom's met your father a couple of times. Purely in a professional capacity. You must be very proud of him."

As the car pulled up at the school gates, Sarah's head nodded, a movement that Kirsty's mother would not have seen.

54

"It's only a bit misty. That's not going to hurt anyone."

Oliver grinned at Becky before bustling down the corridor and up the stairs.

"Come on, Maureen." His voice reverberated through the open door. "Day out, even if it is only in the car park."

The lift cranked into life and drowned out any response.

"You ask him when he comes down. You'll get it out better."

"There's nothing to it. Honestly."

She looked at Liam's face and gave up. They waited in silence at the bottom of the stairs, stepping aside to avoid the carer emerging, back first, from the lift. The man in the wheelchair, head tilted as he was tugged over the lip of the carpet, fixed them with a stare and made a series of low-pitched sounds.

"Yes, they're a lot younger than you, Clive. I don't know what you're worrying about, though - they're a lot younger than I am." The carer smiled at them and pointed to the corridor.

They stepped aside to give her more turning room and the man's sounds continued, each sequence followed by a reply from the carer.

"Intelligent guesswork." Oliver was behind them and had caught the hesitation in Becky's expression. "Like most things in life - and certainly more intelligent than most of our politicians' guesswork. But what can I do for you? You look as if you need to see someone really important."

"We wanted to know how much of the pavement you thought we should use."

"About half - but I'll show you. Nobody minds extra cars parked out there so a few tables and chairs won't be a problem."

Outside, despite the mist, the heat was continuing to build.

"You've got the right idea." He looked at Liam's shorts and flip-flops. "Don't think they'd look right on me somehow. You're Joan Bennett's grandson, aren't you?"

Liam nodded. "I've come here a few times with Dad."

"I know. Joan's one of the lucky ones. Look, grab that shovel, can you?" He pointed to the shed. "Just inside the door." He looked up through the mist and then at Becky. "Not very encouraging, is it? If it stays like this, no-one's going to see you from their cars but you never know."

They had reached the entrance and he grinned at Liam who had caught them up with the shovel. "Lob that in the hedge." He pointed at a pile of dog's excrement. "You wouldn't want to step in that. Neither would the wheelchair. Anyway, you should have plenty of space between the pillar and where the pavement narrows again."

A car edged past them and through the pillars. Oliver waved, unnoticed by the driver whose head leaned forward as if an extra few inches would help his eyes penetrate the mist.

"Look, I'd better go. Can I leave you to it?" Without waiting for a reply, he walked around Liam's shovel and back up the drive, the mist fading him until he disappeared as if he were computer-generated. Behind them, a bus pulled away.

"We can use a couple of those trestle tables. Oh, God." Her last words were whispered as she recognised the shape emerging from where the bus stop must have been.

"Thought you might need someone who could lift. Someone who could push. I thought I'd have to practise on that bus." Briefly a bodybuilder, she flexed her muscles. "It didn't want to go up the hill. Too many people like me on it." She paused for breath. "Seriously, what can I do?"

"I don't really know, Kirsty. No-one's in charge. We're just making it up as we go along. Give us a hand with the tables and the placards, I suppose."

They walked back towards the shed.

"What's your father think about this?"

Becky braced herself for a convoluted answer that didn't come.

"He's why I'm here," were the only words.

"Mr. Wells, do come through." Oliver's voice had the enthusiasm of a dinner party host. "I'm sure it was me you wanted to see."

"Not really, to be perfectly honest. I came to see my father and find him bundled up in a wheelchair, left down here unattended."

"Hardly unattended, Mr. Wells. Anywhere else I'd be using my elbows to get through." With a sweep of his arm, he waved him into the office and shut the door. "Let me clear those things for you." He scooped up a new pile of papers that had found their way onto the chair. "Cup of tea or coffee?"

"Neither. No thanks." He seemed reluctant to sit down. "My father's waiting out there. So what's all this about? Those young people outside - they can't be old enough to work here, surely?"

"No, indeed. One of them's the grandson of one of the residents - the room just along from your father's - and the others are his friends. Come along to help. Their aim's to highlight the situation of people whose health in the past would've -"

"I know all that but my father, and the young lady with him, said that the plan is for everyone to go outside, in all this murk."

"Not for long. The temperature's fine - in fact, the mist is probably a blessing. We've checked it all out with the surgery. Some of the residents, of course, will stay inside but the rest are fine to go out. Dr. Goldsmith was perfectly happy with that and he knows, anyway, that we let the residents choose."

"Then, I'm afraid my father is choosing to stay inside."

He rose to his feet to terminate the discussion. Oliver nodded and opened the door.

"No problem whatsoever. We'll just have a word with him now."

"It was okay a minute ago but now all they'll see is a load of old people going on an outing." Kirsty looked up and realised she was talking to herself. "Still, she said she'd seen Sarah hitching. Oh, God, that poor old dear thinks we're selling something. Give her one of those stickers, Liam. I thought she'd have been here. Just her sort of thing, unless it's overload. She should ask me - I'm an expert on that."

Becky and Liam were kneeling down, laughing with a man whose right foot had been catching on the ground each time his wheelchair was moved. They bent his knee and patted the slippered foot back in place, only for it, involuntarily, to slide off again. She watched as they repeated the process, the man smiling, like a child whose pleasure at the attention he's receiving outweighs the inconvenience of the problem that's creating the attention.

Beyond where they were kneeling, the drive and the car park were filling haphazardly. A huddle of men, dressed for winter in their greys and fawns, one in a wheelchair, two supporting themselves with sticks, waited in the far corner, as far from the women as they could manage - adolescent in their recalcitrance, primary school children in their avoidance of anything female. A young male carer, in shorts and tee shirt, joked languidly with them before moving away to help Liam.

"I don't know who's more awkward, Bill, you or your foot." He adjusted the straps on the foot-rests and smiled at them. "Can't do them up too tight - Health and Safety. It'll be off again in a minute." His glance at them had the resignation of a much older man, quickened by an enforced alertness that carried him after a smartly-dressed woman who was walking purposefully along the pavement beyond the tables and towards the village.

"Vera, come on, my love." His voice carried through the mist, as he placed a restraining hand gently on her arm. "There's much more to look at over here. There'll be a lot of people coming in today."

She had turned without a protest and, as she passed Becky, was talking, her voice precise, a legacy of past influence and probable wealth. "I am sure you are right but I must do these one or two pieces of shopping or we will have nothing in for our visitors." Her face had the rounded balance, the softness, of a contented middle age, the eyes a sparkle that her words lacked. "It may be better if I go later. Ah, there we are." She looked across to where Oliver was standing, arms folded at the end of the drive. "Jonathan will know what to do."

"I'm sure I will, Vera. You come and stand by me and tell me how many people you think will sign this petition."

240

"I will sign it for you. I'm sure it's in a good cause."

"That's good of you, Vera, but that's not really the point. Mr. Cameron can get away with things like that but we can't. Excuse me a second, Vera." He waved one of the carers over. "What is that man Wells doing?"

They watched as he released the brakes on one of the wheelchairs and guided it, gently enough, towards the hedge, away from the cars. The woman he had pushed looked up for some conversation but there was none. Wells returned to the cars and started shooing two of the residents, theoretically mobile but immobile in reality, away from where he had parked.

"He'll never listen. Next I'll have his busy man spiel. No, no, Tony."

The grey-haired man, driven on by Wells, had been walking hesitantly with his stick across the slope of the car park. Oliver guided him to a bench on the grass before turning to Wells and the keys he was brandishing.

"I've got to clear a way so that I can get the car out."

"I quite understand, Mr. Wells, but this is not a forest through which you're trying to clear a path. Is your father inside?"

"He never came out."

Oliver looked at his watch. The implicit criticism registered.

"I would've seen him for longer if it hadn't been for all this rigmarole. I've got a series of meetings scheduled for the rest of the day." He was holding his glasses in his hand to leave his eyes straining, their stare accentuated by the sweat that had formed on his nose.

"I do understand but our residents can only be moved by staff who are trained in their care. That process will take a few minutes, I'm afraid."

"I can't run my life on 'a few minutes', even if you can. I've said -"

A sudden shout, the cutting of an engine, stopped him. Through the thickened mist, Oliver saw, at the other end of the car park, shapes coalescing, their movements blurred into slow motion.

The electrician's white van, lagged in dirt, had stopped, its reversing arc incomplete.

"Eddie's fallen, Eddie's fallen, Eddie's fallen." Barely comprehensible at first, Betty's words, on their final repetition, emerged into clarity.

"Fucking hell, the old bloke's been hit." Kirsty's voice was screaming, her hands waving. "Oh, my God, oh, my God."

Becky, impatient, frowned at her as Oliver spoke to the driver whose head alternated between immobility and a convulsive shaking.

"I know, I know. Just move the van forward again. As slowly as you can."

Even the jolt of the electrician's climbing back into his seat was enough to threaten the body lying behind the rear wheels but, with the uncertainty of a poorly functioning toy, the van at last hiccupped forward.

"Sean, get everyone back inside. Mandy, ring the ambulance. You," he pointed at Liam, "can you help me? He's just breathing."

"Anyone with a grain of sense could have seen this coming." Wells stood over Oliver, car keys in his hand, knowing that a long delay was inevitable. "Anyone without any bloody sense could have."

No words came in reply; no heads even turned in his direction.

55

The school was in its relaxed, end-of-summer-term clothes, the corridors less crowded, Year 10 about to go out on work experience, already believing that their coming role in the outside world elevated them beyond their surroundings.

Their meeting in the hall had broken up, most filing out, their faces a mixture of animation and indifference. At the open door stood Ben Emerton, cajoling, forcing a leaflet onto anyone who would take it. Several of the audience, however, all of them girls, stayed behind to ask questions.

"No, not really. View it as an athlete would. I bet some of you are sporty." There were one or two giggles at King's words. "This is an early season event, with the Olympics a long way off. It doesn't matter if you make mistakes as long as you learn from them. Or like going out with someone at your age." His smile took them all in. "You're not going to marry him so just learn from it."

"What work experience did you do at school?"

"In a pub, strangely enough. Back then, I wanted to be a chef - and I thought in a pub I'd meet lots of girls. I met the girls but I realised in double quick time that if I didn't want to eat what I'd cooked, I couldn't expect anyone else to." The smile reappeared. "The serious point about work experience is that sometimes you learn what you can't do or what you don't want to do. So now I stick to going into a pub to see who I can meet."

Ben was hovering behind him, leaflets in his hand, catching the eye of two of the girls.

"Going cheap. Bargain deal. One for you, one for you ... "

As they took the remaining leaflets, hands stretching out, a conditioned reflex, they glanced at the words in bold - 'C.V. and presentation skills'.

"Is this his number at the bottom?"

"That's what it says, I believe." Ben turned the paper through a full circle, pausing, with an exaggeratedly questioning air, every ninety degrees. "Yes, it looks like a telephone number, it smells like a telephone number - and it is a telephone number."

"So that's where we phone," she was looking straight at King, "if we need help during work experience?"

"No, not during your work experience - that's the school's job. But if afterwards you need any help, give me a ring."

"Clearly a success." Fletcher's words directed over their heads broke the spell. "I could only catch the last five minutes, unfortunately, but this speaks for itself."

Reluctantly, the girls sloped away.

"How did he get to help?"

"He's meant to be paid."

"Ask him. Look."

Ben was running after them, dismissed by Fletcher's stare and a half-nod.

"So what have you got that we haven't?"

In the opposite corner of the hall, Fletcher was ushering King towards his room.

"There's so much enthusiasm there that, as a school, we can really start to tap." He paused to look back, waving at the now empty space. "This cohort – they're a little bit late, unfortunately, but their successors will go through their formative years not seeing this artificial divide between school and the outside world. Both sides helping each other but, most importantly, helping these youngsters."

He closed the door behind him.

"Cooperation is not now confined to the public sector; competition is not the preserve of the outside world. If we fail, we are punished; if we succeed, we are rewarded. Sorry," there was a trace of self-deprecation as he poured the coffee. "I can't shake off the teacher in me that easily."

"Suppose not." King reached for a biscuit. "Have the governors approved that package?"

"Indeed they have. It was all straightforward enough at the last meeting. They got wind of a little disquiet in the usual quarters but nothing came of it. In fact, they added a performance element based on our links with the outside world - very hard-headed, our governors. And that, Martin, is why you're here - exactly what's required."

He pushed the biscuits across to King.

"Everything settled down with your daughter?"

He tried the coffee and nodded. "Seems okay."

"She wasn't involved in this nonsense at St. Budoc's?"

"No, Stuart, apparently not. Probably luck," his words had quickened, "she normally sniffs out a shambles like that."

"It might help to make certain people see sense. A little collateral damage won't do the community any harm."

He leaned back in his chair, stretching his arms behind him.

"Anyway, what about the next stage in your work here? We can't just rely on the trickle-down effect, vital though that is. We need to be proactive. I'm sure you agree."

56

"If he could ring me back. Yes, thank you. And could you stress the urgency?"

Oliver put the phone down and sighed. He swivelled in his chair and flicked the door open with his foot. At the other end of the corridor, Angela was sitting on the edge of the chair beneath the notice board.

"Dear God, can't she get a move on?"

Her words, the Yorkshire accent, penetrated the brief stillness. He watched as Jenny patted her on the shoulder and then walked towards the kitchen. He cut her off as she passed his door.

"A little moan. It'd be a lot longer but we won't get the time. These politicians - they expect you to drop everything but can you get hold of them when you want them? The gentleman in question was here quickly enough when it suited him."

Jenny sat down, not waiting for an invitation.

"They've no idea. We've been complaining about the dogs' mess down our lane. You wouldn't believe for how long. I got a letter at the end of last year - no, it was earlier than that - you know, one of those letters that thank you for your letter. And what have we had since then? Nothing. It beggars belief."

Oliver, attempting to pace the tiny floor area of the office, cut in as she paused.

"It must be frustrating for you." He talked across her attempt to continue. "Yet when there's a death involved, you have to expect much more than this. If you called a doctor - certainly Dr. Goldsmith – you'd get an almost instant response. That's how it should be."

He stopped at the window, his eye caught by Betty feeding the birds in a corner of the car park.

"He always has been brilliant, always like that. When Mike's mother died - I suppose I'm not meant to say this, am I? - he speeded her on her way, you know what I mean. Great with us as well, not like the new one who's just started."

As the flow of words built, eddying, diverting itself at points, Oliver turned back to Betty, his eyes looking through and beyond her battle with a ginger cat that was threatening the birds. So cocooned was he from any sound that he barely registered the ringing of the phone.

"Speaking."

He shook his head in irritation.

"Okay. Just one moment, please." Apologetically, he gestured Jenny towards the door and closed it behind her. "Yes, I was. For the whole period of the incident to which you refer."

He looked down towards his knees and back out through the window.

"It's obviously a time of great sadness for us. Beyond that, there's nothing I'm able to say at the moment. You've clearly spoken to the police and they will have told you that the incident is under investigation."

His hand tightened on the phone.

"No, I've nothing more to say. Thank you."

For a few seconds, he did not move. The closed door offered a brief chance to reflect; it did, however, trap him with the phone. The open door, the contact with chaotic humanity, would be a restorative - and so he walked quickly through towards the kitchen, stepping over the cables that were part of the hairdresser's improvised salon in the dining room.

"Morning, Joan. You look like an astronaut under that contraption." The two women, hearing aids on the converted bedside table between them, smiled uncertainly back at him. "I'll give you the money, Abi, when you've finished. Don't you worry about trying to sort it out."

She waved back over the noise of the hairdryers as he disappeared into the kitchen to make a coffee.

"No thanks, Chris, we're a bastion of democracy." He grinned at the cook. "One of very few left - and one of very few jobs that I can do without creating a crisis. Mind you, that's probably due to you and your endless good humour."

He bent down to open the cupboard door.

"You've heard the news about Dr. Goldsmith?"

He looked up, a sore prodded by her words.

"He's not seeing any patients while they sort it all out."

"What - all this?"

"I don't think we come into it." She turned to check the room was empty. "Groping a patient is how they put it in the shop."

"Dear God. Anyone could tell them ... "

He stopped himself and sighed, the cupboard door left open.

"Sorry. I thought you'd have known. Look, let me make you the coffee."

He moved away, unprotesting, as she reached down into the cupboard.

57

Ben had tried to avoid her, he must have done. School petering out had made it less difficult for him but Trelay was not even a town, anonymity not a mathematical probability. In Whitcross, Sarah had twice seen him on the other side of the street, collar and tie, trousers rather than jeans, before he made his escape. This time, behind her in the queue in the village shop, he had no way out and she waited for him outside in the sunshine.

"Ben, don't go sloping off."

He had turned abruptly left as he strode out of the shop, like a young child who assumes that if he can't see his parent, his parent won't be able to see him.

"Oh!" He looked at her sheepishly. "You want one?" He waved the cigarettes at her.

She raised her eyes at him. "Huh! You haven't driven me to that yet."

A couple hauling their dog out of the car smiled at her.

"Over here." She gestured to the path through the churchyard.

"I haven't ... " He thought better of any protest.

She stopped by a headstone and turned to him.

"Michael Richards." He read the black lettering. "He didn't last very long, did he? Forty-eight."

"Forty-six, actually."

"Just testing." He shifted his weight from one foot to another.

"Your arithmetical skills must be of great use in your new career?" He screwed up his face, a parody of feigned innocence. "With my father. Counting out his leaflets, I suppose."

"It's building up my CV - what the dosser with the DVDs calls 'transferable skills'."

"No money, of course."

He lifted his head, steadier on his feet in the face of anger expressed rather than anticipated.

"Oh, fuck me, don't start preaching at me. It's your family, not mine."

"And you know where I am on that. Do I help him? Do I act like some lackey while a group of girls fawns over him? I've got more pride than that. And principles." He looked away and missed the tremor on her face. "You were with us in what we're doing. You were the one with the ideas but you didn't even turn up when those parasites graced us with their presence. Obvious now. It was just PR all along. That was all you were interested in. Easy transition really - to taking money and dishing out leaflets."

"Suit yourself."

Whatever else he might have said, she didn't hear, jerking her head against the tension of her neck and turning away from him. Her stumble over the serpentine step out of the churchyard barely checked her momentum.

58

It was like the tide: the steady rise in positive comment, almost acclamation, reached its highest point and then a swirl of cross-currents, allegations, disapproval, disciplinary action, magnetic in its inevitability, pulled in the opposite direction. St. Budoc's became, after the death in the car park, a byword not for state underfunding but for public sector incompetence. The cause they had taken up was sullied by association.

"I've batted Oliver away again but not this one. Fifth call of the day. Yesterday's record under threat." Lewis transferred the call.

Andrews gave his well-practised line to the reporter whose name was unfamiliar: a protracted expression of his regret at the fatality, his sympathies for the family, both guaranteed to win a respectful silence, and finally his reluctant concession, before the voice at the other end of the line even asked, that he could make no further comment until the necessary investigations had been carried out.

"That's all well and good, Mr. Andrews, but we have a picture of your daughter at St. Budoc's, on the day of the death."

The man knew well enough how to spring a silence; Andrews knew equally well how to disrupt it.

"Yes, she was with one of her friends there. One of his relations - grandmother I think it is - is a resident. My daughter was very upset by what happened."

"The picture I've got shows her with placards behind her. It looks like rent-a-mob. Not the sort of thing an MP's daughter should be involved in. I'm sure you'd want to comment on that?"

"No, you can add to your piece that I have no comment to make, for the reasons I've already given you."

"She is believed to -"

"I have no comment to make. I look forward to reading your article. No doubt it will be very balanced."

Gently, he put the phone down. His fingers rubbed at a stain on the desk before he rose to gaze from the window. The door opening behind him was unseen, unheard.

"You know how they're going to play it. 'MP's Daughter in Death Home Protest.' An enhanced picture of Kirsty, with, inset, an unsmiling photo of yours truly. Your 'no comment' line in a single-sentence final paragraph, embarrassment implicit in its isolation."

"I do wish, Graham, that you wouldn't listen in on my conversations."

"You've asked me ... but that's beside the point. You saw it coming, didn't you? You said you spoke to her. You -"

Andrews' face was expressionless.

"After the event. She just nodded at each possible implication of her having been at St. Budoc's. All a bit late and - in any case - the stupid girl would do exactly the same thing again tomorrow. She said she knew," his voice was suddenly raised, "that anything she did could have an effect on me."

"But it's not like an adult understanding, is it?"

"No - and I told her I didn't like seeing her dragged needlessly into the limelight. It was the price I paid for being a public figure but it wasn't meant to cover her. All that stuff. Seems prophetic now, doesn't it?"

"It does indeed. So what next then, my dear prophet, now your erstwhile friends have changed their colours?"

59

Sarah knew she ought to get a holiday job. The money would help and it might distract her but, on a day like this, having no commitments had its advantages. Even in her state, the sun was preferable to the mist.

After passing the surgery and waving to the protesters, she kicked a stone into the hedge. Male gesture, her father had told her. All the more reason to do it, even if her aim was hopeless.

She looked back as two more cars were stopped. It was something else she should have done but her mum was probably right. She could not do it all - and they did make it look like an organised outing, a rural routine that in the past would have sustained W.I. coffee mornings. A bit of chaos might have drawn her in.

After an ambulance passed her, no siren but its horn sounding, she turned down the lane towards the park, the top of the scaffolding visible above the rooftops - scaffolding on which no-one moved, pending a legal challenge brought by much the same group that were gently picketing the surgery.

Pushing open the gate, she saw in the far corner two women

sitting in camp chairs on churned ground that had once been home to a basketball net, with, behind them, the piles of concrete blocks, sand and cement, the trenches exposing the outside of the foundations and the 'Danger' warning sign.

One of the women waved to her, beckoning. They looked small against the swathe of new building but at least, even in their boring middle age, they looked finished, rounded. Not like the crude blockwork that reminded her of a holiday in Greece, the houses left jagged and incomplete.

"This, they would have us believe, is more attractive than the glories of nature." Sarah recognised her - the Geography teacher they had all called 'Auntie' who had retired two or three years earlier. "From what I remember, you'd think the same. We could do with some young blood and you wouldn't need a car as they've retreated into the towns and villages now. It's like a military campaign: we've driven them back and although I wouldn't bet against them trying to rip up the fields again, just sitting here - the odd shift - would be really easy for you."

She read the silence on Sarah's face and changed tack.

"You're one of Liam Bennett's friends, aren't you?"

She recoiled at the intrusion into her privacy, the knowledge in a small village that everyone seemed to have of others' business. On a better day, she would have qualified the friendship, marked herself out as different, but the words would not come.

"Yes. Yes, I know Liam."

The woman's expression was kindly, concerned. Her friend was looking past Sarah at the sky, her mouth open a fraction, expectant.

"You know he's been questioned by the police?"

Sarah laughed at the misjudgement. "You must be joking. Liam's never even thought anything that they could question him about."

"It's the incident at St. Budoc's. You were there, were you?" It was the woman's turn to imbue her words with the confidence of a different generation. "He was seen this morning apparently. A public order offence, leading to an accident, in this case a death. It's what they've tried to use at the surgery. They'll try and do the same here," she pointed at the frayed rope that could not prevent the 'Danger' sign from scraping the ground, "the police, the surgery, no doubt acting in consort."

The woman's voice was controlled, the tangential diversion into her own experience brief and in proportion.

Sarah nodded in agreement. "Thank you. Thank you for telling me."

"I'm sure nothing will come of it. Just another example of the scare tactics they're using. It's all the time now."

She turned back to them, a revived animation in her face. "I know." She resisted the temptation to recount her own battle scars and walked back across the park.

"Liam's been questioned by the police."

Becky barely reacted - as if the words were not a headline, more a traffic report at the end of a local bulletin, registered but only subliminally. She raised her finger to her mouth and pointed upstairs.

"Dad's home." She shooed Sarah into the kitchen. "I think he's ill but won't admit it. It may just be everything that's happened - but that can make you ill, can't it? It's the same thing, I suppose."

She closed the door quietly but neither of them sat.

"Liam - he's been questioned over that protest at the old people's home. You were there. What did he do? He couldn't wake himself up quickly enough to do anything."

"No." There was a long, distracted pause. "No."

"So unless someone has made a specific allegation, I can't see why they're bothering."

"He didn't do anything. I was with him all the time, nowhere near the poor bloke who got run over, really." She pursed her lips. "If they wanted to complain about anyone, it was Kirsty - but that was just her being a pain as usual."

"It may just be what those women said, scare tactics, but he's not the obvious target to make that work. I can see why they wouldn't go for Kirsty - or perhaps they would. It depends who's behind it. You'd be a better choice, with the views your dad's got."

The door nudged open and Goldsmith stood, hovering between the hall and the kitchen.

"Oh. I heard voices and I thought it was Mum home early. If you're making a coffee, I'd love one. Sorry, Sarah, forgetting my manners." He turned back to Becky. "Could you bring it up?"

As the door closed, Becky stared out of the window before filling the kettle and listening for his tread on the stairs.

"Don't worry - he wouldn't have heard." Her grip tightened on the cups. "He's not able to go into work - God knows how long for - while a complaint is investigated. 'An allegation made by a woman' is how he described it. He's been going downhill for a while - I just don't know if there's enough fight left in him."

"Oh, God, I'm sorry. Not for your dad - he'll be all right - but for not thinking. Getting like Kirsty."

She watched as Becky, coffee cup in her hand, opened the door.

"It's no different, is it, though? Your dad and Liam. No different."

60

As Beckford's car crawled towards them, the woman put a restraining hand on the shoulder of the boy who had started to step out into the road. 'Boy' is how he must have seemed to her: in his late teens, at least thirty years younger than she was, than all the regulars were. From her friendly but impersonal look, she could not have known him; his resentful but compliant stare confirmed it as he stepped back to join the others who, in the last two days, had started to swell the protest, 'the picket line' as the tabloids incongruously but predictably insisted on describing it.

The easy exchanges between everyone outside the surgery had drifted away as if on an outgoing tide that had left them splintered, divided by age into two camps, the summer breeze like remnants of water between them. They watched as the car slid into the remaining reserved space.

Locking the door, Beckford looked back at the protesters. She hesitated before turning to stride through the surgery entrance.

"Silly time for a meeting, Maurice." He looked at her with the raised eyebrows of mock surprise. "Yes, I'm here. I know you thought I wouldn't be able to drag myself out of bed but if I can be obstructive, that's incentive enough. How you think your guillotine will work, just because we have a waiting room full of patients, I don't know."

"I'm sure it won't be a problem." He held the door open for her. "Just a business meeting."

"Very well put, Maurice - and that is exactly the problem."

A sheaf of papers had been placed in front of her chair. She glanced at the front sheet - and at the others who, having thumbed through the documents, had settled back in their seats.

"Thank you for all making this early start and for running the gauntlet again. I'll obviously make it as short as I can. The key information for today is the second sheet in your pack." His voice, benevolent, hinted at the inevitability of the first interjection coming from Beckford.

"What you describe as a 'gauntlet' - presumably, the reason they're out there is the same one that brings us here this morning?"

"I'm sorry, I don't follow." The benevolence was fading. "You need to be less cryptic, Sheila, for us lesser mortals."

"We are here, as they are, because of the commercialisation of this surgery and, therefore, any decisions we make will determine how long they remain."

"I think you're attributing to us greater power than we possess - or indeed will ever possess. All we can ask of ourselves is that we work logically through the demands being made of us."

"Which includes our patients – who've been order personified in their protests."

"Until the last few days I would have agreed with you -"

"All the more reason, therefore, that -"

"Sheila." Johnson was looking straight at her and then back at Allen. "We've got half an hour at most and we can't keep going over the same old ground."

"I hope you're happy with that, Sheila." He avoided her stare. "The second sheet in your pack is the financial analysis that Martin, who unfortunately can't be here today, promised us last time. It looks at various 'what if' scenarios and shows the financial effect on us of taking varying numbers of patients from outside our practice area. Over to you, Ian."

"Well, first, I think this is very helpful. I also think I know which of the scenarios is most likely for us. But leaving that to one side, the costings will clearly need a bit of additional work. For example, we may well have to take on someone else in the office. And then there'll be issues that are nothing to do with cost - the points that Colin raised at our last meeting."

"And which Colin should be here to discuss now. We're looking at calculations that Mr. King has churned off his computer while one of our colleagues is unable to work. We're getting our priorities hopelessly wrong."

She pushed the papers away from her. Some eyes were averted; others flickered with impatience.

"Colin's situation is our equivalent of sub judice. Unfortunately, therefore, it wouldn't be appropriate for us to discuss it here."

"Oh, come on, Maurice, some of you have clearly talked about it or Colin wouldn't now be stuck at home."

"I can only repeat that comment here is not appropriate."

"Let me, then, ask a simple question: how many people here were party to the decision that Colin is suddenly deemed unfit for work?"

He sighed, his eyes never wavering from Beckford's face. "Some discussion, Sheila, within certain parameters, is possible. The departure - temporary, we all hope - of a doctor creates problems for the day-to-day running of the practice which we can, of course, comment on. Anything else, however, has to remain confidential."

It was her turn to sigh. "Oh, dear me, that's a cheap trick and you know it. We're all grown-ups here and confidentiality is virtually written into our genes."

"Which is precisely why I cannot divulge the detail."

"Fine." She looked slowly around the room. "I'm going to discuss Colin. It may be with myself but that's still a 'discussion'- most of us have had a proper academic grounding - and anyone else is welcome to join in.

"To begin with the allegation itself which this woman has made: couldn't they think of anything more convincing than touching her breast while taking her blood pressure? My training was in the distant past yet my nephew has gone through the same process a couple of years ago and, despite massive updating elsewhere in the course, that's still the stock example given of a situation where an allegation of sexual misconduct is a possibility.

"To add to the glaringly suspicious nature of the allegation, how strange - how ironic, if it weren't so poisonous - that it should come from a young woman at her first appointment with us, a woman who's a beneficiary - one of many, it seems - of this new pseudo-policy of allowing certain outsiders to jump the waiting list queue to boost our finances.

"Finally, from the peculiarities of this young woman's allegations to Colin's situation in general: I saw your surprise, Mark, but I used the word 'they', earlier, advisedly. I am sure our colleague is a victim of forces that are determined to push through supposed reforms and that are quite capable of targeting individuals who are seen as obstructive. Colin has voiced his concerns about the direction in which we're being taken and is now paying the price.

"If it's happening here, goodness knows what it's like in a major city, with a proliferation of Martin Kings ferreting about. Ian, please don't look at me as if I were some kind of barmy conspiracy theorist. Most of what they do is manipulation but it would be naïve in the extreme to think that they wouldn't go further. When they do and when it has a direct bearing on one of our colleagues, we have a responsibility to speak out."

There was the embarrassed silence of parents when a child has misbehaved.

"If you have nothing to say," the anger had flooded into her voice as she stood up, "I'm afraid I will have to share my opinions with people who are prepared to talk. Equally important," she looked at her watch, "I have patients to see in a few minutes."

Leaving her papers on the table, she walked out of a silent room.

61

Kirsty knew his reading habits well enough to realise that it was odd. Normally, he had no newspaper with his breakfast - "one point in the day to escape it all" was the repetitive rationale that he would breezily mutter - or, if there was a key vote or an election was imminent, he would have the broadsheets, squat tabloids, the local rag, every newspaper known to man.

Today, there was just a copy of 'The Sun', her father's inexact folding, perhaps from haste, revealing that it had already been scanned.

"You've become a celebrity." He pushed the paper across to her before she had sat down. "No half measures, either, even if it is the same picture of you at St. Budoc's that they've recycled. Front page as well, with what, in their characteristic manner, they describe as an in-depth exposé on the inside pages."

His summary of what she read, panic obscuring the detail, seemed accurate enough. " 'Drinking what a front row forward would struggle to put away.' 'Crashed-out on the pavement.' 'Gagging for it.' All a reliable source, apparently."

"Oh, God, I'm sorry. Oh, fucking hell."

His lips taut, he scowled at her. "Let's at least talk reasonably about it."

"No, I am sorry. Oh, Christ." She pushed her hands so hard into her face that she sensed her cheekbones were briefly defined. "They'll all have seen it, all think it's bloody hilarious. That's me now, isn't it? One of the fat slags."

"It's true, I presume?"

"Well, sort of. They can't have known what I was thinking, though. They'd know now - whoever's done the talking."

She started to cry.

"Have you thought of its impact on my position?"

She looked back at him, the tears checked, incredulous in her embarrassment and rage at herself. "Of course I have. It's all I ever bloody think of."

"Okay. Okay. Just sit down and we can try and work through this."

"There's no point," but she pulled out the chair opposite him.

"Who would've known enough about you to pass all the gory detail on to the paper?"

"Oh, Christ knows. I don't know where to start."

"It's that public knowledge, is it?"

"What do you think I am?" She went to stand up but his hand, reaching for her elbow, stopped her. "And I'm not a bloody slag. I've really tried."

"All right but what did you mean then?"

"I'd had like a lot to drink that night."

"Only that night?"

"No," she glared at him, "but that's the night we're talking about, isn't it? There were loads of people out. Some I knew, some I didn't know." She started crying again. "And I can't remember a lot of it."

"But people who knew you were 'gagging for it'. Surely there can't have been too many of them?"

"You don't know what it's like, do you? It's not your men's club, with all these suits standing round having meaningful discussions. Sarah's creepy father. Whoever else it is."

"Hang on a minute, Kirsty, it's what happened to you that we're trying to sort out. It's not my 'men's club' that created this mess."

In the silence, she stared at the floor and muttered.

"Is Mum still in?"

"No. She's gone to work."

"And -"

"Yes, she's seen the paper."

She looked grudgingly back up at him. "I could give you one or two names but what good would that do?"

"Very little. Unless it's someone you've spoken to on the phone. You saw that bit on the inside pages?"

"Yeah."

"The extract from a conversation you had with a 'friend'."

"No."

She opened the paper, scrabbling at the pages before swearing and pushing them towards him. "Where the hell is it?"

He found the page in an instant and placed it back in front of her. "At the bottom. Bottom right."

The words stilled her. "I sent this to Becky. I'll check it in a minute. She wouldn't have told them this."

He pulled the paper back across the table. " 'Got turned down by at least three guys last night before 11 o'clock. What the fuck's wrong with me?' "

He refolded the paper.

"I dispensed with the asterisks – we're past the need for the paper's prissiness. Why'd you do it?"

"Drink - and I don't know why I do that either."

"No, not that. The self-advertisement. It's just self-abuse - or whatever name you and your friends give it - in public." She stared at him, a moment's shock, seemingly unnoticed. "Why do you need to tell anyone - it doesn't matter if it's a friend - all this?"

"Everyone does it." Her eyes had dropped in front of her and, flicking her finger nail in a crack in the bare wooden table top, she clenched her teeth - until she shook herself, rubbing her eyes. "But Becky wouldn't have done this. Not ever, but not now she's so upset about her dad." She scrolled through her phone and her face settled into a frown. "She was the only one."

"I know her father slightly. Shame for him - it shows you how quickly a career can be wrecked." He looked at Kirsty's downturned head, absorbed in her mobile. "As for his daughter, I don't really know her - but it seems to me you've got some strange friends."

She caught her ankle on the table leg as she stood up. "I've told you. She couldn't possibly have done it."

"And I'm telling you -"

The anger in his voice drove her out, his words lost as she slammed the door.

62

Tidying up did not come naturally to Pollard. If you were feeling good, there were a hundred and one better things to do; if you were feeling as lousy as she did now, it all seemed pointless. She picked up the debris of what she had eaten the night before - scooping up as well the crisp packets from an earlier evening - and piled it all beside the sink.

There was nothing that he had eaten. There never would have been. It had been better for her that he hardly seemed to eat. The self-discipline that she would have loved in herself, that she was always banging on to the kids about. Self-discipline that had gone out of the window. Not even that trace of him.

It was still worth making the effort. Saturday morning was often when he would turn up unannounced and then stay for the weekend. Or it had been. Friday night, even Thursday, had been the pattern towards the end.

She ran the water into the bowl, scrubbing at something that stained the surface. The last time he'd been there, he had seemed different, oddly caring. Normally, he was so self-contained: no great display of affection, no temper, no demands clawing into her.

And then, that night, he had held her but distant enough to look at her face. Any other night, he would have stayed and yet she had not thought to question it. Not until the look in his eyes - a concern, almost protective, that she would have challenged if it had lingered any longer. If he had lingered.

And that was it. No contact for a fortnight. Nothing. That look of his: was it his way of showing a sadness that she had never let him get any closer; or was it guilt that he knew he was leaving, or that he had found someone else? It could have been both as, either way, it came back to her own inadequacies.

She had rung him, never got through and there was no-one else to ring. Any friends he had - the people he talked about from his past - were miles away. She had no numbers, had never met them - and so the river had dried up. River, stream, trickle, nothing.

She jumped at the sound of the phone. Wiping her hands in a tea towel too quickly, she knocked a dish onto the floor where it smashed, the glass quicker than her rushed steps, a shard already waiting to be crunched underfoot.

Her disappointment at hearing Sarah's voice must have been too obvious.

"No, no, I don't mind at all." She tried to inject some professional humour into her words. "You're still technically one of ours, in any case." It didn't convince. "No, you carry on. Gets me away from the sink."

Most of it was nothing new: Kirsty's front page celebrity had, for a day, been the sole topic of conversation on the streets, in the shops, as the story was swollen by rumour, by reports of people who claimed to have seen her that night, seemingly every other night for a year. Sarah's take on it was briefly more analytical - she contextualised it, even laughed at how typical it was of other

269

tabloid horrors - before changing tone.

"But what she can't make sense of is who told the papers. She's checked out her phone and unless she wiped something while she was blind drunk, she thinks the only ones she's told are Becky and a couple of others. On the phone, anyway. Someone who saw her that night could've done it but not those words. She's too reflective, it's all retrospective, calm light of day, if anything's calm for her. But Becky would never do anything like that. She wouldn't, would she?"

"Of course not. You don't need me to tell you that."

"So then the suspicion goes wider. Kirsty asked me. It was more of an accusation and I suppose you can't blame her for being wound-up. But you know patience isn't my strong point and we've ended up not speaking." She paused. "Don't worry. I'm not asking you to do anything. I'm just sounding off."

There was little more said. There were thanks, the desire to stay in touch - genuine, no doubt of that - before she rang off.

Pollard began picking up the broken glass, composed enough to smile at the absurdity of her being treated as the adult, intact, untroubled. Strange how at that age there was an almost constant falling out, jagged edges, kids tearing at each other, often without even realising it. At her age, the edges were all inside, sealed off from view by expectation.

She knew he wouldn't be back.

63

At least Becky had got him to sit in the garden. That would always have been his own prescription - far more potent, he would say, than any piece of paper he could sign. He was too rational to argue when she quoted it back at him and had brought the papers out with him, dressed as if going to work, the absence of a tie his only concession to supposed relaxation.

As she cleared away the chopping board, she watched him rise slowly from his chair, deep in thought, pen and paper in his hand, and head towards the cellar door. By the time she was carrying the salad out, he was already walking back to the table.

"There's something wrong with those panels. There's a little bit of haze but it's very bright - and yet the meter's changing at the rate I'd normally see at seven or eight o'clock in the evening." He pointed to the detailed, improvised chart in his hand. "This rate of generation is thirty one percent below the level they anticipate for midsummer and over thirty-eight percent below what we achieved last year." She nodded and spread out the cutlery. "I've checked them with the binoculars and there's no problem apparent on the surface. If it continues, I'll have to get the installers around.

Probably next week."

She smiled and pushed his plate towards him. "One advantage, I suppose, of being at home."

As she moved the newspapers carefully onto the grass, she sensed a shift in his introspection.

"You've seen The Best Written, have you?"

"No," she answered with as much conviction as she could muster. "Not yet."

"There are, apparently, three other women who've come forward. Probably a good sign - at least there are no men and three's hardly a flood."

"See - the humour's still there."

He raised his eyes from the ground.

"In all of this," each monosyllable was slow, weighted as if for a wider audience, "what I loathe most -"

" -'is what it must be like for you'. I've told you so many times: there's no need to worry about me. No-one believes it - you should hear Sarah on it."

His expression was hesitant but steady. For a moment, his hands gripped the edge of the table as if the issue were settled.

"I suppose she'd call them a middle-class subsidy?" He started helping himself before her, more of an interest in food than he had shown recently. She looked at the beetroot, the radishes, the tomatoes, puzzled.

"Not them." His smile was briefly as open as it had always been. "You're becoming a housewife before your time. Because of me." A puppeteer's string withdrew the smile. "The solar panels - and I can understand why."

"She probably would but it's not very high on her list of priorities. So she won't be round banging on the door. Have some bread as well."

He acquiesced, taking the smallest piece she had cut.

"She's that organised, is she?" The smile flickered back into life. "When are you going to start getting priorities?"

"Probably when I'm as old as you."

Her voice was flatter than she had intended as the echo of Kirsty's words played in her head: "When are you going to start telling me the truth?" She had phoned in a panic, in a rage - the two were indistinguishable - and had not given her time to start saying anything. Just the accusations.

Goldsmith broke the silence.

"Does Sarah have much to do with her father, do you know?"

"As little as possible. I think they've grown apart."

"Tactful way of putting it." He stretched his hand across to hers. "Not like us."

"Not like us at all. Not her, not me, not him, not you." She looked at his plate, barely touched. "Have you had enough?"

He nodded, distracted once more, leaving her to clear the table.

Opening the door, the plates balanced in one hand, she saw a spider's web of inheritance: for her, a caring uncertainty; for Sarah, certainty, distance, that would stay with her, no matter how much she tried to reject it.

She returned from the kitchen to call out and thought better of it. He was again studying his piece of paper, a preoccupation to stave off the sunshine. She brought the yoghurts out anyway, smiling at the familiar exchange there would otherwise have been.

"What about the boy, Liam?"

"Dad, he's not a boy."

"I'll take your word for it. You consort with criminals now, though, do you?"

"Oh, that. I haven't seen him since it happened but he was

273

only questioned. As a witness but I've got no idea why he was singled out. He certainly won't."

He shuffled in his seat at the sudden edge in her voice. He paused to examine the yoghurt pot, checking the fat content had not changed mysteriously from the previous day, before his free hand pointed to the newspaper on the grass. "The Grauniad's always so discreet but it looks as though I'm not the only one in a little difficulty. Tom Andrews - his daughter was in the same group as you, wasn't she?"

"Kirsty, yes, some of the time."

"They give no detail but hint that the tabloids have got hold of something about her, something embarrassing." He looked sideways at her for clarification.

"She's been having too much to drink again, I think."

"Well, I'm glad you don't but it's none of their business." He pulled the newspaper towards him and then pushed it away. "I'd find that very hard to take." She smiled back at him reassuringly but did not stem his train of thought. "I wonder what he's done."

64

It was much easier than Sarah had feared. Even guessing the password had taken less than five minutes. He had set up the website about two years earlier when his 'business' was starting to take off and so she had looked through her diary for the names of the women who had been brought back to further their careers. She knew that she must have missed several but the fourth attempt, Octavia, no jumbled numbers added, was successful. For him, the irony of a literary allusion.

Or was it even more laughable than that? Had she assumed the name to build a future that had ended on his bed with her legs apart? She was probably thin - most of them had been - and still under thirty, even now. If she had been lucky, she might have an admin job or something in reception. No retraining as a nurse - too long a haul, too mainstream, too passé, too much care.

She thought of her mum, over forty-five and past her usefulness to him. A few nights ago, she had come in after her shift had finished at eight, fretting again that there was not enough food for the two of them but too tired to protest at the tidying Sarah had done when she had let herself in. It was self-fulfilling for someone like him: the tiredness and the ageing justified the callousness.

What had she seen in him? She could not have been just another Octavia - it had lasted too long, certainly by his standards. She looked at his picture on the screen: it must have been taken six or seven years earlier. The relative youthfulness could have been down to enhancements that he had got someone to make for him but she recognised the open-necked shirt that had long since disappeared from his wardrobe. He almost looked 'dashing', an image that could have adorned the trashy novels in the newsagent's.

Perhaps that had been the other side of the coin. A romantic side, a left-over from his childhood, that set her mum on a pedestal, and when that failed, when reality - his and hers - intruded, life was transmuted into a sequence of relationships, each a brief idolatry.

Too kind: he could only be judged by the here and now, to use his own criterion. "It's what you do that counts, not what you say," was his pet aphorism, never grasping that words were themselves actions.

The picture cried out for alteration but that could wait. Something more discreet was needed as a test to see how thoroughly his latest conscript checked the site's content. Probably just counting the hits, answering the enquiries.

She looked at the section grandiosely titled 'Current Projects.' 'Contributing to change in the public sector' would do. 'Contributing to and gaining from': her additions would not jar and might escape detection.

Before signing off, she came back to the picture. A minor change would complete the test: she removed a bush, its colour enhanced, that had helped to frame the naturalness of his setting.

She shut down just in time. From the window, she saw his car pull up on the drive. Only the one door opened: whether that was preferable she could not say. Packing the laptop away, she winced and flopped down on the bed as the phone rang downstairs.

She heard him unlock the door - with hindsight, that must have put him off - and rush to answer the call.

"No - no problem. None of her usual mess. You carry on."

65

Opening the door, Liam's father grinned at her.

"What are you going to get him into this time?"

"Nothing" - and then Becky realised the defensiveness was unnecessary. "I don't know how all that happened."

He ushered her in. "Well, he's survived. Like everything else. It just seems to wash over him - same as this course they've talked him into doing." He pointed towards the stairs. "Go on up."

Liam, who must have heard the door, was already coming down the stairs.

"Oh, I didn't think it -"

His father had looked quickly up at him. "I'll leave the two of you to it." He spoke with a warning in his eyes, before turning away. "But show Becky into the sitting room."

He walked awkwardly in front of her, avoiding the settee that faced the television, and offered her the other armchair as he sat down.

"Sorry, you know - all this that's happened to your dad."

"He'll be all right - it can only be a mistake." She sat on the edge of the chair as if visiting her aunt. " But what did they do to you?"

"That was a mistake as well." He seemed to relax, with a story to tell. "They knocked at the door, just like you did. Two of them, both taller than me. The one who was in charge … "

She tried to stop her face from setting into the resigned patience that Polly would assume when one of the Year Sevens came stuttering into the room with a message. She waited for the preamble to finish.

"But why did they interview you?"

"I don't know. They asked me what I saw through all that fog for a bit. Then they asked me how much of it I'd organised." He looked up at her from under his hair, amused still at his disbelief. "God knows where they got that idea."

"You were the only male there."

Her comment eluded him. "They knew I'd produced the poster thing. But when they asked me about the politics of it all, they figured me out pretty quick. All they then did was ask me about you and Kirsty. Why you were both there. What you had to do with anyone at the home."

"What did you say?"

"That you'd been to see Gran and I didn't know about Kirsty. They knew whose daughters you were."

"What do you mean?"

"They wanted to know if your dad had been there that morning. If he'd spoken to me."

"And that was it?"

"Nothing else." His voice had grown bored, dismissive.

"And what about Kirsty?"

"They kept referring to her as 'the MP's daughter'. I think they thought one of you could be the ringleader. They kept asking who'd put me up to it. I think they got the message in the end."

She glanced at her hands before looking up at him.

"You know all the stuff about Kirsty in the papers. Did they ask you anything about her? What she's like. You know what I mean."

"No, nothing. They just said that neither of you would end up building for a living."

She turned as the door opened behind her.

"Haven't you made this young lady a drink, you dipstick?" She nodded in agreement to his father's offer. "And what about you, Becky? Have they tried to get at you as well?"

66

Seeing him, finding him, was pure chance. Pollard had grown so tired of her own company that she had invited Charlotte down. Her sister for whom nothing ever went wrong and her public school husband who was marked, like a stick of rock, by his upbringing - and who loved it.

After a late breakfast of obliquely patronising comments about the size of her flat, he opted for a walk that took in Penalwick and the chance to see some of the characters who had been in the TV programme. All reduced to a miniature village and sunny weather - but acquiescence was the easiest tactic.

Walking down the hill, she drew away from his wittering, all, anyway, intended for Charlotte, trapped in a bubble of domesticity. They were like the trippers who shrouded themselves in plastic on the beach, half windbreak, half tent, keeping the sun out, keeping the world out.

Switched off from them, she was shredded by rage - less from his disappearance than from everything Sarah had said. How every moment she had enjoyed, had recalled, was now coated with deception. Any question that should just have been his gentle creation of his image of her past, her hopes, was instead a probing of anyone associated with her. A means to an end.

And there he was, at the bottom of the slipway, helping to drag the boat up, talking to the fisherman, no doubt wheedling everything he could from him. She pointed her sister towards the pub and turned off onto the head of the slipway. His back turned to her, he had no sense of being like a dog trapped in a corner: the sea beyond him, the cliffs on either side, the only possible escape route past her.

She stood, the chains, the nets cluttering the cobbles and watched him: the casual bearing, the diffident dipping of his shoulders, all so familiar. The antennae as well that sensed her watching him, all part of the training - and, as he turned, the tremor, perhaps guilt, in his face as he saw her.

"I think you owe me a few minutes."

The fisherman smirked and stared at her as Kew walked slowly up the slope. No public scene: she would have to keep her temper in check or the schoolteacher's tantrum would be around the village by the end of the day and vibrating through the school at the start of the new term.

"I'm not even going to throw at you how you've treated me, how you left me without a word, like being raped by a ghost, because that's a side issue, isn't it? That was all I was, wasn't it? But -"

"That's not true. And that's why I couldn't come back to see you." His eyes did not leave her face. "I had -"

"But you warned me off all the action against Toad. Who was paying you to do that?"

"No-one."

"Oh, of course not. This new generation of philanthropists that you've joined."

His stare faltered. "That was for real. You don't seem to realise. They're not mucking about."

"And I am, I suppose? All my little playing about, all my pretend activism? While you do the serious stuff, the man's stuff."

He started to edge up the slipway, past her, his head shaking, but her arm across his chest stopped him.

"Were you the only one? Or do we have to look at anyone as another you? It shouldn't even be 'we', should it? We all have to be an 'I', don't we? It's like living with the Stasi."

"If you stop and think about it, I didn't have to warn you off like that. It's up to you whether you believe it but I did that for you."

"Crumbs from a rich man's table. How kind! No crumbs for the poor sods at St. Budoc's. Did you hire the fog? Was that driver one of your colleagues?"

He lowered his head in frustration.

"There's no point in all this hysteria, Emily." He took her arm and forced it down. "People are looking. Don't make things worse for yourself."

She swung her free hand at him and missed. "Oh, fuck off." Her voice was suppressed, hissing, as she tugged herself away from him. The flickering of public humiliation made her stand aside.

As he walked up to the village, he turned to wave, more of a salute, to the fisherman who had started coiling rope, slowly, carefully, so that he could follow Kew's sudden drama on the slipway above him. He would have seen Pollard staring at the back of the retreating figure before she turned to gaze past him and out to sea.

She stood for five minutes, ten minutes, bracing herself to rejoin her sister. She watched two girls from her Year 7 class pulling stones gently out of a pool, having recovered from the giggling at seeing a live teacher outside the school cage. They bent and then raised their heads, shrieking at a movement in the water below them, absorbed in the moment.

In fifteen years, would they be like her? In four years, would they be like Sarah who had arrived, energised, at her door two nights earlier? She, too, was relying on external injustice for a purpose: there was no innate equilibrium. A father who had fucked her up, that she still felt she would escape. If only she knew the queue of successors there would be.

The animation, however, had been there as she stepped inside, past the hoover and the black bin liners. Animation that she had tried to check, like a river in flood. The anxiety in her eyes had been the look of someone who suddenly felt herself an equal. Her words, however, tentative, had trickled out.

"Did you know what's been going on?"

"About Kirsty, yes. And Becky. Only what you told me on the phone."

"Not that, no. Well, it might be. Your man - Andy, wasn't it?"

At the hint of tension in Pollard's expression, Sarah had squeezed the bridge of her nose between her thumb and forefinger and taken a deep breath.

"He's been working for my father."

"But you knew that. You told me."

"But I didn't realise what work. I thought he was just someone cheap doing glorified work experience. Internship was the name they gave it. And all along he was a plant. In any group he could work his way into, so that he could report back. To my father, of all people."

Pollard's face had set.

"You wouldn't believe what he'd found out. I overheard my father on the phone to him. Any protest we'd run, St. Budoc's, you name it. And he'd seemed so plausible - afraid that I'd tell my father what he was doing." She hesitated, perhaps sensing that while she was still the pupil, the woman in front of her was no longer the teacher. "Am I speaking out of turn?"

"No. You carry on."

"I've contacted the press."

"You've what?"

"Anonymously. I didn't have the guts to give my name but I thought I had to let you know before it all comes out."

Pollard's eyes were almost closed. "Please. Can you get on with it?"

"I couldn't tell you everything. You know what it's like when you just listen to one end of a conversation. Well, you probably don't - but that must have been how Ben got turned, not that he needed much turning. That stunt in Whitcross did get a lot of publicity. It was just a joke but they had to shut even that down."

"Did you hear anything about school?"

"Well, what I've just said." She stalled, puzzled. "Anything that we were planning. I know it wasn't just our school but they probably couldn't run to a plant everywhere."

"Not that. What about the school itself?"

"How do you mean?"

"It doesn't matter." Her face had set. "So what about St. Budoc's? Was it just a question of tipping off the newspapers?"

As Sarah continued, back on surer ground, the link between eyes and brain had severed. She listened as she would read after a full evening's marking, registering the syntax but not the meaning.

Now, as the girls ran past her, shrieking when a safe distance behind her, she felt the downward pull of introspection, compared with which even the constant irritation of her brother-in-law was preferable. Barely noticing the kids' sudden acceleration as they feared they were being followed, she turned to stride up the slipway.

67

Her mum had put on a good appearance of being untroubled by it all. With her usual briskness, she had dismissed it. "It's despicable but it'll get sorted out. You don't need to worry." She had put her arm briefly around Becky's shoulders and then carried on preparing her packed lunch.

In his own, very different way, her granddad had been his usual self for an hour or more in the garden, with his jug of water, ridiculing the grounds for the surgery's action, praising his son's record. When he assumed that she was reassured, he had ended as calmly as he always did. "He'll see this through, he's stronger than they are," his fingers gently tweaking her cheek. "But don't forget to look after yourself."

Reassured, however, she was not - and between them, they had left her as her dad's carer, not that he would have admitted the need. Being at home had a psychological impact that she could not define, other than his detachment from some of the routine essentials of life. He needed no reminder to shower or to dress smartly, probably because those were parts of his pre-work, early morning ritual. Eating, however, had never fitted into that category

- he would eat his sandwiches at any time of day, in his car or in the surgery, whenever an opportunity presented itself.

Now, there was no incessant rush from which a moment had to be seized and, left to himself, no food would have been prepared or eaten during the day. At least, that was her fear - and that was where she came in. Fortunate that it was the holidays, fortunate too for him that while her friendships weren't disintegrating, all of them - Sarah, Kirsty, Liam and the rest - weren't around so much, either from the fall-out of the incident at St. Budoc's or trouble at home - one problem or another. And so she made her dad's lunch and regular cups of coffee.

It also won her time to think. She had never really bought Sarah's cynicism, her seeing the political undercurrents of conspiracy everywhere, but recent events had made her a more receptive listener. Liam's questioning she could have brushed off but the stories about Kirsty were totally different.

Her thoughts kept drifting back to questions her dad had asked her, never consecutively to suggest any great concern, more an occasional pebble dropped into the water. It had always been his way, masking adult reality from her, preserving the innocence of her childhood as far into her teenage years as he possibly could. But a question about Sarah's father, bland enough but curious, dissonant, in its context, had cropped up three or four times: what Sarah felt about him, how her politics had developed, how long they had lived in Trelay, when the marriage had broken up.

He had seemed like someone returning to a jigsaw at one or two day intervals and attempting to build up one corner of the picture without anyone noticing. She had, however: not just the recurrence of Martin King but the absence of any reference to his own work, either as it had been or as it now was. It was as if the one replaced the other, as if the one was the other.

With something impersonal, he would have asked for her help. In any research, his one-finger typing speed as laboured as a child first holding a pen, he would stumble his way through the internet, avoiding all available shortcuts to slow himself even further. He always acknowledged it: with his self-deprecating smile, he had turned to her with a written list of questions before they had installed the solar panels - how the angle of their roof would affect their output, the relative merits of the different panels in the quotes he had received, along with nine or ten issues, all beautifully phrased and logically sequenced - and had watched as she threw up enough data to trigger another set of questions the following day.

But this was too personal for that. He was searching for something in his own supposedly secretive way that he lacked the computer skills to conceal from her. On the history, she had found Martin King's website, EZN Consultants and a range of blandly named bodies that the website listed him as having worked for, as well as NHS action groups, even UK Uncut. Despite her uncertainty and the strain of witnessing her dad's preoccupations, she still smiled at the notion of him, immaculately dressed but chained to a lamp post outside Top Shop.

She had no idea where it might lead - and, almost certainly, neither did he. She could have helped, could have asked Sarah. She was the obvious source but to ask, to assume disloyalty, might have strained even the distance of that broken relationship. It was one thing to listen to Sarah's complaints but quite another to take them as a given.

She heard the post drop through the letter box. As she opened the door from the kitchen, her dad was already bending at the front door. She watched him sift the letters and then scrutinise the postmarks of two brown envelopes.

He got no further than the first before he turned, sensing her presence. He held up the letter in her direction, unaware that the envelope had fallen to the floor.

"You'd think I'd applied to open a bank account. Or to close one. 'Our statutory obligation ... We will write to you again within twenty-eight days of the date at the top of this letter to inform you of our progress in dealing with your case. We have to emphasise that it is rare for a case to be concluded within those twenty-eight days.' They're stalling deliberately. It's just a ploy to keep me out of the way."

He shrugged his shoulders, placed the letters neatly on the chest beside the door - and walked slowly upstairs to his room.

68

For a few days, Sarah saw the British press in action. There were so many angles, competing, contradictory: all of the tabloids still looking for salacious detail on 'turbulent teenagers', most of them seeking some grime with which to smear Tom Andrews and one or two of the broadsheets digging for more detail on Andy Kew.

For her, the reality was less clear-cut than she had expected. A reporter from 'The Sun' had stopped them in the street, had told them who he worked for and, with no aggression, no slime, had asked them what they knew of 'the MP's daughter'. After three or four unanswered questions and realising he was getting nowhere, he had thanked them and gone on his way.

The woman from 'The Guardian', however, perhaps guessing that Sarah was the source of the anonymous tip-off, had staked out the house and, for a day, had stopped her at every point she had gone out, asking her about her father, about the work that Kew had done for him. Deadbatting the questions was difficult - she had felt that fusion of pride and a surging need to talk that she remembered as a child when she had gabbled to her friends about a fire engine she had seen hurtling down their road. It was a huge step, though, from an anonymous phone call to an interview out of which comments attributed to her would appear in print. The woman's manner - treating her like a child - was the final factor, checking the bile that she would have loved to spill into the paper, confirming her in what felt like cowardice.

The reporter must, however, have known her stuff. There were so many gaps in what Sarah had overheard, so much guesswork, and yet here the woman was, after only three days in Trelay, running the same story and more - a lot earlier than Sarah had anticipated. It was Becky's call that had sent her down for the paper but that revealed nothing. "I'll let you read it yourself," as if the details of her lottery win were hidden in the pages and the suspense were not to be spoiled.

No wonder, though, that her voice had sounded so agitated on the phone. Here it was, sharing the front page with the latest casualties from Afghanistan: "Protest group infiltrator believes he is 'one of many'." The picture of Kew was passport-like: head and shoulders only, square to the camera, unsmiling, as if he had been convicted of an offence.

"Andrew Kew, the man accused of infiltrating a student protest group in Cornwall, has, in an exclusive interview with 'The Guardian', named Martin King, a self-styled management consultant, as 'the man pulling the strings' but would not comment on the political motivation behind the operation."

There was, in what followed, no word from her father "who was unavailable for comment" - nor from the surgery "for whom he had been working on a consultancy basis. The nature of the consultancy remains unclear. King's website lists a number of organisations on whose behalf he has worked but none would appear to have a natural connection with a surgery or the new commissioning process."

The calculatedly cryptic comment diverted her momentarily into checking the website: the bush was still deleted, her minor addition still intact. She smiled at the scope, childish, on another day, to bite back at him.

It would be, however, a mere pinprick beside the paper's stab wound. Her smile faltered. A wound to her father; a wound in her, the shame, that balanced her delight at his exposure.

69

Beckford now made it a point of honour to talk to the protesters. On driving into work and on leaving, she always stopped, with her window wound down. At least once a week, she arrived early enough to give herself time to park, time to walk back out and talk before she started work.

She had to concede Johnson's point: there were new faces, unfamiliar ones, standing there, no doubt drawn in by the latest newspaper revelations. Hardly the Molotov cocktail brigade but they did avoid all eye contact with her while the others talked. Their posture spoke impatience, implied that she, from the other side, was not to be trusted or spoken to.

The regulars, though, were different. They voiced their concerns, some right, some wrong: the rationing of treatment; the number of 'incomers' they had seen in the car park; Amy Goddard who remained a running sore; what was happening to Colin Goldsmith; rumours of charging for treatment. Sometimes they would hand her a petition or a newspaper article.

Most of the time, she could have been someone from a PR department sent to smooth things over. She knew what she was going to hear and just listened. This morning, however, was different. John Alexander, a quiet man in his early fifties whom she, more often than anyone, had seen on his rare visits to the surgery, was standing to the side, with the air of one of the backroom staff. The others, however, beckoned him to the front.

"Show Dr. Beckford that analysis you got hold of, John."

His face showed the embarrassment of the plodding researcher who is taken aback when his findings are suddenly centre stage.

"Well, you know the government was supposed to be clamping down on doctors who have a financial interest in private health providers."

"Yes. To eliminate any conflict of interest."

He nodded as if to reassure her. "Well, after several Freedom of Information requests, Bring Back the NHS has produced a list of GPs who still have such a financial interest. Two of your colleagues - Mark Stanley and Ian Johnson - are on the list because of their wives' shareholdings."

She studied the printout he passed to her.

"It's not right." She did not take her eyes from the page as the woman at the back of the group, one of Johnson's 'intruders', raised her voice almost to a shout. "Is it any wonder everyone's being referred on to that place in Plymouth and not The Royal?"

"We must keep this in perspective. It's not everyone." Her voice remained unusually emollient as she looked up at Alexander. "Is this a spare copy? Can I hold on to it?"

He nodded.

"And what are you going to do about it?" It was another voice from the back this time.

"What I can, of course."

"Fucking politician's answer."

At the glares of those around her, the voice ebbed into silence with a few muttered protests.

"What I can is all I can." Her voice refound its sharpness. "I'm no Messiah." Softer again, she turned back to Alexander and the woman next to him. "Thanks for this." She glanced back as she turned away. "Keep up the good work."

With evening surgery drawing to a close, she had been more assertive than usual in dealing with successive patients. Two recurrent headaches and one badly swollen ankle were swiftly dispatched. Sandwiched between them was a man whose skin was again showing early signs of a potential cancer. He seemed reassured once he was referred back to reception for an appointment to have it removed. In-house: no great cost, no conflict of interest.

It left her time to hover, time - as someone who never waited around for a chat or a cup of tea - to create a tremor of anxiety in Maurice Allen and each of the other doctors, as they passed her. She must have been waiting in the corridor for almost fifteen minutes before first Ian Johnson's final patient and then Johnson himself emerged.

"No home to go to, Sheila? There must be better places than this on a Tuesday evening."

"There are indeed but before I depart for my spinster's bliss - that word is supposed to be pejorative but I think I'm growing into it - I wonder if you could spare me a couple of minutes."

He nodded and smiled, that mixture of boyishness and professional charm, as he ushered her into his room and closed the door.

"I hope you've had a better day than I have. Twenty-five minutes with Mrs. Emerton, most of which, in her usual mangled way, was probably saying that she thought she too might have been molested by Colin. I have to admit, it was beyond my powers of deduction to ascertain if there was a medical reason for the appointment. Church work yet again."

"I know - and there'll be more and more of that." She returned his smile, only, abruptly, to switch it off. "But that's not why I'm here."

"Don't tell me. Martin King - and how you were right all along."

"No, not even that. Our register of interests - the new one, the one that was brought in six months ago - it doesn't anywhere record that your wife has shares in Acavo International."

"Look, Sheila, I assumed that your conversation would be about the practice, not my own financial arrangements."

"Unfortunately, it appears to concern both. If your wife does have those shares - and, of course, in normal circumstances, I wouldn't dream of prying - I think you have to declare them." She leaned forward, anticipating his reaction. "I'm saying this because you're a colleague. It's help."

"I don't doubt the intention but you need to look at the facts. My wife has had those shares for - it must be at least twelve years, long before the company had any involvement in healthcare."

"But they are now operating hospitals, including Glenfine. I don't know what your referrals have been but the practice as a whole has sent eleven patients there in the last month."

"My understanding was that shareholdings of family members didn't have to be disclosed even if the company in question had an involvement in healthcare."

"Oh, Christ, Ian, it's not bloody 'healthcare' - and you must know a defence like that isn't going to stand up. Look, this information is out there now - it's on the internet and the people at our gates have got hold of it. They've been incredibly restrained thus far. Colin's windscreen, whenever it was, and that's about it. The mood's getting uglier now, though."

He sat back, forced patience lining his face.

"It's a matter of principle, Sheila. We can't just cave in to pressure."

"No. I can see that." She stood up, looking past him at the line of family photographs. "You're right, however. It most certainly is a matter of principle."

70

"I presume you'll soon be a racehorse owner. That is, if you haven't already cottoned on to that little wheeze."

King looked blankly at Marriott whose eyes relished his easy superiority.

"Do you never read anything? The latest product of these groups - the ones dear Mr. Younger calls our fuckus groups. Enough people in Newmarket said that the racing industry was struggling, so what do they do? Bring in a tax change that makes owning a racehorse a better proposition than thirty years paying off a mortgage. And then they're surprised that not just the proles, but our Mail-reading former supporters, are up in arms."

He pushed the paper towards King.

"The upshot of it all is that we don't just have Cameron with his head in the trough; we now have the car salesman with his head in a nosebag. In my era, long before you attained even your present level of awareness, Maggie said - a little clumsily but one could forgive her such a rare failing - that every Prime Minister needed a Willie; now, sadly, as Mr. Younger once again put it, all our current dear leader has, for company, for advice, is a prick.

"There's no money to make a significant impact anywhere so they just look for ways to tinker. No judgement - just picking up the mood from these groups and misinterpreting it. Someone says that the military needs redefining for the future; Cameron cuts defence spending. Could you imagine their conduct of a real war?"

King was still smiling at the front page, unaware that the question was not rhetorical.

"Well, could you?" He stood up, exasperated at the grinning silence opposite him. "Perhaps that is why you've wheedled your way into your current work. Consistency: bungling at the top; bungling at the bottom."

King's face drew back, a cobra without the menace.

"This is a fine mess you've got yourself into. Oh, for pity's sake, stop reading that, man."

As he sat down, he pulled the paper back across the desk.

"Who's spoken to you so far?"

"They've spoken at me - the journalists from the tabloids, not that one," he pointed to the desk. " A couple of them were pretty aggressive but I didn't say anything."

"What about the police?"

"No, why should they? Whatever I've done, it hasn't been illegal."

"And the surgery?"

"Oh, God, no. Nothing illegal there."

"No, not that." His hand, impatient, rubbed his eye. "What have they said to you? How've they reacted to this publicity?"

"No idea. I'm only in there once every couple of weeks now and nobody's rung me. Probably glad to see the back of me - some of them anyway, the pious ones. And the feeling's mutual."

A smile resurfaced, widening as Hannah opened the door after a quiet knock. He watched her as she passed a piece of paper across to Marriott.

"The address you wanted, with a map - which is probably advisable."

Marriott's face showed the gratitude of someone who was becoming forgetful. He nodded as she edged her way back out of the room, glancing at King before she closed the door behind her.

"Simon Younger has been in touch. He thinks it's better that you lie low."

"I know. That's what I've been doing."

"But not around here. Not out of the country, but a good few miles from here. He thinks you're a bit accident prone. I don't know where he got that idea."

"No problem. If it's a good hotel -"

"You'll have to leave your daughter on her own. Will she be all right?"

"Ditto what I said about the surgery. I think she'll welcome the breathing space."

"And - to extend the analogy - so will you." He pushed the slip of paper across the desk. "The place you're staying is clear enough - and Younger's got what he called work for you marked in blue." He anticipated King's question. "He implied it was in the 'change is as good as a rest' category but don't ask me what."

"What about timing?"

"Straight away - and I don't know how long your little holiday will be." He smiled at King's shifting in his chair, as if he were going to stand up, before subsiding again, the fingernails of one hand scratching his eyebrows. "Anyway, you be grateful you're not in as big a mess as dear Mr. Andrews. Good job done on him, Younger seems to think."

"No need for Andrews to lie low. He'll get out of it. They always do."

"Perhaps - for once, very perceptive of you - but not yet a while. He's made his bid for freedom and now he's been reeled in."

King shook his head. "It'll -"

"Again, you're probably right. I daresay your new employer will choose to soften the blow. Sooner rather than later. He might even, at the end of it all, find a little perk for you."

71

It was early evening when Kirsty heard his key in the door. As she came out of her bedroom, she saw him drape his coat hurriedly over the banister - loosely, to be regathered a few minutes later and put back on, regardless of the haste, the collar turned up with precise informality.

As she walked down the stairs, she double-checked her reasoning for the thousandth time. Not Sarah, too old and disapproving. Becky, Ria, Lily - they were the only other ones she could possibly have told and their reaction was genuine. They could barely remember it: one of many like it or perhaps they had not even bothered to read it.

All she remembered was a hand in her pocket, the inevitable but minimal pressure on her thigh. As close as she'd got for a while, the body remembering if the brain did not.

"This bloke Kew - what did you know about him?"

Her father looked at her, his blankness the sign of disapproval, of a confrontation to come. She steeled herself for it.

"Quite a lot, thanks to the investigative powers of our splendidly impartial press."

"No. Before all that. What did you know then?"

"Very little. Nothing. But why are you asking?"

He stared at her as if she were a child who, inexplicably, has, out of the blue, uttered a swear word.

"Oh, come on, please. What does 'very little' mean?"

"And I need to know what lies behind all this. I've interrogations enough on a daily basis, without having another one in my own home."

"All the crap that's been thrown at me -" She checked herself. "Anyway, they seem to have run out of steam now and I just need to work out how it all started. I think Kew had something to do with it. That's why I'm asking you. You move in these circles. You know how these people work."

He pushed the papers on the table into a rough pile and picked up an A4 envelope.

"I would hesitate to describe my work as moving in those circles but, setting that to one side, I can tell you what I do know. For years, governments have used plants - they're often glamorised as spies - to find out what the opposition, protest groups, underground movements are up to. That, it would appear, is what your Mr. Kew was doing. That," he glanced at her face, the lips she kept rigid, "is the unpleasant side of politics."

"You think I don't know that? Look, what I want is - what was that lovely expression of yours? - a bit of public self-abuse." She kept her eyes off the table as she had planned. "What I asked you was what you did know - not what you know now. Like you warned me off any of those protests you knew about. That's not your normal style."

"Careful, careful." He glared at her and hesitated. "Being in a coalition is not 'normal'. There are constraints on what you say, what you do, that were never there before. It was against that background that -"

"So you knew there was an undercover operation in place and tried to keep me clear of it all?"

"That's not what I'm saying. My point is that if you know the way the world is, you try to keep your family out of potential trouble."

His smile was reassuring; her words were not.

"So Kew's being just around the corner from your office in the middle of the night is pure coincidence?"

72

Sarah heard his clumsy attempts at quiet packing: the light footsteps on the stairs, desperate not to wake her; the heavier tread each time he had forgotten something, his face, she imagined, contorted by the conflicting pressures of haste and anxiety.

When to open her door was hard to judge: turn the handle too late and she might even miss him altogether; do it too early and she would be subjected to the aftermath, his self-justification prolonged as he ransacked the house for more aftershave and deodorant. Catching him as he was heading for the front door was ideal, the confrontation crisp, explicit, in his interest as well as hers.

She stepped past her own bag at what she took for the signs of imminent departure and turned the handle. He froze momentarily at the bottom of the stairs before looking away.

"Where you going?"

"Work again."

"Another offer you couldn't refuse?"

He was bending to zip up the flap of the suitcase.

"When you're older, you might understand a bit better. You

can't just pick and choose the work you do."

"Why not?"

"I'm not getting into one of these discussions." He stood the case on its end and moved it towards the door. "I've left money by the kettle."

"Is that how you treat all the girls?"

He took a jacket from the arm of the chair and checked the pockets.

"Is there anything that doesn't just come down to financial calculation?" She caught the look in his eye. "No, I'm not talking about me, not even about all the women you fuck - but the supposed work. Your little spy network, messing up Miss Pollard as a bonus, the undermining of the surgery, the destruction of Becky's dad's job - you did that, didn't you? - a man who's a hundred times anything you'll ever be ... " She paused, hearing her own voice, knowing that she had failed again, her tirade giving space that should have been denied him. "Money, jealousy, insecurity - what else is in there?"

"Not all prim and proper like the heroic doctor. Just me, I suppose - but I'd rather be where I am than where he is. At least, I've still got a job." He opened the door. "I don't know when I'll be back."

"A job where you have to run for cover, where you can't even stay in what masquerades as a home."

"A job all the same and it keeps you in money."

As he hurried down the drive, head pivoting like an iguana's against the threat of non-existent reporters, she checked the urge to have the last word. A slanging match in the open air would be one humiliation too many.

Her slamming of the door would, however, have shown the neighbours how fragile her self-control was. Still more the pace at which she strode from room to room, despite the rigidity of her body, until her eyes fixed on the kettle. The money, more than she could possibly need, unless he really was anticipating an absence of months, was bulging from a brown envelope, probably the same one in which he had recently been paid.

She picked it up and examined it as a police officer might have done. Apart from the tear along the top, nothing: no name, no address, not even the grease marks from where his hands would have held it. She dropped it back into the puddle of water that had spilled from the draining board and watched the dampness seep through the envelope and into the notes.

She had forgotten that her mum was having a holiday. A break, a few days away, was what she preferred to call it: three days in a B&B in Exeter with two other nurses was hardly what the brochures would call a holiday. Two days would be given over to the union's regional conference; the rest of the time to shopping and walking by the river.

Even that, on the morning her father disappeared, was a source of annoyance. Her usual respect for her mother's resilience, her commitment, returned by lunchtime but was no help to her immediate plight. She should not have left it so long. In a couple of days, she could stay with her mum but, in the meantime, she had to find somewhere else, free of the stain, the residue of her father.

Would leaving the house be leaving home? The concept was elusive. She scanned the room: the worn, comfortable settee, the desk that only she had worked at, even the box-like CD player that seemed to have been there from her childhood. All of them should have been part of that mosaic called 'home'; all, instead, were his property, marked by memories, subdued in colour like a garden on a dreary day.

Not that they had a garden worth speaking of. She looked out at the poorly-tended oblong of grass at the front. She had despised the regular weekend strimmers of lawns and cleaners of cars, all the little, bourgeois people, but what if the alternative were not spontaneity? At least an effort had been made.

She was not alone, she knew that. Few seemed happy - and Kirsty had the glare of publicity on all her failings. Becky was the exception: a family diverse, under strain but cohesive, a home where order and freedom were not mutually exclusive. Becky who might offer sanctuary.

'Sanctuary' - she surprised herself in her choice of wording but that was how it felt. The relief of someone being taken in when Becky said she could stay. No ifs and buts, no time limit established in advance, no need to check for the approval of adults. Just the usual laugh.

The laugh, however, must have been a little forced. As the door opened, it was not Becky but her father standing there.

"Come to lighten our mood, young lady?" He looked back diffidently to Becky appearing in the kitchen doorway as he ushered her in. The smile was genuine. "Please do stay as long as you need to. Or even as long as you want to. That sounds better, doesn't it?" The question hung in the air between the three of them. "I'll leave you to it. Might even pick your brains later, especially with those results you've had."

She smiled back.

"And Becky - but it seems ages ago already."

As he walked upstairs, she faltered on the threshold.

"My bag."

She glanced behind her.

"Well, don't leave it there."

Sarah stooped beside the front door.

"Is that it? It's not just one night you're staying, is it?"

"Couldn't find anything else. He'd taken anything decent." She laughed at the canvas bag, its broken zip. "Would one night be best?" Her voice was a whisper.

"No, no." She beckoned her through into the kitchen and closed the door. "You've misread it. He really does want you to stay." She raised her finger to her lips and nodded. "Why not go down to the beach? Leave your bag there and I'll just tell Dad what we're doing."

They never got as far as the beach, sitting instead against the hedge in the lee of the wind - her idea, to hear more clearly what Becky was saying, not to have to wait.

"It's not his clarity of thought that's gone. He's as analytical as he's always been - about the surgery, about the procedure they're subjecting him to, about ... anything really. I suppose it's a bit hazy at times but that's only a by-product of how he now sees himself." She threw some grass into the air behind her and watched it blow back over them. "Even the way he speaks can show it. That's why you mustn't worry about staying. The words come out the wrong way sometimes. He's like a child learning to walk who has got as far as the middle of the room, looks around and suddenly sees where he is." She pulled at another clump of grass. "I think he's an example of what they keep banging on about in PSHE. Self-worth, self-esteem."

"It's hardly surprising. Everything they're putting him through. Anyone -"

"That's not it. It's awful and it gets him down a fair bit but he knows he's done nothing wrong. Most of the time, it's another thing to be methodical about." She almost smiled, picturing him

310

with yet another piece of paper in his hand. "But that's not the point." She shook her face, as if trying to clear a headache.

"No, the real root of it goes back a couple of months. You remember all that rumpus over Amy Goddard. Steph tried to get you involved, didn't she?"

She saw the surprise in Sarah's face.

"No - the rumpus I'm talking about is all the campaigning, not what the poor woman must have gone through. And Dad thinks he didn't deal with it as he should have done. He was sitting in the garden - he'd finished his cup of coffee when he started talking about Amy. I didn't realise it at first and I can't recall his exact words. He's normally so clear and precise but this was a bit of a jumble. Basically, he thinks he helped to deny her, on financial grounds, treatment that might have made a difference. He said he didn't realise it at the time, called it a form of doublethink, but it's what he criticises the rest of the surgery, other surgeries, for doing. He was close to tears because he can't bear hypocrisy in himself and then it clicked that he shouldn't have said anything about it." She suddenly realised her own culpability. "So don't say anything, will you?"

"Oh, God, no."

"That's what I meant about self-esteem. I can't really talk to Mum about it. I don't, anyway, know how much she knows. She's all right but sort of in the "pull yourself together" camp. And that leaves him: it's as if he's a building that's shaking because some blocks at the bottom have been pulled out."

"It's your own tears now, isn't it?" Their hands touched as Becky fell quiet like someone bracing herself for a funeral. "I know it hurts but in a way you're lucky because you can still admire him. His principles determine what he is, for better or for worse, not like my father. Any mess he finds himself in is just a predicament to wheedle his way out of. No reflection, no learning from it, either."

She risked a smile, sensing that Becky's eyes were looking out, not in.

"Be honest - you still wouldn't want to be me, would you?"

73

Becky was outside with Liam, standing below his father on the ladder. She came in once or twice to shut windows that could have been hit and smeared by falling cement but, otherwise, turned her dad's anxiety about the upstairs pointing into an opportunity.

Sarah watched her talking to Liam, a one-way conversation that, through the closed window, seemed like a segment from a silent film. His eyes stayed fixed on the ladder unless they were drawn up by some muffled comment from his father above him. When he had to adjust his position to avoid the glare of the sun, he shuffled across, stumbling in his effort to avoid brushing against her.

Why he came in, she couldn't say. Perhaps his father was, by now, standing on the flat roof over the dormer window, secure enough to work and talk continuously to Becky below. He used the loo and then hesitated before opening the French windows.

"I didn't know you were here."

"No. I thought I'd be in the way out there." She put her book down.

"When did you come?"

"I'm staying here, only till Tuesday."

She watched him struggle, unable to formulate the question that surfaced and then froze in his eyes.

"I'm moving in with my mum then. Probably better for college."

She should have led up to it, fed him that information in bits to which, like a fish reacting to the twitching of a line, he could respond. Too quick for him and all he could say, after a painful pause, was, "I'm sorry."

"No need. What about you? You're going to start it, are you?"

He nodded but just stood there. In looking back on it, she realised it must have been the lesser of two evils.

"What's your dad doing out there?"

"Repointing - and there are some cracks that need looking at."

He was like a tap that is briefly turned on - and she was unsure how to keep the water flowing.

"What's 'repointing'?"

"It's where the cement has fallen out or is about to." She felt his pleasure at, for once, having knowledge that she lacked. "You have to clean it all out and refill it."

"Is that a long job?"

"Could be. Depends."

Still he stood there, untroubled by the imprecision of his answer, looking past her but, at least, his eyes were off the floor.

"Are you not needed out there?"

"No. She can do anything I can do."

"Why don't you sit down then?"

The sweep of her hand, her intention, must have been too obvious, too quickly past the single chairs and finishing for too long, like the final advert in a commercial break, on the space on the settee beside her.

His eyes dropped, one foot already in retreat.

"No, no. She won't ... I'd better ... "

If his tongue could not find the words, his feet made certain that nothing more needed to be said as he was gone back out through the French windows. She sat there, book closed on her lap, head thrown back in despair at her own folly. The light rain flecking the windows, thankfully, brought none of them back inside.

Her fingers were unnecessarily hard on the keys: the laptop, like everything else in the house, worked perfectly. Becky's shower would be the same so there was no time for false starts, for dithering.

His picture would take too long to doctor and, anyway, on second thoughts, she wanted there to be no problem for anyone trying to identify him. She clicked, instead, on 'Martin's Life' and there, in 'Likes and Dislikes', she scanned, in the positive half of a column that could have been lifted straight from 'Hello' or 'Take a Break', an unrecognisable range of reading, of esoteric Eastern and European food, a million miles from the Tesco ready meals that provided both his sole reading matter and his regular, unhealthy sustenance.

Below it, she clicked on 'Distinguishing Features': blue eyes, a small scar on his nose - 'the legacy of too much enthusiasm on the rugby field' that she had never heard mentioned before - and more self-deprecation in 'curly hair originally black and still, miraculously, curly'. She added reality: 'pimples on both buttocks; right foot, a verruca below the big toe.' She checked the impersonal and she was right - nowhere, in the original either, was there a 'me', a 'my', an 'I'. The language elevated him beyond himself, like the self-reference to 'Martin King' which she had heard so many times on the phone.

He had never used those words to her. At least his delusions did not extend that far - or perhaps he had never bothered because there was no financial profit to be made from her. Rejection in another form: too young to be of any consequence to her father; too ugly, too intimidating to be of any interest to Liam.

Hearing a footstep in the hallway, she clicked 'Complete' and looked up to see not Becky, but her grandfather.

"I thought it might be you. Fancy leaving you on your own."

She smiled back at him.

"Becky's just having a quick shower and I never mind my own company, anyway. Oh, sorry, I didn't mean it like that"

The feigned affront on his face vanished as quickly as it had appeared.

"Don't worry. It's what you're supposed to do when you're my age - speak your mind - isn't it, so why shouldn't you get in some practice early?"

"But -"

"She's not happy, is she, Becky? Hasn't been for a while now."

Sarah looked at him more closely. Patient respect for someone older was turning into an attentiveness tinged with apprehension.

"No, I suppose not but -"

"It's the boy who was around here today." His eyes didn't leave hers. "The one you were talking to. I know it really shouldn't be anything to do with me but she's got enough on her plate at the moment."

"I understand all that but you ought to ask her. She'll tell you that Liam wouldn't touch me with a bargepole. It's really not an issue."

He hesitated as she stiffened.

316

"I'm sorry. I shouldn't have presumed to talk like that."

She got up, dislodging the laptop with her hip, catching it before it hit the ground, blurting her words out with her head at knee height.

"Please. Just take my word for it. It's not an issue."

She restored the laptop to safety and, with a grimace in her eyes, walked past him to her temporary refuge upstairs.

74

The start of term was always like this. A brief period of congratulation on a set of results that in some obscure statistical way had set another record and then the planning for another cycle was underway: tinkering with approaches to kids in the middle – still them, despite the changes that were coming - to squeeze out the tiny improvement that would turn a 'D' grade into a 'C'; a system of monthly monitoring, another 'mechanism' that made the job sound like a branch of engineering.

With only a term to go, to Pollard it all seemed even more of a façade, an irrelevance. One, no doubt, that would be foisted upon her in a new job but an irrelevance all the same. She sifted the mound of data that had been distributed earlier in the morning. Into the bin went the latest attempt to rank the school in a European league table. The tentative, almost apologetic tone of the document was the inevitable introduction to the certainties of two or three years' time when its statistics would be definitive. Now, Trelay School had slipped forty-one places from the previous year, perhaps, the report opined, because of an unusually gentle winter in Poland and repatriation policies in southern Europe. No direct criticism as another statistical tier slid into place.

Not fair to knock it all. On the background sheets on the new Year Sevens were the behavioural problems, the family circumstances that you would not find out in any other painless way. She was slotting them into her main folder when the door opened.

"On my tour of duty. Checking all is well. Everyone as happy as Larry."

She looked at Fletcher patiently, willing him on his way.

"An eventful summer." The door clicked shut behind him. "Not just the results but the resumption of our all working together."

"Not difficult when we're all on holiday, I suppose."

"You may be right but hot weather can ferment - or should I say 'foment'? - the wrong ideas." She looked down at her desk and brushed a biscuit crumb onto the floor. "They were brewing well last term and yet you, I'm surprised to say, stayed out of it. I won't ask why but it's a good sign, especially as we now have the power to reward that any company in the real world has had for years." He stopped, ostentatiously. "You're not saying very much."

"I'm listening very carefully."

"You probably should. The question of your replacement has yet to go to the governors. No-one knows of it beyond our management team and I've been greatly encouraged by your recent behaviour. I could take the matter no further and you just stay in post."

"Interviews being an expensive process - and I, of course, am cheap."

"You're still there, aren't you? You're right but only so far. You wouldn't necessarily be cheap for ever. I'm not going to twist your arm, it's not my style, but I do think you should consider it."

Non-committal, she waited.

"We've had no recent requests for a reference so I presume you've nothing lined up. Surely my offer has to be given serious thought especially as - I don't really like touching on this - you may need a bit of stability in your life. It's hard when a relationship breaks up and people need around them as much familiarity as they can muster."

She looked at him with incredulity.

"What's that got to do with you? We're not feudal, for Christ's sake, not yet anyway. Stuff your fucking job. I won't tell you where. Use your own scrap of imagination to work that out. Now will you leave?"

She stared until he turned and let himself out, a minor victory squeezed among so many defeats.

75

At half past nine, when the man with the Geordie accent started swinging his sledgehammer, King's eyes were briefly held by the jagged cracks appearing in the wall - before concrete, lump by lump, was dislodged into the former kitchen where he stood. A shout warned him off as he bent to clear the first debris.

What followed were the regular thuds - and the wait, with dust coating the cupboards and the unused kettle. He watched, his face strained, until the Geordie propped the sledgehammer against the door, reached into his pocket for his cigarettes, waved his hand at King without offering him one and walked outside.

After five minutes of delicately shifting the rubble, one lump at a time, into the wheelbarrow outside, he was stretching his arms back and peering down to the van - but all in vain. His lifting slowed, his cut hands were checked as often as his watch, like a child in a classroom, until the pauses became longer than his attempts at activity.

Twenty-five minutes had gone when the Geordie returned, with Younger standing in the doorway behind him, polished black shoes on a threshold of dust.

"A hive of industry here."

King ignored the voice and continued his improvised stretching exercises.

"Only a month until we need to be ready for our new guests."

King's eyes were closed, an accompaniment to the exertion, but as the sledgehammer swung into action again, he threw up his hands in despair.

"He can't bloody talk - too many fags stuffed in his mouth." He gestured to Younger, as he pushed past, to follow him outside. "Christ!" Head bowed, he grimaced. "Keeps your shoes clean, I suppose, like the rest of you."

"Now, now: personal abuse isn't going to help you. Remember you're not in the best of situations."

"Oh, bollocks, it's as bad for you lot as it is for me."

"Surely you're not stupid enough to believe that. As another famous prole once said, the posh boys can always blame the servants."

King grimaced again. "But this isn't what I'm any good at."

"A bit more realism, please: you've hardly covered yourself in glory in your normal duties." He watched King stretching again. "We're not going to pay you for doing nothing. That part of our PR you can believe. Time to show your flexibility."

"Look, I've got to sit down." He perched briefly on a window sill before wincing and easing himself back into a standing position. "What's all this in aid of, anyway? Marriott didn't tell me a thing." He waved at the mound of shattered concrete in front of him. "It's got the lot. One minute I'm just standing around and then -"

"James knew nothing about it - and who said it was all about you?"

"- five minutes later, my arms are dropping off and my

322

sciatica's kicked off again."

"Have you finished? All part of the collective effort. In four weeks, as I've said, this mini-terrace will no longer be three run-down houses but one - let's call it a hall of residence. Twelve bedrooms, I forget the number of bathrooms, one communal living area, one communal kitchen."

"But who'd be your takers? There're no bloody students around here."

His eyes, derisive, locked on to Younger's.

"You're in danger of completely overstepping the mark. Have I got to say it again? Just remember who you are and where you are."

"No problem working that out," he kicked into the layer of grit in front of him, his voice reduced to a murmur. "Fucking asshole."

"Your vocabulary is certainly as extensive as James described it. If, however, that's what I am, I'm not as pretty as yours, by all accounts. That part of your anatomy, we now know, is, to coin a new verb, bepimpled."

King shook his head, dismissive, exasperated.

"She doesn't like you much, does she?"

"There's no -"

"Nonetheless, not as clever as her publicity would suggest. What we thought - the wait was hardly necessary. Conference League stuff." He looked at King's lowered head. "All gone now, though. Mummy's made it better. And, for Christ's sake, stop muttering. You've got work to do."

"Is that what you call this? Gove building a new university down the road in three weeks? That'd be a record, even for him."

"First of all, the government wouldn't do the building itself, as you well know, and it's not," his voice slowed, parent talking to

323

child, "actual students we're talking about. These are the skivers who can no longer afford to live in London and whom we, very kindly, are housing in this shit-hole. A shit-hole with no middle class fussing over planning regulations - and a constituency we haven't got a hope in hell of winning." His face was contorted in distaste. "Look at what's around here. Run-down factories - you'd have seen it all on the way in. They don't look after anything. Ideal for us: we've just got to be careful to do the building work in dumps like this. A lot of them - so until things quieten down, you'd better practise that little kick of yours. There'll be plenty of dust to get off your shoes."

They moved away as the impact of the sledgehammer grew louder.

"Don't ask. You still do have a brain in there, ticking away. Suffice it to say, the owner's someone with similar views to mine. Similar views to yours when you're not feeling sorry for yourself."

"Well, I hope they've done their sums." The tone of flailing complaint returned. "And there's not a woman worth looking at anywhere. Anywhere at all."

76

It was one of five pieces that Lewis had highlighted for him. Not even an article, just an obituary. In a matter of weeks, Irene Croft had gone from cause célèbre to a death that was barely noticed. The issue, the tarred association with the institution, disappeared with the body.

"Why've you picked that out?" At her voice, Andrews looked over his shoulder. "You weren't even there."

"Well, I'd been at St. Budoc's earlier. On one of my visits. She was someone I'd been campaigning for."

Kirsty edged away, the scepticism in her eyes unnoticed.

"Can't we just have a pleasant chat?"

"Course we can." She talked to the cupboard door as she took out the tin of crunch bars.

"No interrogations on either side?"

"Whatever."

"Was today okay? The bus not too much of a pain?"

"No. Overcrowded but I get on near the start on the way in so it's not too bad."

"And what about college? Very different from school?"

"One or two mess-ups. Two classes in one room and, in the afternoon, no lecturer turned up."

"They'll sort that out quickly enough. It must be a massive thing to get right. Less than two weeks, I suppose."

When she, chewing quickly, turned to tune the radio, he filled the empty space,

"I'm in Whitcross the day after tomorrow. You'd said about getting Mum's birthday present. We could do that in the afternoon if that fits in with your timetable." He pushed the paper across to her and pointed. "Briggs have got a sale on."

She carried on chewing. "You seem to have forgotten. That's a bit upmarket for me."

"Hang on - just look at the prices. I know they're only examples, the best ones, but you should be able to get a scarf or something for her quite reasonably. Anyway, set your own limit and I can help with the rest."

"Okay. I'll be free from 2.30, I think. I'll get the bus in and meet you there."

"I can -"

"No, no, it's simpler and it's free. Plus it's being independent which you always wanted me to be."

There was a first hint of a smile in her eyes. Ironic perhaps but a smile nonetheless.

"I've got some news as well which you'll be the first to know. Not even Mum knows yet."

He missed the curtain being drawn, the smile disappearing from her face. His head was raised; he was talking to an imaginary audience.

"I'd no idea it was coming. I'm being made PPS - Parliamentary Private Secretary - at Transport. I'm meant to counterbalance the Tory, at least in presentation. It's my first promotion, a big one, even though the odds are it won't last. Not beyond the next election."

"So despite everything that's gone on around here, they can still do something like that? Or is it because of it?"

"It's never that straightforward, Kirsty." His words may have been softened by the back of her head which was all he could have seen as he turned in her direction. "There are so many factors they have to take into account. I hope one of them is my ability but no-one's perfect. I'm glad you see things the way you do because you're young - but, unfortunately, the world isn't that black and white.

"And I do have a specific contribution to make. There are local transport issues - the rail network, rural bus services - where I'll really be able to influence the key decisions. For instance ... "

Her head turning, the tremor of her lips, stopped the flow of his words.

"It's always about you, isn't it?"

77

Their tactic had worked. The second letter, a virtual replica of the first, arrived. The stalling continued. The letter might even have been generated automatically.

' ... Following our earlier letter of 11 August 2014, our consideration of your case is continuing. We will write to you again within twenty-eight days of the date at the top of this letter to inform you of our progress ... ' The same concluding paragraphs that said nothing and covered backs.

It was two days before Goldsmith showed it to Mary or Becky. Two days in which he ignored it as a linguistic concoction on a par with the shower of information that accompanied any new drug, anticipating every eventuality but never intended to be read. Two days in which it had the same impact as those information sheets that had always drawn him back obsessively to check in case there was a single detail of relevance to one of his patients.

By the time he did show it to Mary, like a cancer that recurs, it had eaten into him far more than the original letter. Time was key, widening the wound left by Amy Goddard: each month took him further away from the reality of work, the self-reinforcement of the contact with his patients; each month intensified the introspection, with the confines of the house and the first, occasional warnings of autumn deepening his gloom.

The obsessions grew. With so much time on his hands, the trivia of every day were swelling until they provided the structure for the hours he had to pass. Technology was the principal predator: the solar panels that had arrived on the roof as a common-sense investment had become a source of analysis on the hour when he would glance at the meter to determine the density of the clouds above their heads; tidying the arrangements for their online banking had seemed simple housekeeping, a way to occupy himself through the days of waiting until an online request necessitated a phone call that in turn, four days later than had been promised, produced a letter that included the wrong passcode - and then the whole cycle started again.

Every demand on his time became a potential trigger for frustration that only a burrowing attention to detail on his part could avert. Life was a complex exercise in staving off calamity. And yet he was still sufficiently self-aware to respond on a Saturday when a watery sun had risen and Mary had thrown him the sloppy green jumper in which he used to garden.

"Stick that on and find yourself some jeans and a T-shirt. I've made a picnic so the work clothes will have to take a rest on the chair for a day. Becky's idea - gave me a lecture - so you wouldn't disagree, would you?"

Too fragile to protest, he found himself in the front passenger seat of the car, pretending to unravel the knots in his shoelaces until the changed rhythm of the engine told him that they were clear of the village. He pushed himself back in the seat, tugging at the jumper around his neck before winding down the window.

"I'll have to contact them before the end of the week if -"

"But not today." She stroked his leg. "I thought that Sandcombe walk would be lovely on a day like this."

And so it was until they parked the car: each time his agitation surfaced, his sentence was diverted like a stream. He then was loaded with a rucksack whose weight in other times would have elicited a protest and, as they walked, an hour inland across rutted fields and over hedges where the stiles had been obscured, to swing back to the coastline, he felt his mind clearing in the sunshine.

"We could do this every day, I suppose?"

"Remember ... " And then she changed her mind. "Perhaps not every day because I'd still be working."

"You could work less. You ... " He checked himself, surprised at the casual, almost flippant, tone of his words. She put her arm around him, slowing their walk.

"Anything's possible, I suppose. Money's certainly not an issue, is it?"

"I'd have to check it but I wouldn't have ..."

His words drew back, overtaken by his thoughts, and they walked on.

Sitting on the rocks, their lunch finished, she repacked the rucksack while he stared out to sea, tracing the progress of a small motor boat.

"See, that looks fun but we wouldn't need anything so ostentatious."

She followed his gaze as the boat moved away, invisible to anyone else but them.

"One of my problems is that people don't retire at my age. I know it wouldn't be retirement in the conventional sense but that's what it would feel like. I'd be withdrawing, saying I was no longer useful."

"That's not the case. People would know why you were doing it."

He saw her eyes flicker at the misjudgement and his thumbs pressed against the bridge of his nose.

"That's the other part of it. All the speculation will start up. 'Did he jump or was he pushed?' That'll be their line, won't it? I just don't want them to win. Yes - and I don't want them to be seen to have won."

"It depends what you class as 'winning'. Is it 'winning' to allow them to keep you dangling in limbo when you could ... Not something like this every day, all right, but still deciding for yourself how your days and months should be spent."

"But you can't escape your past, can you? How would I handle that sense of failure?"

She took his face in her hands, stern and smiling, matronly.

"Because you're too well-balanced, because you'd put this episode in context, because of your success as a doctor that you know, that everyone else knows. Why are you the only one that patients wait three weeks to see?"

He smiled back, the compliments like the breeze brushing past him.

"That should be past tense, shouldn't it?"

78

The blockage in the hoover was simple to fix, only because Sarah had done it six times already in as many minutes. She resigned herself to another forty seconds of activity before the next blockage.

At least the room was small, with the rest of the flat uncarpeted. As the hoover cut out again, she moved the hexagonal coffee table that had been her grandmother's. The polished oak surface blended with nothing else in the room: the solitary piece of pine on which the lamp stood, the chipboard shelving secured by metal struts that looked like remnants from a meccano set - and most of the rest concealed by drapes.

She lifted the table back into place, the weekend papers sprawling, read casually in fragments until another Saturday arrived. They covered, in part, minutes of meetings and cuttings from the local paper. Her mum had brandished one at her the night before, the usual aphorism - 'national news is local news; local news is national news' - a brief tirade before the self-deprecating apology for the digression.

After two more interruptions, she cut her losses and stowed

the hoover back in the cupboard. It was time, anyway, to get the bus. A late start two days a week was not what she imagined it would be: the vision of morning hours spent engrossed in reading recommended by inspiring lecturers had been replaced by domestic chores that seemed preferable to the texts, some of which repeated the final year grind at school. A veneer of disillusion coated everything, its source untraceable. Her father, no longer physically around, was not so easily cleared away from inside but there had to be another reason. As she walked to the bus stop, her head flitted from symptom to possible cause and back again, until all - perhaps it was her father - blurred like trees, shrouded in mist, indistinguishable.

An hour's Psychology done, she was ahead of the rest in the queue for the canteen. She saw a cluster of them, only one or two familiar from the year before, sitting where they always sat - and then Becky waving, two or three tables along from them. The coffee paid for, she headed for that vestige of school, where her sandwiches, her buying only a drink, would not draw any comment.

"You all right?"

She nodded to Becky's question and to the others at the table, sensing, as they coalesced into a new group, that her appearance was no intrusion.

"Same as usual, I suppose." Her nervous smile relaxed, the other heads, the other ears at the table sealing her out.

"And me. Same as usual but moving on, if you know what I mean."

"I could guess but you're going to have to tell me."

"It's my dad ... he's resigned. Mum told me first."

Eyes turned at the shock on Sarah's face but drew away again once they replayed the words that had just been spoken, dull in their irrelevance, a generation too old.

"He didn't say anything to me for a couple of days. I don't think Mum twisted his arm but he doesn't seem sure about it. I know it's a stupid thing to say but he just sat like someone making a resignation speech on television. You know - the brave face, the body too rigid. I asked him what he was going to do instead and he didn't say anything - couldn't say anything, I suppose. I think he's like someone in free fall who finally pulls the parachute - only that's meant to be exhilarating, isn't it?" She smiled, despite the tears that were starting to form. "I never could get my similes right, could I?"

They touched hands, clenched fists briefly interlocking.

"Did he seem better?"

"The words, yes, but not the way he looked. You know, when he stopped talking, when his face set. He's been beaten down, found the bottom of what he can stand." Her words had momentarily again roused the interest of the rest of the table. "But he's too strong not to lift himself. I'll tell him to ask you for advice."

She took the hint, the feigned humour.

"Can't he do any better than that? He could give me an injection of something in return. I've only been here a couple of weeks and I feel I need a break. Pathetic, isn't it? I ought to eat these, I suppose." She tugged at the cellophane on the sandwiches. "My attempt to emulate Goldsmith organisation. You want a bit? No, not very tempting, are they?" She looked around, chewing slowly. "I'd better go over and see them in a minute." She flicked her head towards the nearby table. "The college action group. The college inaction group."

"Don't let me stop you."

334

"Oh, there's no rush. Duty really, sticking with things. Admirable adult qualities." She pushed down one corner of the sandwich where the drying bread was defying gravity. "I still think it's appalling that the people who lose out in this are the ones with integrity." The generality of her comments, her soapbox delivery, drew no eyes from the rest of the table towards her. "The manipulators, the duckers and divers, that's what he'd call them, skate through it all. It's the same at the top. That's the only way this trickle-down crap of theirs actually works: the bland and the devious, a success to emulate."

"You're on the wrong table." Her words had carried over indifferent heads to an audience. "I recognised the voice, knew it was you. One of our veterans now. Knew what we've been missing."

"I'll be over in a minute. Got a few things to sort out first."

"Like the world?" He glanced at Becky. "Why don't you come over as well?" The words were an afterthought before he walked away.

"Lenin's gone - and Stalin and Trotsky as well. I don't know what you'd call him - one of the apparatchiks that got killed ten years later. One of the leftovers."

"Looking to you for inspiration, looking at me as another appar - whatever you called it. Well, I can boost the numbers as well as anyone. You go over there and I'll join you."

The girl next to them had, once more, fastened on to their conversation. "Fancy a bit of skank, do you?"

Becky raised her eyes.

"No. Let's go over there together. Now."

79

Sarah had heard nothing from him. No concern, no checking to see she was all right - but she had never expected that. What she had hoped for was an explosion about the website - and that never came, either.

Scanning www.martinking.co.uk had given her an immediate explanation: the pimples, the verruca had all disappeared with an ease that doctors and potions from Boots had never managed. She had tried to reblemish that sanitised image but had been rebuffed, all access denied. Someone was the keeper of the keys, someone whose imagined appearance she winced at, someone who would have been replaced in a couple of weeks - and who knew nothing about her predecessors, her successors, her simultaneous rivals for his attention.

He, she was sure, had never even seen her attempt at sabotage. Face to face, she had known she could barely touch him; now the same was true of any attempt in cyberspace. Another failure, more wasted spleen, worse than the tinkering with Wikipedia, more personal.

He had never understood her attempt at anything. Her mum

had just shrugged that off as a statement of the obvious. "Don't forget the papers, though," had been her smiling, parting shot.

She looked at herself, puckering her lips. The light above the mirror, she told herself, was the source of that greasy sheen on her nose. A spot on her right cheek, that she had not noticed the day before, drew her eyes as the central character draws the camera. Was it the external sign of his revenge?

She knew what she would tell anyone else, how brisk she would be. Time to break the tyranny of perception. She dabbed at her nose and watched the slight reddening. Worse on balance: why was it always the same? She tried some of her mum's face powder but that only made her nose look as though it had slipped on an overcoat.

Wrenching herself away from the mirror, she spread everything on the floor and the edge of the bath: two other pairs of jeans, a yellow top that her mum had given her for her birthday and that she had never worn, a necklace, a pendant, a handful of rings that lost themselves against the denim. Nothing there to lift the soul. So little to show for sixteen years - but it didn't matter.

She pushed everything into a pile and sighed - what she was wearing would have to do. The magnet in the mirror drew her one more time: she gave her hair a final brush, as pointless a preparation as all the others.

The wind, cool but chaotic, hit her face when she opened the door. It sharpened her mind, if not her appearance.

"You know what you said about your dick?" Sober, the morning after, she could not believe she had said it. The crassness, the mimicry of Ben's own language but, at the end of it all, the fact that she had joined the club. She touched herself under the sheets, the slight soreness, the matted hair, a confirmation that it had happened. Public enough – she'd heard them laughing just as she had hoped; public enough as well for her to shed that tag, 'icicle', 'ice queen', whatever it was they called her.

Whether it was all drink - or alcohol accelerating a latent intention - she couldn't say. She remembered goading him although at first it had been straightforward abuse: him as brainless, him as a turncoat, him - worst of all - a lackey of her father's. Each barb, though, he had enjoyed, relishing the contact, the chance to be the clown inside the camp again. And with the drink, the words became flirtation, each insult's cutting edge blunted by a smirk.

Pushing against him, supporting herself against him on an outstretched arm, she must have waited for the circle to draw in, to focus, maximising their attention as Polly said she always did, subconsciously. And then her words, those words, came out. He undid his zip, expecting her to stop him but she hadn't - and he stood there, flicking it, big but not erect, talking through it like a ventriloquist's dummy, making it recoil in mock shyness at some imagined affront.

She remembered that and the guard of honour which formed as he pulled her towards the back door and the garden. So many gaps in her recollection: the door may have stayed open or been shut, there may have been faces, an audience, staring out into the darkness, the moments before her jeans were around her ankles.

What did she remember? The uneven stone wall that she was pushed against - her fingers touched tentatively the bruise on her hip where the skin may have been broken - while her head flopped forwards onto his shoulder; his head boring into her neck; that thrusting between her legs that seemed, separated from her by the discomfort from the wall, to be happening somewhere else, to someone else; his words, joking, predictable, at the end - but he hadn't rushed back to the house immediately. She remembered the dampness, the stillness.

She heard the front door pulled gently shut. She could not find her watch on the floor but it must have been her mum setting off for work - or she might just have popped out to the corner shop. Better, either way, to be quick: after one final stretch under the quilt, she swung herself onto her feet and headed for the bathroom.

80

"Oh God, did I make a complete idiot of myself?"

Her enjoyment of her own embarrassment shone through the surface of the words.

"No, it was just a bit out of character. More than a bit, I suppose." Becky smiled and pushed Sarah towards the window to let the others pass without catching her shoulder. "Don't know what Liam made of it, standing there half-asleep. You've cleared the way for me - at least in theory."

"I was never any obstacle." Her laugh was a mixture of elation and self-deprecation. "He's his own biggest obstacle. It's nothing to do with you."

"You've turned agony aunt now, have you?" She leaned across Sarah and, as the bus slowed, wiped away a patch of the condensation that the chill of autumn had produced. "Oh no, it's her. Now anyone on the bus who didn't know will get it in stereo."

"She had a clear view, did she?"

"Not as clear as you had but -"

The rush on the metal stairs and Kirsty was sitting in front of them, body swung around, squashing a waif of a girl against the window.

"Why's it so full today? Sorry." She pulled her bag closer to her. "Usual fucking luck, I suppose." She apologised again to the girl and swung herself in the opposite direction, her legs in the gangway. "I nearly didn't bother but hadn't had enough to drink. Seemed better than sticking at home." She looked at them both before screwing up her eyes and turning back to look in her bag.

Becky raised her eyebrows to Sarah, getting only an amused grimace in return.

"Are you all right?"

The tap on her shoulder turned Kirsty again. "I thought I'd lost my fucking bus pass. Crisis over - and I'm not bothered about you getting off with Ben. We've all done it. It's like finishing school - that's what my mum would call it."

In the silence, with Sarah stiffened against the window and Kirsty fidgeting, Becky reached into her pocket for her mobile.

"Well, I must be one of the few who hasn't."

"Keep hoping. Trouble is you could wait twenty years for old pretty boy. He would be old, wouldn't he, and probably not so pretty."

Becky passed her mobile to Sarah who looked puzzled at the text and then feigned interest when Becky clenched her teeth and stared at her.

"It should be a good offer. It's half what I'm paying now."

"Christ, it's awful at home at the moment. Not between Mum and Dad - she's in training to be on the steps of Number 10 - but between me and them it's heading towards frosty." She caught the others' glances. "I know you think it's all down to me but it really isn't this time. It's down to you," she looked at Sarah, "more than anyone else."

"How come? Some form of contagion?"

"No, I'm being serious." She pushed herself back and knelt on the seat, pleased to have, once more, their attention. "It's him as well, the way he ... but it's you banging on all the time about the government. I suppose I'm getting older - no, I don't suppose, I *am* getting older - but the things he says and does, they could all be taken a different way. Or some of them could. He's got some new government job," she attempted a whisper, "and I know he's good at what he does but I can't help wondering why he's been singled out. I can't prove that he knew about that bloke, the good-looking one, or that he was linked up with your father in some way. I sound like some silly Enid Blyton kid, don't I, and there should be some stunning revelation any minute, shouldn't there?"

"But there won't be." Sarah's voice failed in its attempt to rise above an adolescent disillusion.

"Nothing's worked out, has it? What difference has anything you've done made? All that ferreting around, all those demos?"

"That's what I've just said." She put her thumbnail to her mouth and teased her teeth with it.

"But you're - we're - keeping going." Becky looked puzzled. "That massive conference. This weekend."

"Habit - but worth a go, I suppose."

"Course it is." Becky looked at Sarah for approval, for confirmation of what she was about to say. "You ought to come as well."

81

Two months earlier, Beckford would have grimaced at the prospect of another meeting. Now, she had gone beyond the reach of discomfort, like someone who has resigned her job and has a few sacred weeks when no-one, nothing, can touch her. Her weeks, though, would be years, at least, and the anger might ease or be trampled into an actual resignation - but not yet.

Calling in to see Colin had been more difficult than she had anticipated. On issues of principle that he could separate from his own predicament, from his recent decision, he was as lucid as ever. He gave her ammunition like a civilian volunteer alongside a gun battery.

She, in return, tried to paint his fading link with work in positive colours - but without success. The letter from Jonathan Oliver to the surgery, praising his thoroughness, his 'ethical solidity' - a strange phrase, she conceded - was batted calmly away in a few words: "From one near-convict about another."

On his own health, his own feelings, he produced only uncharacteristically bland expressions - "I'll be fine", "I'm viewing it as a new start", "I think Mary and Becky are finding it harder than I am." His defences were too secure for her, too secure for his own good, and her skill in teasing out the truth from a patient was of no use on a man who was more professional colleague than friend.

Just once, when he elaborated on the morality of their new procedures for determining when patients should receive expensive treatment, did he pause, as if rocks were puncturing the still surface of the sea. Thereafter, his voice, which so many patients had found reassuring in its gentleness, resumed, a monotone emerging from his mouth but from a distance.

On leaving, she promised to keep him in touch and he fixed her with an affectionate stare.

"Not too much editing?"

"Only the tedious parts: Maurice's grandiloquence and that little man's banalities unless they're really risible - assuming, of course, that he's allowed to put in an appearance again."

He shook his head, reflecting, incredulous for a moment.

"We were right about him, weren't we? They'd have to acknowledge that, if nothing else."

She nodded and bent forward to kiss him on the cheek but, like a diffident child, he nullified the attempted warmth by looking down at the floor. He, instead, proffered his hand for her to shake.

What he would have made of her behaviour at work, she could only guess. She had not told him about the way she sought, like a thwarted adolescent, an opportunity each day to refer on a patient for hospital treatment, to punch a legitimate hole in their budget. Today had been no more successful than most other days. The closest she had got was a woman with persistent vertigo but there was still one approach, a new drug on the market - admittedly, pretty expensive - that had to be tried first.

She made her way down the corridor, determined not to be the last to arrive. She sensed Johnson's footsteps behind her but looked straight ahead. Only when she pushed through the part-open door did he confirm that she had been right.

"Punctuality this time, Sheila? Trying to beat me to the best seat?"

"Hardly, Ian." She headed for a chair as far from Allen as possible. "You mustn't read competition into everything."

The pile of papers in front of her was higher again than the tower churned out for their last meeting. More spreadsheets, 'a position paper setting out revised guidelines for updating the register of interests', recommendations on how to manage 'out-of-practice-area' patients - and so it went on. As she skimmed the pages, she found in thirty seconds four agenda items, each of which deserved an hour's serious discussion and an hour's careful thought in advance.

She reached for the water as Allen set the meeting underway.

"Ladies and gentlemen, what a good sign. Thank you for your punctuality. I appreciate these longer evening meetings make significant demands on our time and energies but we do have issues of substance to work through - and, now, we may even finish before nine o'clock." He looked at no-one, as if his words were destined for a television audience.

"To that end, perhaps we could start with the usual formalities. Minutes of the last meeting: I trust I can sign these as a true record?"

"Not as they stand, no. I remember a discussion, largely with myself, on Colin's situation which hasn't been minuted."

"I believe, Sheila, that the meeting to which you refer was in late July. The meeting, the minutes of which we're now discussing, was approximately two weeks later and was one that you didn't attend."

"One that I didn't know about."

"I hate to correct you but it does appear on our annual calendar and it was highlighted at the end of the previous meeting which you, unfortunately, left early."

"But there's always a written reminder circulated two or three days in advance."

"At the same meeting, we decided to dispense with that convention as a sensible cost-cutting measure. I can, of course, at the end of the evening, provide you with a copy of the agreed minutes of that July meeting."

"Which should have been circulated long ago."

"Again, we agreed, in the interest of operational effectiveness, to change our procedures and, instead, to distribute minutes at the following meeting." He held up his hand to silence her. "I'm sorry, Sheila, but we have to move on. Can we agree these as an accurate record?"

Heads nodded, some tilted down, others raised, exchanging impatient glances.

"Thank you. I assume that there are no matters arising, in which case we can move on to our major item of business - our own charging for minor operations carried out in situ. You have before you a distillation of the issues raised at the last meeting, with some initial conclusions. Sheila?"

"I know I'm repeating myself, and I know I'm irritating the life out of some of you, but papers like this should be circulated in advance."

"It's a fair point you make, Sheila, very fair in normal times, but we agreed at our last meeting, because of the pace at which change is now forcing us to move, that it wouldn't always be possible to distribute papers as far in advance as we've always tried to do in the past. We did, however, consider the possibility that important items of business might, as a result, receive less scrutiny than was ideal and that is why we've scheduled this longer meeting for today. Perhaps we can move on?"

She brushed away the conciliatory tone in his voice.

"So who is the company referred to here? Trelay Care? Where have they come from?"

"Sheila, we need to have the item introduced properly. Mark, over to you."

Mark Stanley pulled his papers towards him.

"I'm sure I don't need to read to you what you're perfectly capable of reading for yourselves, so I'll just highlight the salient points. The key element in the background to these suggestions is the often lengthy delay our patients are subjected to before they're treated for relatively minor conditions. Trelay Care are, most importantly, in a position to cut average waiting time to almost nothing, in a way which is also financially beneficial for us as a practice. Firstly, the cost of those minor operations is removed from our balance sheet. Secondly, Trelay, in carrying out the operations, would pay us an hourly fee for the hire of our premises until their own are available."

Johnson cut in before Beckford. "There's also a major gain for our patients in that there's greater continuity in their treatment. Many - particularly the elderly - would also welcome their operations being carried out in a familiar, local setting."

"But who - or what - is Trelay Care?"

"I'll come to that in a minute, Sheila, but I can't overstate the benefits to our patients. They will, in most cases, have the operations conducted by someone who's personally familiar with their medical background. The need for those initial questions to put flesh on the medical records will have gone."

"But who is this new organisation?" Her voice, oblivious to Johnson's words, sounded like a recorded message.

"A number of groups have been formed, involving local practitioners, to deliver a range of services to the community."

"In other words, it's you."

"I am involved, yes, because of the benefits we can bring our patients."

"Benefits such as," she glanced down at the pricelist in front of her, "£119 for a skin biopsy, £389 for a lipoma." She shuffled on her chair, contemplating another early departure, before fixing herself as if with nails.

"I can't be bothered to ask what this 'one stop' claptrap is supposed to mean - but how on earth are you proposing to do all these other operations 'under local anaesthetic'? You're not just talking about cutting off a wart in Alison's room: you'd need a fully equipped operating theatre, for heaven's sake."

"Two, actually." Johnson's voice implied he was correcting a minor error. "Both available in 2016, once planning objections have been overcome. Overlooking the park which, of course, has the added advantage of being within walking distance of where we sit."

"So you don't just corrupt traditional medical practice; you capitalise on these parallel plans to massacre the green belt?"

"It's hardly a massacre for us to demolish ramshackle outbuildings and to add to the cleared land a small section of the park - but that's an issue for another arena."

"Not according to them it isn't. Planning, health, education - you name it - it's all meant to fit together. And it does, so that people like you can profit."

"I'm sorry, Sheila, this is the reality of the world in which we now live. We may not like it but we either work with the new system - or we allow others who don't have the patients' interests at heart to come in and run the show."

"And 'show' is exactly how it's now -"

"Sheila, Ian is just using a form of words." Allen was leaning forwards, demonstrating how patience and urbanity were still possible in the most trying of circumstances. "This is a -"

"This is a betrayal of everything some of us have ever stood for. And I'm now reduced to a role somewhere between participant and spectator." She paused, as uncertain as those around her. "But I'll stay and say my piece. Have we finished with demolishing that cornerstone of our work? Why don't we move on and look at this revised register of interests? You really, however, ought to rename it. 'Register of self-interest' would be much more accurate."

82

The day - the weather, at least - promised so much. From the windows of the bus that trundled on its way, they saw the blue streaks emerging in the sky and beginning to shrink the pools of mist that lay, unnaturally even, in every valley, as if poured there. A rare weekend day when the dreariness of the week's journeys was transformed, a hope that a trace of summer would survive into the autumn.

"It only starts at midday?"

"That's the scheduled start, Kirsty."

"So why the hell are we so early? I could've had a proper lie-in - and all the excuses would've been a lot simpler."

"Because there's no point in getting there after it's started." Sarah looked out of the window, trying to conceal her exasperation.

"So, we stand there for two hours like old biddies organising a fucking village fete while I could've been lying in bed, thinking of ... all sorts of things. Safer to do it that way - you don't have to realise what bastards they are."

Becky, grimacing, flapped her hands downwards at Kirsty and

spoke softly as Sarah prolonged her stare from the window. "They'll be there long before twelve. Some of us just make our presence felt; some do the talking, the persuading."

"More chance of me getting off with Liam than -"

"Christ, you said you fucking wanted to come. Get off the bus if all you want to do is moan."

They sat briefly in silence, the bus shuddering up the hill - shuddering as it usually did, until a surge in the engine, a jolting, jerked them forward, before it stilled and the bus, angled in to the hedge, pulled to a gentle halt.

"Look, it's not that I want to moan."

"This is the third time it's happened this week."

Sarah glanced at her watch.

"All I'm saying is -"

"Oh, forget it. At this rate, we're not going to get there before it's over, anyway."

* * * * *

"It's just him trying to get back to normal. Or what's left of normal when you no longer go to work. Mum's idea of rehabilitation."

Becky had winced when they waved and called her over as the three of them rushed past the museum, just after their eventual release from the bus. Her dad's considered curiosity at what they were doing, the others' impatience, checked by respect, at the delay - both had been neutered by her breezy smile that he would have seen through.

"You don't have to do this."

"I know that, but I want to. More than ever now, it's not just something to do - and I think he'd probably approve. Will approve. I must stop talking as if he's not here any more."

351

"Get a move on." Sarah turned to shout at Kirsty. "Christ, she's hopeless."

"I'm sorry I roped her in. It just seemed a good idea at the time but -"

"It doesn't matter. It's a high price to pay for the irony of it all, though, and she -"

They turned the corner and the noise, a blaring of horns, the chanting, was suddenly released on them and growing with each rushed step forward that they took.

"Sounds more like it." The frustration of the journey ebbed away in the buoyancy of her voice. "Look at that."

Before them, enclosed by a tight horseshoe of police, a discreet distance in front of the conference building, was a mass of colour, some from union banners that for so long had only seen the light of day once a year, some from recently improvised flags, childlike in their vibrancy.

"God, this is what it should've been all along."

"What you mean? Is this all there is? They filled the whole square for that pasty tax march a couple of years ago." She sensed their annoyance. "Well, that's what it looked like on TV. Hard to tell, I suppose ... " Her voice trailed away.

"How are we going to join the others, Sarah? For a start, I can't see -"

"Look, over there." They followed Kirsty's outstretched arm. "It's Polly - and she's got a load of Year Tens with her." They cringed at Kirsty's waving but, at least, it brought Pollard over, the Pied Piper detached from her retinue.

"You never did this with us."

"No. I probably should've done, Becky, but things are different now. Glad the fire's still burning. I thought Sarah'd be here but not -"

352

"Parental influence, all indirect."

"I heard. I'm sorry."

"She's the catalyst as usual. We wouldn't have been here otherwise."

Sarah stood back, like a mother listening to the prattling of her children.

"I'm going to have to get back. It's hardly loco parentis but all the same. I should be able to see you later."

As she edged away, Sarah followed.

"You've gone out on a limb, haven't you?"

The smile she got was adult to adult. "It's called having nothing to lose. It took me more than ten years to reach the point you got to a few months ago. No moral in it, no moral at all. We must talk about it. Somewhere quieter. I'll give you a ..."

Her words were lost in the surge of noise when the double line of police in front of them was suddenly broken. A man, a shaven head with letters seemingly scored into it, burst briefly through before being pulled to the ground, at first in slow motion, by the two policemen, his body braced as if in a tug of war and slowly yielding, until the film accelerated into normal speed and his head hit the ground with a crack, like stone on stone.

The horseshoe reformed, amoeba-like, save for the two policemen weighting the man's shoulders to the ground, his legs twitching - whether in protest, or convulsively, they could not tell.

* * * * *

"You've got her ready, have you? We don't just want the TV footage."

"All done - couldn't be bloody easier for her - but he's going to be late, isn't he?"

Younger ignored the bitterness in King's voice.

"He's never punctual. We've allowed for it. Standard procedure now."

"Cock-up, in other words. That's their only standard."

"Our, not 'their', little man - so silence, please. There's a middle tier that knows what it's doing, even if you and the great leader don't. The groups all have additional material. Their move into the main hall could be any time between twelve and one."

"I need something to eat."

"And you'll have to wait. You may be back in place but it's only a brief respite - so don't push your luck. Come in with me -" He hesitated, flicking the sheets over on his clipboard. "No, not that room. This one along here. Plenty of fanny in here. Should keep the wolf from the door - and dear old James, who wouldn't have liked all this, said you needed a bit of a bonus."

He walked quietly down the corridor, beckoning to King to draw closer as he pushed at the half-opened door. Inside, he nodded to the man, upright but relaxed, beside the projected image on the wall and stood - with King next to him, acclimatising himself to the near-darkness - behind the gently curving semi-circle of chairs, the attentive heads, two male, six female.

In front of them, the first seconds of an urban scene played out - quiet streets, no children, isolated adults, brisk and as drab as the sky above - before the cameras cut to the interior of a warehouse. In the background, two men stacked boxes, only their backs visible, their jeans and their jumpers, while, in the foreground, at an improvised desk, a young woman checked the slip of paper pushed in front of her. Her smile was reassuring as she gestured across to one of the men behind her.

"No," she waved him back, "one of the bigger ones - those over there."

The reporter's question sounded unobtrusive as the camera scanned the contents of the box - bags of pasta, an array of tins and plastic packaging.

"They all need a referral and they've gone up sixty percent in the last six months."

Her voice continued as the man before her lifted the box in both arms and head down, pushing his back against the door behind him, was gone.

The silence was allowed to thicken before a subdued lighting was restored.

"That's the context. Any comment?"

"It's hard to tell from such a short clip," King moved to his left, away from Younger, eyes straining, for a clearer view of the face of the woman who was speaking, "but it ties in with other bits I've seen on the news. It doesn't somehow seem right in this country."

"I don't think anyone likes seeing it." The voice of the man next to her was considered, non-confrontational. "But it's still getting the job done, at no cost to the taxpayer. If it wasn't, there'd be even less room for tax cuts."

"What do you think, Mike?"

The other man in the group appeared reluctant to be drawn out.

"It would've been interesting to know where that was filmed and to hear what some of the customers - I know that's not the right word - thought. It obviously wasn't somewhere like this. I don't know what I'd feel if it was on my own doorstep."

"But it is." The woman looked to the front for confirmation that did not come. "Spotlight, the other night, said there were more and more of them right across the West Country."

"In any case, as a nation, shouldn't we be taking a broader

355

view than that? It's part of our values to look after each other. It's not mollycoddling and I thought Cameron's comment, whenever it was, about these volunteers being a sign of The Big Society working was really unfortunate."

There was a lull for reflection before the man at the front picked up the reins again.

"How, then, does the government appear on this issue?"

"Neutral, if that film is all that's ever shown, but for me - and I guess for a lot of people – it'd be very different if you also showed the wealth of the few at the top."

"But you need to know about the individuals as well. Some of them've existed on handouts for years. All this is doing is changing the source."

Younger turned and stiffened at the sounds, a brief, renewed shaft of light behind them.

"What, then, if this were the case?" The man, after briefly turning to the screen, sat down before continuing. "The usual, unnecessary health warning: the people you're about to see are all actors."

On the wall, a new warehouse appeared, almost identical to the one they had just seen: two anonymous men stacking boxes; a patient, good-humoured woman at the makeshift counter; the pasta, the tins, the cheap packaging; a man retreating through the door, bent double by the box he was carrying.

"Let me replay a section of that and see if you can spot the difference."

Five seconds at most: the woman checked the referral slip and pointed to the screen; the man nodded in acquiescence.

"What's shown there isn't just a sharpening of the administration but an integration of the food banks and the welfare system. A price is placed on the food and that's deducted from his benefit."

There was no immediate reaction.

"What difference does it make to your perception - not of the food bank but of the government?"

Again there was a reflective silence.

"What about you, Pauline?"

"I'm not sure. It depends, I suppose, on how much it costs them."

"Up to a point, yes, but it does have an element of fairness. We've all got to pay for food out of the money we earn."

At a voice behind him, King's eyes turned slowly away from the heads of the focus group: a voice little more than a whisper but a voice recognisable, in its declamatory certainty, from countless television soundbites.

"That'll do for us. I couldn't have put it better myself."

* * * * *

A first wave of police vans, with their dogs, had hurtled into the square and, with the now closed horseshoe of police watching, had driven any bystanders along the streets, away from the conference.

The square had become an exclusion zone into which more vans surged. The horseshoe had opened at its narrow end like a sphincter muscle and the kettled protesters were driven, as the horseshoe tightened, through the weight of their own numbers into the waiting vans.

Only then, with police blocking every entrance onto the square, had the message gone out through loudhailers for medical help, for a doctor. Becky had heard it when she was washed up, half a mile away, as the pressure of the tide driving them from the square had ebbed away and as she saw her dad standing, nonplussed, in the doorway of a mobile phone store, at the chaos spilling past him.

"You should've seen it. You wouldn't believe it - but you'll have to go. Some bit of good for whichever poor sod it is."

Her words replayed themselves as he looked down at the skinhead, with her, a trainee nurse for the day, at his side.

"I need a blanket, a cushion, anything, to put under his neck."

The policemen, young, uncertain, looked at each other and shrugged.

"Have my bag. Better than nothing."

The man, barely conscious, responded as they tilted his body.

"Is he going to be all right?"

Goldsmith nodded, almost imperceptibly, to her, unseen by the two men, before looking up. "We'll need an ambulance and I'll monitor him continuously until then."

"We won't get one through."

"Of course you can. It must've been planned for."

He watched as one chewed his lip and thought of asserting his own competence, before reaching for his radio. Both moved away to make contact unheard.

"One advantage of age. He didn't know enough to argue." He laid his hand on the skinhead's forehead. "You're going to be fine. No need for an ambulance, really. It just stops them throwing you into one of those vans."

He gazed around the empty square, the police line at every entrance, traces of litter swirling, the man on the ground, his daughter.

"We won't see this on the news tonight."

She said nothing.

"So this is what ... "

She looked at him, unsure from the flatness of his voice if he was about to ask a question.

"Not much, is it? For them," his arm waved, perhaps towards the conference hall, perhaps towards the police, "for me, for you? For all of you."

* * * * *

The speech neared its end, to decorous applause triggered, at regular intervals, by the reassuring phrases - 'the debt inherited from Labour', 'a fusion of public and private', 'the strivers', 'a system that traps people in poverty', 'hard-working families', 'a world where no-one is owed a living' ...

"But we are at the beginning of a new phase for the government. We have taken the country through difficult times. Doing the right thing. Making difficult choices. Almost as difficult as the range of pasties I had to choose from when I arrived."

The chameleon relaxed visibly at the laughter from the audience, his colour waning, his head less angled as if there was no longer an immediate threat he had to evade.

The photographer, the purple fading in her hair, caught him three times as his head tilted again to one side. Power in the image; power in the words.

"A new phase." He paused, a practised moment of reflection. "A new phase but the same principles. It's time to restate why we're in government. And why we will continue in government. We are a party for all the people. Yes, we are Conservatives. But, first and foremost, we are compassionate Conservatives."

Printed in Great Britain
by Amazon.co.uk, Ltd.,
Marston Gate.